At Home in Adelbury

TESS BARNETT

Cover Art by Siobhan Chiffon
www.siobhanchiffon.com

His Princely Delicates
An Imprint of Corvid House Publishing
Fantasy and Science Fiction Gay Romance Novels
Pensacola, FL
http://www.hisprincelydelicates.com

ALSO BY TESS BARNETT

Tales of the Tuath Dé
Those Words I Dread
Because You Needed Me
To Keep You Near
It Ends With Us

Devil's Gamble

Starbound

Domesticated: A Short Story Collection
In collaboration with Michelle Kay

Left Undone

Turkish Delight

AS T.S. BARNETT

The Beast of Birmingham
Under the Devil's Wing
Into the Bear's Den
Down the Endless Road

The Left-Hand Path
Mentor
Runaway
Prodigy
Disciple
Apostate

A Soul's Worth

1

Ethan Kwon had his entire life packed into the back of his SUV. The landscape outside the windows had long ago shifted from skyscrapers to suburban sprawl to farmland, and now he was driving alongside a wire fence and seemingly endless fields of freshly-plucked cotton. The trees had grown taller than the carefully manicured and engineered green space of the city he was used to, and the sky seemed greyer and clearer all at once. He would have been enjoying it—if he wasn't waiting in the dread silence his editor had left hanging in the air of their phone call.

"You did *what?*"

"Well," he began, trying to sound calmer than he ever was in the woman's presence, "you know how hard it is to find a place downtown like mine, so it didn't take long to sublet—"

"What I mean is, you didn't think to tell me you were *moving* until you were already there?"

Ethan cringed and gripped the steering wheel a little tighter. "It was sort of a...last minute thing? And it's just for six months—my new landlord and the guy I sublet to both know. And anyway, I'm actually not *there* there, I'm still a couple hours—"

Her deep sigh sounded through the car speaker. Deianira Grivas was not the warmest person on her best day—if Ethan had to describe her, he might do it in terms of weather rather than personality traits. She was a little like the sea. Sometimes smooth and calm, so you'd never guess the depths of what went on underneath, and sometimes stormy and frightening. Right now, he'd guess there were clouds on the horizon.

"I'll still be working, Dee, I promise. But I think this will be good for me, you know? You said yourself you thought I needed a new perspective."

"On your *art*, Ethan, not the view out of your goddamn window." She gave a soft, faintly rumbling sound of resignation. He could picture the soft black feathers at the backs of her ears fluffing in irritation. It happened a lot when she was talking to him. He was lucky to have one of the top editors at Wendigo Comics helping him—even if she didn't feel the same way about having him as one of her artists.

"Just get me some new pages by the end of the month," she said with inarguable finality. "And you'd better pick up your phone more often if you've taken away my option of showing up at your apartment."

"I will. I promise."

"Enjoy your farmhouse," she finished archly. "I'll call you if anything comes up."

"Thanks, Dee."

Ethan let out a long breath as she ended the call, and he relaxed into his seat and adjusted his round, wire-rimmed glasses. This was going to be what he needed. Adelbury had a population of just over 2,000 people, and the pictures made it look like an Old West town in a John Wayne movie—sweetly painted wood-plank buildings lined up in a neat row along a main street just waiting for a Fourth of July parade. And just outside the town itself, rolling fields of flowers, clear lakes, and snow-capped mountains. Like a postcard.

It was going to be a total phase-shift from his tiny apartment on the 12th floor of an interchangeable grey building in the city, and he would finally be able to breathe and get his inspiration back.

That's what he was hoping, anyway.

At the command of his GPS, he turned up a long dirt drive, and at the top of the hill, a pair of buildings surrounded by wide, grassy fields came into view. The red barn caught his eye first, but there beside it, the little farmhouse that was going to be his new home sat waiting for him. He parked in the worn grass beside the porch and climbed out of the car to get a better look.

It was the coziest-looking place he'd ever seen. It was a small, two-story design with a double window in a gable above a covered porch. A little run-down, maybe—some of the wooden slats making up the front had peeling paint, the screen door had been patched, and the porch railing had seen better days—but it was exactly what he wanted.

As if summoned by the slam of his car door, a voice sounded from around the far corner of the house, calling Ethan's name amid a hurried thump-thump-thump of hoofbeats. A centaur with tawny skin and a red roan flank appeared in the yard, the canvas tool belt around his human waist clinking and clanking as he moved, and he skidded to a stop nearby, drawing up dust around the dark stocking marks on his legs. His t-shirt had a few holes in it, and he'd obviously just wiped his hands down the front of it. He took a moment to push a mess of black curls out of his face, his wide smile plumping his freckle-covered cheeks.

"Ethan! You're Ethan, right?"

He nodded and smiled as he craned his neck to look the centaur in the face, resisting the urge to take a step back from his bulky body.

"I'm Carlos! We talked on the phone! I was just—" He turned to point back at the house, and he whipped around so quickly that his precariously-dangling hammer fell from his belt. "Oh, shoot. I was just—I was fixing the shutter at the back, there—" He shifted and began to widen the stance of his front legs while he was talking, trying to shimmy low enough to be able to reach the ground when he bent over to retrieve the lost tool. "We had a bit of a nasty—" He grunted as his fingers brushed the grass, and he wiggled and stretched into his front hooves to get a little deeper.

Ethan fought to keep an anxious grimace off his face. Should he just pick it up for him? Would that be rude? He'd met and been around centaurs before, of course—but he'd never been super close with any, and he definitely didn't want to offend his new landlord on his first day.

"—storm the other day," Carlos went on, undeterred, "and the one shutter came loose, so before you got here, I—ha!" He scooped up the hammer and did a little hop to straighten back to his full height, a beaming grin on his face. "Anyway, it's fixed now. Welcome to

Adelbury! Let's get you inside!" He tucked the hammer more securely into his belt. "How was your drive?"

"It was fine," Ethan answered, a little overwhelmed by the centaur's enthusiasm. He scooted past him toward the back of the car and lifted up the trunk door, but Carlos was immediately beside him, ready to help carry things. Ethan had never had a landlord in his life who did more than show him the door and wish him good luck—this one wanted to help him move in? He hesitated, then awkwardly handed Carlos a duffel bag and hefted his own suitcase out to carry it up the porch steps.

The screen door gave a long, satisfying creak as Ethan swung it open. He turned when Carlos tapped his shoulder, and then the centaur dropped a key into his hand—attached to a carved wooden keychain that read "Welcome Home" in a fancy cursive script. Carlos watched him with such expectant eyes, clearly very pleased with himself, that Ethan couldn't help returning his smile before he opened the door.

Inside, the house looked like the pictures Ethan had seen online— mostly. The living room furniture and floor were covered in drop cloths, there were paint cans in the corner, and, at the far side of the room, a door was off its hinges and leaned against the doorjamb. Some of the baseboard seemed to be missing, too.

"Oh, shoot," Carlos said from behind him. "Hold on! Sorry!" He dropped the duffel bag just inside the door and set off across the yard at a canter, leaving Ethan to set down his suitcase and take in his new surroundings.

He was definitely sure all the doors were on in the pictures. The kitchen, open to the other end of the living room, looked more normal—but there was still a heavy-looking toolbox on the counter.

Carlos reappeared before Ethan could get too far in, his hooves clattering awkwardly on the wooden porch as he tapped them like he was wiping his feet. The centaur hunched through the front door with a wicker basket in his arms, piled with fruit, hand-labeled jars, and a loaf of crusty bread. He cradled it in one arm and tugged the dropcloth off the coffee table with the other so he could set it down.

"Sorry about this," he said, already winding the rest of the dropcloth up around his arms and scooping up the next to reveal an aging green sofa. "I was trying to get the rest of the painting done and cleaned up before you got here, but then I had to use the cart yesterday, so I was late getting back, and then that darned shutter—anyway, I got you a basket!" he finished with a smile. "Oh—and I'll fix that door today; promise. It needed sanding on the bottom. I was waiting 'til the painting was done, but I'll get it back up."

"That's—it's okay," Ethan promised, lifting his hands in an attempt to ease the worried hunch in the other man's shoulders. "Thanks for the basket."

Carlos positively beamed. He tucked the rolled-up cloth under one arm and stepped closer, seeming to have some difficulty navigating the relatively narrow spaces in the living room designed for humans. "Tia made the preserves herself; you'll probably meet her soon. They're really good. And Ophelia baked the bread! I almost didn't want to give it to you. She makes the best bread. The fruit is from Marcus's orchard. Oh, and there's some chocolate in there too. That's just from the store."

"Thanks, Carlos," Ethan cut in. "You didn't have to."

"Of course I did! I want you to feel welcome. You're going to love it here. Everybody's so nice. I mean—not *literally* everybody, you know, it's a town—but it's a great town!" He edged by Ethan and hunkered his way out the front door again. "Let's get your stuff! I'll just—pass it to you from out here, if that's okay."

Ethan sighed softly, but he couldn't help his faint smile. Carlos was a lot—he'd gotten that impression on the phone—but he seemed so legitimately excited for Ethan to be there that he didn't have the heart to send him away.

So he collected boxes and bags from the porch as Carlos unloaded them from the trunk, and between them, they were able to empty the car pretty quickly. Once Ethan had packed up all his things, he'd realized how little he actually had, aside from his art supplies. Actual unpacking would wait—right now, after two days on the road, Ethan just wanted to sit on his hand-me-down grandma couch and eat that entire loaf of bread for dinner. But when he leaned out the front door to thank Carlos for his help, he didn't get to speak first.

"Ethan! You probably don't want to cook tonight, right? Let's go into town! We can go to the Little Goat! Ophelia will cook you something special for your first night, for sure."

Ethan tried to restrain the grimace he felt pulling on his lips.

"Thanks, Carlos," he started, hesitating half a second while his brain scanned for a good reason to decline, "but I really don't think I can deal with getting back in the car today."

"Oh, no worries!" Carlos's tail flicked excitedly, and his front hooves fidgeted. "I'll give you a ride. It's not that far."

Ethan froze, his hand tightening on the handle of the screen door. "A...ride? Like a...ride ride?"

"Sure!"

"That's not—I'm sorry," he said with a deepening furrow in his brow, "I've never—I mean, it's not...rude?"

Carlos laughed. "It would be rude if you tried to just hop on, but I'm offering. Don't worry about it."

"But I've never ridden any kind of...anything. Anyone. Any—living thing or person."

"Aw, there's nothing to it," the centaur assured him with a bright smile. "Let me just change, and I'll be right back!"

He turned without leaving any room for a "no," and Ethan waited awkwardly on his own front porch while Carlos trotted over to the red barn across the yard. This was not the first day he had planned. But this was what he'd asked for, in a way, right? Small town living. That meant people were going to be more friendly than he was used to.

A few minutes later, Carlos came in a hurry back to the house, now wearing a dark green waffle-fabric henley with the sleeves pushed up to his elbows and a dark grey fanny pack fastened around his waist. He came to a stop at the porch steps and offered Ethan his hand.

He accepted with an uncertain grip, and he did his best to try to hop onto the centaur's back while Carlos helped lift him by the arm. After a bit of unstable wiggling, Ethan was able to settle himself, but the first time Carlos moved underneath him, he gave a short shriek and clamped his legs so tight around the centaur's middle that he chuckled.

"Just hold on," Carlos said. "I won't go too fast."

"Hold on to what?"

Carlos reached back for Ethan's hands and placed them casually on his waist, but Ethan immediately retracted them and took hold of the back of Carlos's shirt instead. Way too weird to hold some dude's waist the day you meet him. Carlos seemed to accept this, but when he started walking, Ethan almost slid off the side of the centaur's flank, stretching the shirt in his grip until Carlos could twist around to help him back up. He smiled over his shoulder at Ethan as he paused and held his hands at the small of his back.

"Come on," he said, wiggling his fingers until Ethan relented and took hold of them. Carlos gave him a firm, gentle squeeze as he started off again. "Just hold tight with your legs. It'll help."

This was weird. It was so weird. But if Ethan said it was weird, that would make it even weirder, wouldn't it? Small town friendly was one thing, but he had definitely not expected that to include a horseback ride from his new landlord. While holding his hands.

Ethan puffed out his cheeks in a sigh he hoped Carlos didn't hear. He was at least able to keep his balance a little better after the first few minutes.

He barely had time to think about the awkwardness of the ride after that—Carlos didn't stop talking long enough to let him. He talked about the mountain and how pretty it looked, how they didn't expect snow for a few weeks more yet, and how much he just knew Ethan was going to love it here. He pointed out when they rode by the orchard owned by Marcus, who Ethan absolutely mistook for one of the trees when they spotted him in the field. He was a treant, with thick, bark-covered limbs and worn denim overalls. He raised a rough hand in a wave when Carlos called out to him, then carried on his slow stalk through the rows of trees—he was almost as tall as they were. Who better to take care of an orchard, Ethan guessed. He definitely had seen very few of them in the city. Accommodations were made in most places for most body shapes, but some types of people were just too large to have an easy time managing subways and elevators.

Downtown Adeulbury hardly deserved the title, really—when Carlos spread his arms to indicate they'd arrived, he was walking down a two-lane street lined with quaint little shop fronts and painted wooden signs, just like the photos Ethan had seen. A handful of cars sat parked along one side of the road, and wooden lamp posts stood at intervals down the street, holding up banners advertising a "Big Bad Pumpkin Patch" for all of October. People strolled the sidewalks, greeting each other and carrying bags of various goods. Most of them smiled or waved at Carlos. With the autumn breeze chilling Ethan's skin through his baggy flannel overshirt, and the sky beginning to take on the soft orange of the approaching sunset, the whole atmosphere was...charming. More charming than he'd expected.

This part, at least, was exactly what he'd wanted.

Carlos came to a stop outside a green building with a windowed front and a sloped roof over the porch. Wooden lettering above the roof spelled out "The Little Goat," and a neon "open" sign flashed in one of the windows. Ethan couldn't help the smile on his face. It was too perfect a vision of a small town diner.

He slid down Carlos's side with a tight grip on the centaur's hand, stretching his toes toward the ground as he eased down to the sidewalk. At Carlos's urging, he headed to the door and pulled it open by the worn metal bar, causing the bell overhead to tinkle softly.

Inside, the diner was like somewhere a nice young couple might go for a malt–after a football game, maybe. Booths in brown vinyl lined the wall across from the long bar counter, and tables with smooth Formica tops dotted the yellow linoleum between, with a number of patrons both human and not chatting over meals on thick ceramic plates. Stools with cracks in the cushions lined the bar—there was even a glass display case housing half a pie. It was too much. Rockwellian. He wished he had his sketchbook.

"Ophelia!" Carlos called from right behind him, startling him out of the doorway.

A sepia-skinned figure behind the bar turned to answer the call, her bountiful brown ringlets bouncing with the movement. Long, rounded ears pierced with thick gold hoops perked up as she smiled. A pair of gently curling horns were half-hidden by her curls, and light tufts of dark brown fur peeked out from the sleeves of her apron-covered button-down. The soft click of hooves as she bustled down to the end of the counter gave her fully away—she was a satyr.

"Oh, hello! Is this him?" She smiled brightly at Ethan, her broad nose wrinkling. "You're Carlos's new tenant?"

Carlos was already settling himself at the counter, dropping down onto a long cushion on the floor in front of a lowered section of counter—clearly intended for his use. He patted the stool closest to him, so Ethan moved toward it while he answered.

"Hello," he said with an awkward half-wave. "I'm Ethan, yeah."

"That's right! I'm so happy to meet you, Ethan!" Her accent had a subtle, pleasant twang to it. "We don't get new people in town very often. I'm Ophelia, obviously," she added with a small laugh and a gesture toward her plastic name tag. "This is my place. That's my daughter, Zoe," she said, waving out toward a small booth, where a younger-looking satyr in a slouchy knit hat was refilling someone's water from a pitcher. "We're open for breakfast, lunch, and dinner, so anytime you get a rumble in your tummy, you just come see me, okay?"

"Sure," Ethan agreed as he slid onto the stool. This woman's whole aura was welcoming—she had a soft, curvy figure and a round face with full lips and the faintest wrinkles at the corners of her eyes. She looked like she would read Ethan a bedtime story if he asked.

"So," she began again, "what do you feel like? Something special for your first night?"

"Ophelia," Carlos cut in, his tail flicking against the tile floor as he leaned his elbows on the counter, "do you have sweet potato pie today?"

"Do I have sweet potato pie," she echoed with a sly smile. "Of course I do, sweetheart. But Ethan probably doesn't just want pie for dinner, do you?"

"Uh—what do you have?" Ethan looked around for a menu, a board, or anything with a hint as to what his options were, but Ophelia waved the question away.

"You know what? How about I just make you my specialty. Allergic to anything? Dietary restrictions?"

"Um. No."

"You like eggplant?"

"Sure?"

"Oh, you'll love it," she promised him with a nose-wrinkling smile. "Zoe! Get these boys some cider, will you? Thank you, dear!" She carried on without time for the girl to answer, and she bustled away through the swinging saloon doors into the kitchen, her fluffy tail twitching between the hem of her shirt and the knot of her apron.

Carlos's fingers drummed on the counter during their wait, and he yammered endlessly in Ethan's ear—about Ophelia's pies, Zoe's last birthday party, the list of things still yet to fix in Ethan's house—until someone set off the bell at the door, and he stopped short to wave them over.

"Tia! Tia come meet Ethan! I told him about you!"

Ethan turned and found himself faced with an ethereally beautiful young woman with platinum blonde hair falling loose over her shoulders. Black jeans hung from her petite hips, and a knit sweater hung loose around her torso, exposing one shoulder. Behind her, a pair of shimmering, pale green wings fluttered gently, flashing a matching set of gold and black eye spots. Ethan had never seen a fairy with wings like this before—like a moth. Her smile was just as glittering, and when she put an easy hand on his shoulder, Ethan fought the urge to pull away out of...respect? Intimidation? It was hard to say.

"Well aren't you the cutest thing," the fairy said. "That's lucky; there's a shortage of available young men in this town."

"Uh," Ethan started, but she didn't seem to be waiting for an answer.

"I'm just picking up my call-in." She waved at Zoe when the young satyr approached and stepped behind the bar to grab a to-go box, and she smiled over her shoulder once she had it in hand. "Nice to see you, Carlos. Ethan, I hope you like the preserves." She winked one mint green eye at him and wiggled her fingers in a wave, then almost seemed to float out of the diner again.

"I told you she was nice," Carlos said brightly.

A loud crash sounded from the kitchen, then a roar of fire that seemed much too large for the stove of a small diner. Pots and pans clanked, and a rapid scraping skittered on the tile as the small, scaly body of a red drake swung butt first into the space behind the counter, back arched like a cat.

"Kylos!" Ophelia shouted from the kitchen doorway, one hoof giving a solid clacking stomp on the tile as she leaned out. "How many times have I told you to stay *out* of the fridge? We have orders!"

The drake opened its toothy mouth wide and snapped it shut again as if in protest, hopping up to stand stiff-legged on all fours.

"Don't you give me that. Get back in there before I decide you need a good scrub instead."

The creature snorted out a puff of smoke, its long tail flicking against the floor in irritation, but then it marched itself back into the kitchen.

Ophelia sighed, offered Ethan and the other patrons an apologetic smile and wave, then disappeared herself, her next scolding swallowed by the sound of flame bursting back to life.

"That's Kylos," Carlos explained unnecessarily. "He helps cook.

Don't worry—he always washes his hands."

"Good to know," Ethan answered.

Ophelia appeared shortly with two plates laden with some sort of eggplant, cheese, and tomato dish with a name that Ethan didn't catch, and Carlos seemed more excited for the meal than Ethan had ever been for anything in his life. He couldn't deny how delicious everything was, though—the apple cider was crisp, the eggplant was rich, and the sweet potato pie was actually the best Ethan had ever tasted.

He answered Ophelia's dozens of questions while he ate—she wanted to know where he came from, why he moved, what his work was. Maybe he ought to send out a newsletter so he didn't have to answer these questions a hundred more times during his stay here. When he mentioned he'd published two graphic novels and was working on a third, Ophelia leaned on the bar to look more closely at him.

"Ethan, that's incredible! I want to read them!"

"They're not very good," Ethan mumbled down at his empty plate, and he got a soft, scolding tut and a swat to his hand in response. "They're just, like—kind of folksy, whimsical adventure comedies for kids. I guess."

Ophelia gasps lightly. "Maybe we could get them in the library here! It's just down the end of the road. You should talk to Nareth; he's the librarian. Pan knows we could use some new material in there."

"Oh," Ethan said, "that's—the publisher would normally—"

"Well, you take your time settling in, anyway," Ophelia cut him off, reaching across the counter to pat his arm. "Don't let Carlos bully you too much!"

"I'd never bully anyone!" Carlos said, a little too loudly. He actually seemed hurt by the accusation, but Ophelia just gave him a warm, knowing smile.

"Anyway," she went on, "we're glad to have you, Ethan. Don't be afraid to ask if there's anything I can do to make things easier on you while you get situated."

"I will," he assured her with a nod. "Thanks."

She smiled at him. "You look beat, hon. Carlos, get this boy back home and leave him be, you hear me?"

Carlos laughed out an agreement and steadied himself on the

counter while he pushed up onto all four hooves. Ethan tried to pay, but Ophelia shooed him away with a grin and insisted he think of the meal as a housewarming gift, so he thanked her again and followed Carlos back onto the street.

"Well, I wanted to give you a tour," the centaur sighed, "but I guess you probably do just want to get home, huh?"

"Please," Ethan admitted with a laugh, and Carlos smiled.

The ride back wasn't as awkward—Carlos raved about the pumpkin patch and named at least a dozen townsfolk that Ethan almost immediately forgot. Back at the house, Carlos made good on his promise to hang the bathroom door again.

"I'll come work on a few other things tomorrow," Carlos said as he hopped down from the porch into the yard, bypassing the steps completely. "Oh, but—shoot, I forgot to tell you," he sighed. "They still haven't gotten the Internet hooked up over here yet. They were supposed to come a few days ago, but they didn't, and I had to keep bothering them. You know how cable companies are—and it's even harder to get them to come all the way out here. It should be soon, though! And there's the library in the meantime. See, you were meant to talk to Nareth," he added with a smile that looked like he hoped to be forgiven.

Not having WiFi access was ridiculously inconvenient, but Ethan only nodded. What would complaining fix? "Don't worry about it. I'll check out the library. Oh, and—is there a mechanic in town? My car was making a weird noise for the last couple hours of the trip."

"Oh, for sure!" he answered, pointing down the road as if Ethan was likely to take off walking. "Rob and Luke will help you out. It's a block past Main Street, on the corner. You can't miss it."

Ethan nodded. "Thanks, Carlos."

"Have a good night, Ethan," the centaur said with such sincerity that Ethan almost felt bad. "Welcome again."

Ethan returned his wave and shut himself into his new home, letting out a long, heavy sigh as he stood in the quiet living room. He would have to make the bed, at least. And he'd have to text Maya—if he went to bed on his first night in a new town without letting his best friend know he was safe, he'd be hexed into a toad.

But he was here. And it was going to be good.

2

By the time Ethan rolled out of his floral-blanketed new bed around the middle of the next morning, he was ready for a breakfast of fresh bread and preserves. The elderberry jam really was amazing—he was going to put on weight if everything here was this good.

The upstairs bathroom didn't have a showerhead, and the bottom of the cabinets were chipped. More improvements Carlos had meant to get to, Ethan guessed. He washed himself in the single pour of water from the pipe sticking out of the wall and dressed in his usual jeans, t-shirt, and baggy flannel. The air had a chill in it, so he tugged on his pale blue beanie as well and pulled it down over his ears, then dug through still-packed boxes until he found what he'd need to do some work. He'd have to go to the library, he guessed—he just hoped it wasn't as busy as the one back home was. The times he'd been, he'd had to find himself a corner of a table among chatting college students and city residents filling out job applications. He was grateful for libraries as a concept, but they weren't always the best setting for quiet work.

He expected to be roped into conversation as soon as he set foot out of the house, but Carlos was nowhere in sight. That was a relief. He liked the centaur already, but he had a lot more energy than Ethan was used to being around. He dropped his laptop bag into the passenger seat of his car and pulled out onto the long dirt lane, driving as gently as possible so as not to aggravate the warbling squeaks coming from his engine, even louder than before.

The mechanic shop wasn't hard to find, as promised. It looked like it had once been a gas station; part of the large concrete yard was covered by a roof with bolts sticking out of the spots in the ground where pumps should have been. The store had been converted into an office, by the view through the front windows, and a long garage had been built onto the side. Two sedans sat parked under the covered portion of the patio, and the rear of another was visible inside the open garage door. Ethan parked his own SUV off to the side of the lot and approached the office, where a small brown tabby cat lounged in a sunbeam. He smiled, but it rose and walked casually away from him when he approached it.

"Rude," he chuckled to himself as he turned to the door. The lights were on inside, but he couldn't see anyone—were they open?

He heard a clang from the direction of the garage, so he leaned back to peek toward it and walked over. A pair of Dickies-covered legs ending in thick black boots extended from the underside of the jacked-up two-door inside, moving subtly in time with a wrenching sound from underneath.

Ethan knocked on the wall near the open garage door. "Hello? Excuse me?"

The sound stopped, and, after a brief pause, a pair of hands appeared at the lower edge of the car. In this light, they almost looked green. The wheels of the creeper underneath the legs ground on the concrete as it moved, and as a young man appeared and sat up, Ethan swallowed hard at the sheer size of the body that just revealed itself. He *was* green—a pleasant, muted green, with black hair shaved close to his scalp except for a mess of waves on top and falling back from his forehead, pale amber-yellow eyes, subtly pointed ears, and a pair of short, curved, tusklike teeth jutting out from his lower lip.

An orc.

An orc with an offensively pleasant jawline.

"Hey," he said, unexpectedly softly for someone his size. "Can I help you?"

Ethan took a moment to find his voice. "You're the mechanic?"

The orc paused for a moment, then looked down at his oil-stained jumpsuit. He made a show of noticing the patch above his chest pocket that read "Damox Automotive," and he pointed at it as he looked back up at Ethan, blank-faced. "Huh. Would you look at that? I guess I am."

Ethan's face heated instantly. Of course the first thing he'd say to the small town's hot orc mechanic was something stupid. "Sorry. Uh. I just moved here yesterday, and when I was coming in, my engine started making this weird noise."

"Oh, you're Carlos's new captive, huh?" He laid a hand on the side of the car and got to his feet with a small grunt of effort, then leaned over to snatch a rag from the nearby rolling cart and wiped his hands.

Ethan opened his mouth to answer, but when the other man took a step toward him, he backed up on instinct. He barely came up to his chin. Ethan couldn't be called tall—he was 5'7" in the right shoes—but this mechanic was well over six foot and built like a linebacker. And now he was looking down a long Roman nose at Ethan and lifting one thick black brow in a silent question, and Ethan was just standing there, wetting his lips and staring like an idiot, trying not to let it show on his face that he'd just imagined being thrown over the orc's shoulder like a sack of flour.

Great first impression.

He always did this. Anytime he was around someone attractive—and this man was stupid attractive—he clammed up and stared like the teacher had just called on him to explain string theory.

Not this time. This time he was going to talk like a normal person and have a normal conversation. He took a deep breath and said, "Are you Rob or Luke?" Then he almost vomited into his own mouth. Yeah. Just like that. Great work.

"...I'm Luke," he answered after a heavy, awkward pause. "Rob's my uncle."

"Great," Ethan said, so quickly he began before Luke finished. "I mean, it doesn't matter. Carlos just said that both of you were here, and he said you were the mechanics, and here you are, so—I'm Ethan," he finished, feeling the bile of shame rising in the back of his throat.

Luke finished wiping the grease from his hands and stuffed the rag into his pocket, his expression unreadable. "Why don't you just start the car for me, huh?"

Ethan turned away from him and squeezed his eyes shut in misery for the few steps back to his car. Good. Excellent recovery. Very normal. He slid into the driver's seat and started the engine, then leaned down to pop the hood when Luke gestured to him. The whole car shifted with the orc's weight as he leaned on the front of it, and Ethan waited anxiously while the mass of man stood to listen. After a few seconds, Luke waved at him to shut the engine off, and Ethan obeyed—and a moment later, he was trapped as Luke came around and leaned an elbow on the open door to talk to him. He looked even bigger, looming over Ethan like this.

"Sounds like you're about to lose a belt," he said with a small shrug. "Pretty easy fix. I'll check it out and replace it—I've got one that should fit already. I've got people ahead of you, though. Think you can come back for it this afternoon?"

"Oh—yeah, no problem at all. I was going to go to the library for a while, anyway."

"Great." Luke gave the top of the car a light slap as he pulled away to let Ethan out. "Leave me the key, and I'll take good care of her. We'll call it a hundred bucks if that works for you—that'll account for the part."

"Sure!" Ethan clambered out a little too quickly, coming to a short stop as his flannel got caught between his supporting hand and the seat. He stumbled to his feet and dropped the keys into the orc's waiting hand, unable to keep his mouth from carrying on without his brain. "I never have any idea what to expect when my car acts up, so that's kind of a relief, actually. Thank you."

"Sure. Wouldn't want to fleece the new guy too bad on his first day in town." He tucked the keys into his palm and retrieved a small flip notebook and pen from his chest pocket. "So, can I have your number, Ethan?"

His heart stopped. "My—uh, but I—you're, uh—I mean, if you—"

"So I can text you when the car's ready," Luke said evenly, his interruption like a mercy killing.

"Yes," Ethan breathed. "Thank you." He was already circling the car to grab his bag and make his escape while he called the numbers out, and once Luke nodded at him, he took the longest strides possible away from the shop and down the sidewalk. Maybe a truck would hit him on his walk, and he'd never have to look Luke in the face again. That would be preferable.

Why did this have to happen? This place was supposed to be

relaxing, inspirational, a new page—not the same flustered bullshit as always. Why did Luke have to be so big? And so hot? And so hot and big?

He frowned, his steps slowing to a more sane pace as he got some distance between himself and the shop. Was this racist? Was *he* racist? Was he fetishizing this stranger just because he was an orc? Ethan snorted and tugged the strap of his bag a little tighter over his shoulder. No. No he was not. Because if Luke had been a human person that size, Ethan's reaction would have been exactly the same level of stupid. He knew himself well enough to admit it.

The big teeth were pretty cute, though.

Ethan groaned out a sigh and rubbed the skin under his nose pads with his free hand. Just get to the library. Get some work done.

He walked by the library twice before he realized he'd been looking for a much larger building than the one actually waiting for him. The building he wanted was a simple white house with columns supporting an upper level above the porch, where black painted letters read "ADELBURY LIBRARY," and a small round window sat in a slatted gable. The stone steps up to the porch looked well worn, and on one of the columns, a little painted sign displayed the library's hours.

Ethan smiled and took a few steps back to take a picture of the building on his phone. It was perfect for the kind of small-town aesthetic he was hoping to harness for his next book. He ought to remember to take a few pictures of the diner, too, if Ophelia gave the okay. He never would have found places like this in the city.

The library door stuck a little when he pulled, but then it swung outward and let the morning sunshine into the building. It was just as small inside as it looked outside, but it was neatly organized—two rows of shelves surrounded a long conference table in the center of the room, and a short set of stairs led up to a mezzanine of additional shelves. Right at the knee wall of the staircase, barely out of the way of the entrance door, sat a desk, cluttered with books, folders, a barcode scanner, and a computer monitor and keyboard. And at that desk sat a man who almost looked like a negative of Ethan himself—his skin was grey, almost a true black, and his messily-styled straight hair contrasted sharp white against his dark face. He looked up at Ethan with warm honey-brown eyes behind round wire glasses, the delicate gold chain hanging from the arms and the gold pendant earrings in his long ears swinging subtly with the movement. His white eyebrows lifted as he took Ethan in, as if he wasn't expecting anyone to actually come into the library.

"Good morning," he said, his voice rich like warm coffee. "Can I help you?" He had an English accent. This was bad. He looked young, though with elves, dark or otherwise, their youthful faces were almost always deceiving—but he had sharp cheekbones and thick, pale eyelashes, and there was an attractive aloofness about his expression as his slim, gold-ringed fingers drummed once on the desk, as if Ethan was already taking too long to answer.

Really, God? Ethan had been sent from a burly, soft-spoken mechanic to a beautiful elf who looked about to scold him? With his shirt unbuttoned and delicate collarbones showing? Did Ethan really deserve this? To make an ass of himself in front of every person in town, one by one?

"Hi," Ethan said, confident in his start, at least. "There's no WiFi hooked up at my place yet, so I was hoping to just leech for a while, if that's okay." Great. So far so good. Sounded normal.

"Ah. The new transplant," the elf said dryly. "Mr. Morzillo's tenant, yes?"

"Uh, yeah." Ethan twisted the strap of his bag between his hands. "Does...everybody know about me already?"

The librarian straightened in his chair and reached to pluck a folder from a metal sleeve on the wall behind him, tapping it lightly on the desk once he'd turned back. "In a town this small, nobody farts without their neighbor three doors down knowing about it." He inhaled through his nose and looked up at Ethan over the gold rims of his glasses. "You ought to have a card. There's a form," he said simply, and he tugged a piece of paper from the folder and laid it on the desk in front of him.

Ethan dutifully took a pen from the nearby cup and bent down to fill in his information, but he paused when he reached the blank for the address. "Uh, so...my ID still has my old address on it, and I don't have any mail or anything yet. Don't I need to prove I'm a local to get a card?"

"Hm." The elf paused a moment, considering, then rose from his seat with a kind of smooth grace Ethan would never even dare to dream of having himself. He was slender and lithe, with his dark button-down tucked into his grey trousers and held in place with a black leather belt. He flowed a few steps over to a small display near the window and chose a sunbleached postcard from one of the slots, then returned to his chair and slid it across the desk to Ethan with splayed fingers. "Put your new address on this. As if you were mailing it to yourself, please."

Ethan frowned, glancing between the card and the librarian's face uncertainly, but he did as he was told. As soon as he finished, the man across the desk scooped up the card and held it in both hands to wait.

"Now there's mail with your name on it. Carry on, please."

A laugh fell out of him. "What? Really?"

"Hold on," the elf said, holding up a finger and lifting the desk phone receiver to his ear without dialing. "Let me ask my supervisor." He let a single beat pass before continuing. "Yes, hello, me? Me again," he said with ingratiating cordiality. "Do I have my approval to run my library as I see fit? Oh I do. Ta." He hung up the phone and looked back at Ethan as he folded his arms on the desk, a sly smile playing on his dark lips. "He says it's fine."

Ethan couldn't help returning such an infectious smile. A stripe of heat licked up the back of his neck at the lingering stare of the elf's warm eyes, and he forced his attention back to the paper in front of him. He signed the bottom in more of a scrawl than usual, handed it back, and waited while the librarian scanned his work.

"Mr. Ethan Kwon," he said, and he bent down to tug open a stubborn drawer and returned with a plastic card bearing a colorful logo of a fox and an open book, which he scanned with the reader on his desk and offered up between two manicured fingers. "You're a card-carrying member of the Adelbury Public Library. Leech away. I'm Nareth, if you need anything further."

"Thanks," Ethan answered, and he took a step back from the desk with card in hand, but then he paused—the only other place to sit in here was at the long conference table at the center of the room, the near corner of which was no more than two feet from the corner of Nareth's desk.

Oh no.

If he took the first seat, he would almost be within arm's reach. But if he went too far down the table, wouldn't it seem like Ethan was purposely trying not to be near him? How many chairs were there? Five on each side. Great. Right in the middle. The middle is good. But should he sit facing the front desk, or away from it? If he faced away, Nareth will be able to see his screen—that wasn't good. But if he faced him, he'd be staring right at him every time he looked up. Was that worse?

He'd definitely already stood here too long thinking about it. It was getting weirder every second.

It would be weirder for Nareth to be looking over his shoulder, Ethan decided, so he took the third seat down on the side of the table facing the desk and tried not to notice how close to the hot librarian he still was while he unpacked his tablet.

Once he'd settled down, the library was dead silent except for the occasional sound of Nareth's keyboard and the soft tick and scratch of Ethan's stylus on his tablet screen while he sketched. It was unbearable—so Ethan pulled his earbuds from his bag and plugged his ears with music instead. He had always felt awkward drawing around other people—especially strangers—but he had just about perfected the art of tuning out the world around him and focusing on the lines on his screen instead. He let his hand do whatever it pleased, shaping some of the people and places he's seen since arriving, testing different designs for possible characters, but when he happened to briefly glance up, Nareth seemed to sense it. Their eyes locked for a moment, and then the elf winked at him, causing Ethan to slouch lower into his seat and hunch his shoulders to hide the warm flush he knew showed up so easily on his pale skin.

The Internet at his house had better be hooked up by tomorrow.

Ethan eventually fell into his work despite the enduring presence of the attractive elf across the room from him, and he soon found himself deep into a landscape, focusing his attention on the nooks and crannies of the mountain peak in the background and letting the music in his ears wash out the room around him.

Then he felt something.

He turned his head, and Nareth was bent down behind him, almost cheek to cheek with him as he stared down at the tablet screen. Ethan's skeleton tried to leave his body, and he slid halfway out of his seat, his tablet clattering to the table as he gripped the arms of his chair to keep from hitting the floor.

Nareth seemed unperturbed by the sudden movement; he just turned to look down into Ethan's panicked face. He said something, but all Ethan saw was his mouth moving, so he pulled out one earbud and reached for his phone to turn off the music.

"What?" he said, sounding more out of breath than could be reasonably justified.

"I said, is that meant to be our mountain?"

"Oh. Uh. Yes—kind of? More like—inspiration, I guess."

The elf gave a soft hum. "It's nice. The drawing, I mean."

"Thanks." Ethan slowly straightened himself and swallowed in an attempt to slow his racing heart, but Nareth didn't seem to be leaving.

"Is this what you do for work, then?" the librarian asked. "You're an artist?"

He nodded, and Nareth smiled.

"How romantic."

"It's really not," Ethan shot back with an unintentional snort, shifting in his chair and pretending not to notice the way Nareth had leaned his hip against the edge of the table to talk to him. "I make comic books—not, like, Renaissance oil paintings."

"Well just being from somewhere other than here makes you the closest thing Adelbury has had to culture since Ophelia canceled trivia night, so I'll take it."

He frowned. "Why did she cancel trivia night?"

Nareth gave a quick, haughty sniff and folded his arms. "Some people, as it turns out, are poor losers." He glanced sidelong at Ethan and threw him a mischievous smile that turned his insides gelatinous. "Not me, of course. Only because I'm never wrong."

Ethan chuckled on purpose, hoping that was a normal response. "Of course."

The elf watched him for a moment, then tilted his head toward him with a soft, pensive hum. "Have you been given the grand tour of the town yet? Not that there's all that much to see here, but...I could be persuaded to show you an entertaining evening."

The low, almost purring timbre of his voice shot through Ethan like a nail gun to the chest. He kept his eyes anywhere except Nareth's patiently waiting face, trying to force an answer out of his throat. This town was going to be the death of him. He opened his mouth once, then twice, hoping to make some sound and failing. Was he trying to say no? Why would he be trying to say no?

"I'm asking you on a date," Nareth added, his long ears twitching upward just faintly as he took up the plush Molang keychain attached to Ethan's bag and turned it idly in his fingers. "In case that isn't clear."

An embarrassingly loud laugh exploded out of Ethan before he could stop it. "Uh, yeah, I—thank you," he stammered. "A *date* is—my car is at the shop, so I'll need to—you know, later—"

"Goodness," the elf chuckled, "but you're all atwitter, aren't you?" He leaned one hand flat on the table and reached for Ethan with the other, stilling him instantly with one grey knuckle under his chin. "I'm through here at four. When you're done leeching, meet me at the Crystal Lantern Pub, across from Ophelia's. We'll have a drink, see the sights...and I'll take you to get your car in the morning," he finished with soft promise.

Ethan was going to pass out. He was barely breathing, but he nodded, and Nareth retreated from him with a smirk on his lips, returning to his desk across the room as if nothing had happened. Ethan sat motionless for a few awkward seconds, then began to scramble, stuffing his tablet and earbuds back into his bag and slinging it over his shoulder while he was already walking.

"I'll see you this evening, Ethan," Nareth called as he reached the door, and Ethan offered him a half smile and another weird, forced chuckle, and hit himself with the door before he made it out onto the sidewalk.

He was *such* a loser.

Ethan was now out a place to sit and work that had WiFi access—at least for the rest of the day. Not that he thought he'd be able to face Nareth after whatever was going to happen that evening, either.

He slowed to a stop on the sidewalk and pressed his bag tight to his face to muffle his private scream. He was going on a date? With that person? With that English-accented, tousle-haired, jewelry-wearing librarian who looked like he'd stepped out of a catalog? It must have been because Ethan was new. New people seemed to be rare in this town, so he was probably just looking for someone new to...

To what?

I'll take you to get your car in the morning.

Oh, god. Ethan's fingers curled into the bag against his face. Oh, help.

"Ethan!"

He dropped his bag as he jumped, and he whipped around toward the voice to see Carlos in the street, wearing a pale blue, short-sleeved button-down with a US Postal Service patch right above the chest pocket. The drawstring of his dark blue sun hat was pulled up snug against his chin, tensing with his grin. A heavy canvas saddlebag was strapped just behind his forelegs, and he held a padded envelope in both hands.

"Sorry," he said with a small laugh. "I didn't mean to startle you. Are you exploring?"

"Sort of, I guess." Ethan let out a long breath and settled his bag on his shoulder again. "I took my car in, and I was working at the library for a while, but uh...I had to go."

The centaur frowned and moved a step closer to him. "Was Nareth rude to you? He can be really rude."

"No no," Ethan promised. "He was—not rude." He scratched at the hair at the back of his neck. "He sort of...asked me out?"

Carlos visibly perked up, eyebrows disappearing beneath his curls, and then his shoulders lowered into a conspiratorial hunch, and he held his parcel close to his chest as he leaned in. "Did you say yes? I mean, are you—not that it matters, I just didn't know, you know—"

"Am I gay?" Ethan laughed as his hand dropped back to his side. "Yeah. I...figured it's usually obvious," he added with a small shrug.

"Well I don't like to make assumptions. People can look like anything and still be themselves, can't they?" Carlos smiled. "Anyway, that's great! Nareth is...nice."

"Didn't you just say he can be really rude?"

He fidgeted briefly, front hooves clicking on the asphalt. "Well, about the library. I just...well, I try not to judge anybody. It's none of my business. I'm sure he'll be nice to you, since he asked you out."

"That's not super encouraging, Carlos."

"I'm sorry!" he laughed. "I don't mean to gossip. Nareth isn't a bad person or anything. I'm sure you'll have fun!" He looked down at the envelope in his hands as if he'd just remembered it. "I ought to go. I don't want to get behind. Oh! I'll come over tonight and replace that kitchen faucet; I got one of those nice ones that you can pull it down on a hose and there's a button and it sprays and stuff."

"Do you happen to have a showerhead for upstairs, too?"

Carlos stared at him blankly for a moment, and then his expression fell, his eyebrows knitting into deep concern. "Oh my gosh, Ethan, I'm so sorry! I took it off to clean it and—oh, I'll bring it back tonight too! I'm sorry!"

Ethan waved him away with a smile. "It's fine. Really."

"Tonight, I promise!" He started to turn away, then stopped again. "Oh—if you're...going to be home tonight? I have to give you twenty-four hours notice if I'm going to go in when you're not there, and you just said you have a date, so—"

"It's totally fine," Ethan cut him off, laughing softly. "You're already the most considerate landlord I've ever had. And I don't plan to be out all night."

"Oh! Sure. Of course. I'll see you later then!" Carlos gave him a wave and one last bright smile before turning away, his long black tail swishing idly as he continued down the street.

Ethan stood for a minute once Carlos turned the corner, looking up and down the street. He couldn't go too far without his car, and if he tried to sit in the diner to work, Ophelia would definitely want to talk with him—and after last night, he already knew her well enough to guess that would mean zero work done. It would have been nice if there was an actual coffee shop or something—anything with a little anonymity, where he could have just disappeared into a corner and been ignored.

But that was city thinking, wasn't it? In a town like this, everybody knew everybody—so everywhere you went, you were with people you knew. That was comforting in a different way. At least, it probably would be to someone who was actually from here. Carlos seemed to be among friends no matter where he was. For Ethan, it was a little harder to adjust.

He wandered for a little while without any destination in mind, and before long, he found a small park—just a grassy field with a gazebo and an aging, abandoned playground. He settled himself on a bench and propped his tablet on his knee to do a bit more sketching. Fat squirrels seemed to have taken control of the vicinity, and they weren't shy about approaching him. One even put its little hands on his shoulder as it perched on the back of his bench. They must have been used to people feeding them. He wished he had something to give them. Without any offerings, they soon distracted themselves by chasing off the few plump little mothbirds encroaching on their seed-hunting territory.

At the edge of the treeline, he even spotted a pretty maitake doe, her soft, green moss-covered body peeling at the shoulders and haunches into fans of yellow-brown fungus, and he managed to get a decent picture of her before she ambled away into the woods.

His phone vibrated in his hands while he was trying to zoom in on the picture, and a text notification dropped down from the top of his screen.

Are you full of inspiration yet? Ready to come home?

He smiled. Maya had thrown a fit when he'd told her he was leaving. They'd been best friends ever since they met in the 9th grade, so leaving her had been hard for him too—but he felt already it had been the right thing to do. He'd been going to the same cafes, getting the same takeout, and seeing the same people for years. How was he supposed to tell new and interesting stories if nothing about his own life was ever new or interesting?

Not quite yet, he typed back. *But I got a date.*

The answer came immediately. *Shut up. With Farmer Joe?*

His name's Nareth. He's the librarian. A dark elf.

Sounds hot. Are you gonna be okay? Is he hot?

Yes and yes.

So one of those is a lie because if he's hot, you're not gonna be okay.

Excuse you, Ethan typed back with a frown. *I am a grown adult person with grown adult functionality.*

Sure sure. Hey, so what color are his lips?

What? Normal? Why?

Because a guy's lips are the same color as the head of his dick.

Ethan choked on his own spit and almost dropped his phone while he coughed. He stared at the words for a long while before he was able to form a response.

That's not true.

It is so! It's true for you.

Ethan paused with a frown on his face. Was it? He knew Maya had gotten a look at him once at a college party when she helped hold him up to pee behind someone's house—she'd teased him about it for weeks—but he didn't expect she'd been paying enough attention in the dark to remember the *color.* With a disbelieving furrow in his brow, Ethan turned on his front-facing camera and stared at himself.

Holy shit, he typed back a second later. *It is. Why would you tell me that? Now that's all I'm going to be able to think about!*

Uh, that's why. Send me a creeper shot of him when you get a chance.

No promises.

They shot back and forth at each other for a while longer about some of the townsfolk Ethan had met, how ridiculously folksy everything seemed, and some ideas he was mulling over for his next project—he sent her the photo he'd taken of the library—until he realized it was almost four. He shoved everything back into his bag and jogged back toward Main Street, slowing as soon as he spotted a wide, dark window with the name "Crystal Lantern" painted in swirling white script on the glass.

Okay. Ethan drew in a steeling breath and let it out slowly. A date. Just a date. A normal date. A normal date like normal people go on. This was good. Definitely good.

He gripped the strap of his bag in both hands and stood facing the door, trying to will himself to go inside. He had almost managed to hype himself up enough to put a hand on the door when something tapped his shoulder, and he yelped and spun on his heel.

"I like a man who's punctual," Nareth said with a smile as Ethan focused on him. "Come on." He opened the door and held it until Ethan moved, and together they stepped into a warm-looking room, all dark wood and brass. Polished lanterns hung from the ceiling, bathing the room in soft purple and pink light that washed over the heavy wood tables and chairs. Nareth led the way to the bar and took a seat on one of the leather-cushioned stools, so Ethan took the one beside him, a few seats down from a human woman and a man drinking from a glass of suspiciously thick red liquid.

The man behind the bar smiled as he approached them, already laying out a pair of napkins for them. He was slim and blond and exceptionally pretty—soft features, glittering rich blue eyes, and a single mole at the corner of his eye. The soft flutter of flecked brown wings at his back caught Ethan's eye.

"You're a new face," he said cheerfully. "We don't get many of those. But I see Nareth sniffed you out right away, as usual."

"I don't appreciate your tone," the elf said dryly as he leaned one elbow on the bar. "Ethan, this is Piri, who is much prettier on the outside than he is inside."

"Love you too, sweetie," the fairy answered. "But you're Ethan? You met my sister yesterday. Tia?"

As soon as he'd said it, Ethan saw it. The same white-blond hair and perfect face, and the same bright smile. "Oh—yeah, I did. Tell her thank you again for the preserves."

"Sure will." He set a lowball glass in front of Nareth and poured gin and dark juice over a bit of ice without even being asked. "What can I get for you, Ethan?"

"Oh, just a—scotch and soda, please."

"Mm, classic. Manly. I like it."

"Wait your turn," Nareth muttered with a teasing smirk, lifting the glass to his lips, and Piri tutted at him.

The fairy turned back to the shelf to choose a bottle, revealing softly textured brown wings flocked with grey, outlined in a pale cream and marked with a pair of black-ringed eye spots. Another moth, of course. They were beautiful. Maybe Piri would let him take a picture.

"I'll give you the good stuff, since Nareth's paying," the fairy said with a wink as he set down a glass for Ethan and began to pour.

Ethan whipped around to look at Nareth. "Oh you—you really don't have to—"

"I invited you," the elf said simply. "It's only polite."

As soon as Piri finished topping off the glass with soda, he excused himself to the far end of the bar with one final flick of his eyes over Ethan's awkwardly hunched body on the stool.

Ethan scooped up his glass and took a large gulp, hoping the liquor would calm his nerves. Nareth didn't speak for a while, seeming content to give Ethan the time he needed to settle, and when he did, it was with a smile. He asked about Ethan's books and listened with more than polite interest while he explained them; he recommended some middle grade novels he'd come across that sounded like the same sort of adventure-whimsy Ethan was looking for and promised to put them on hold for him. They talked about their favorite books—Nareth preferred true crime or thrillers, while Ethan was more interested in fantasy and science fiction.

The elf didn't seem so intimidating like this. He was just a person, sat beside Ethan in a dimly lit bar, having a drink and a normal conversation—but sometimes the curl of his dark lips or the look in his eyes when his gaze wandered gave Ethan a nervous shiver.

His phone buzzed in his pocket—and when he checked the screen, he found a text from an unknown number.

This is Luke at Damox Automotive. Your car's ready.

Ethan hesitated. If he left now, Nareth would definitely think Ethan was ditching him. And...he didn't particularly want to go. So he typed out a quick reply. *Is it okay if I pick it up in the morning?*

The only response was a thumbs up emoji, so Ethan pushed his phone back into his jeans pocket.

When they'd finished their drinks, Nareth paid their tab despite Ethan's protest, and they moved onto the street. Nareth hooked his arm into Ethan's while they walked, and he pointed out some of the more interesting things downtown had to offer—a secondhand and vintage store, a farmer's market, a little candy shop. They wandered for a few minutes in the secondhand store, which was helpfully marked with "Cursed" and "Guaranteed Non-Magical" sections, but nothing caught Ethan's eye. The large front window of the candy shop did, however, and Nareth followed as Ethan rushed inside. They were welcomed by a pair of women, one with red skin and horns curling from her temples, the other with shimmering pink scales on her cheeks and hands. They each had strong opinions on which candies Ethan would like, and they bickered like birds about it, but Nareth chose for him in the end—a bag of sour hard candies that sparked in your mouth if you bit them. They were surprisingly good, and Ethan promised the women he'd come back.

"Do they always argue like that?" he asked once they were back on the street.

"Do you know a married couple that doesn't?" Nareth answered dryly, and when Ethan frowned, he gently shooed away his worry with a gesture. "Don't feel sorry for them. They're disgustingly in love in private. I think they just enjoy it."

Ethan laughed softly. "I guess so."

Most of the people they passed on the sidewalk seemed to know Nareth, and by the time they reached the end of Main Street, Ethan had been introduced to half a dozen people. But there was one shop Nareth hadn't pointed out—a small wooden door by a window with a dark curtain, and hung above, swinging and creaking under an overhang, was a sign that looked like it was made of wood hacked from a tree by hand. The words "Rocks and Roots" had been drawn crudely in white paint.

"What's this?" Ethan asked, pointing up at the sign, and Nareth's lip curled.

"A catastrophe. We're not going in there."

"Why? What is it?"

"It's an apothecary—ostensibly. Herbs, crystals, healing magic, et cetera. In reality, it's a heap of junk."

Ethan glanced to the painted door, considering. Maya would ask him if there was a decent shop in town—he mostly knew what to look for, having been to at least a dozen different stores with her over the years. He looked back to Nareth. "Can we look anyway?"

The elf gave a long-suffering sigh and gestured vaguely toward the entrance, so Ethan pulled the door open and stepped inside. The interior of the shop was lit entirely by two ceiling fans with bare bulbs and a single string of fairy lights drooping on the wood slat wall above the register, and there didn't seem to be a single flat surface left vacant in the whole place. Glass cabinet counters and shelves made of what looked like driftwood lined the walls, and tables draped with rough-hem cloth filled what little walking space remained. One of the shelves at the back seemed to be made out of half a pickup truck bed. The whole shop was a clutter of baskets, bins, and buckets, filled to the brim with different colors of stone and crystal, bouquets of incense, and piles of bones and antlers, each with an index card taped to it with a price written in marker. Dried and drying herbs hung in clumps from the ceiling, and, in one corner, a whole flank of bright red gumball and candy machines waited for quarters. By the register, a produce scale hung from an iron hook.

Nareth held out a hand toward the disorderly collection, as if it spoke for itself. "Satisfied? We should go, before we have to—"

"Well hey there, Nareth!" a scratchy, Southern-sounding voice called from the back of the store. A tall, lanky elf appeared from behind a dusty curtain, wearing tan work boots, jeans with holes at the knee, and a red flannel button-down with fraying sleeves cut off at the bicep. As he stepped closer, Ethan recognized the typical traits of a sun elf—shining blue eyes, faintly glimmering bronze skin, and pale blond hair. The difference between this sun elf and others Ethan had met was that this one's hair had been cut short at the front and left in a curly, truly luxurious mullet in the back. "Haven't seen you in a dog's age!" He shook Nareth's reluctantly-offered hand with a few energetic pumps, showing a tattoo in black Elvish script on his inner bicep, then turned to Ethan with a bright smile. "Who'd you bring me?"

"Ethan Kwon, Jorendriel Wyndan. *Proprietor,*" Nareth added dryly.

"Call me Joe," the sun elf said, taking Ethan's hand in such a strong, exuberant shake that he wobbled on his feet. "Great to meet you, Ethan. You a new arrival? Just visiting?"

"Long-term visiting," Ethan answered, matching the other man's friendly smile on instinct. "I'm staying at Carlos's?"

"Oh, that's you! All right, all right." Joe put his hands on his hips to give Ethan a proper look. "Well, look, you need anything healed, balmed, charged, uncursed, unlocked, or otherwise unfucked, you bring yourself here, you get me?"

"Uh. Yeah, I think so."

"Tell you what," he went on, barely waiting for Ethan's answer, "I think I know just what you need. Come on over here and get you a little welcome to town present."

"Oh, you really don't have to," Ethan started, but Joe was already heading for the counter, so, with a quick glance back at Nareth, he followed.

Joe ducked under the fold-up door in the counter rather than lifting it and popped up on the other side with a single clap of his hands. "Now," he said, rubbing his palms together, "tell me what ails ya, and I'll get you right lickety-split like."

"I don't really have any ails," Ethan said, and Joe gave a friendly scoff of disbelief.

"Everybody's got ails, young'un. You ain't gotta be shy. Go on now." He leaned one hand on the counter and cupped the other around a long ear.

Ethan stammered for a moment, and Nareth spoke up behind him.

"Just tell him you have a headache so he can shake some deer teeth at you," he said, picking up a leather-bound fan of dark feathers with two fingers.

"Now I heard that, Nareth!" Joe answered back with a solid slap to the wood countertop. He pointed a finger at the other elf, but despite his intensity, there wasn't a trace of actual malice in him. "I done told you before, deer teeth are for stomach troubles; for a headache, you'd need *coyote* teeth." Joe gave a sad tut and shook his head as he returned his attention to Ethan. "Nareth's real good at some things," he said in a conspiratorial half-whisper, "but when it comes to healing treatments, the boy don't know his ass from a hole in the ground."

"Right," Ethan said, fighting a smile, and when he glanced back at Nareth, the dark elf had one white eyebrow sharply arched as he stared at Jo, but he didn't bite back.

A small thump sounded on the floor somewhere behind the counter, and Ethan jumped as a large, brown hare leapt up onto the surface and settled into a long-legged seat, its nose twitching as it stared at Ethan with intense bronze eyes. He paused. Not a hare. Pale pronged antlers grew alongside its tall ears—this was a jackalope.

Ethan took a small step backward. Jackalopes were wild and supposedly dangerous. This one was easily the size of a small dog, its antlers came to sharp points—and it didn't take its fierce, feral gaze from Ethan's face.

"Ah, don't mind him," Joe said. He drew a small glass bowl from the other side of the register and took a bottle of whisky from beneath the counter, sloshing a pool of amber liquid into the bowl. The jackalope hunkered down on its slim front legs and lapped rapidly at the alcohol while Joe stroked him, its muzzle quivering with the movement.

"He's...yours?" Ethan asked, and Joe grinned as he bent to put away the bottle.

"We been pals for years now." The elf leaned in closer with a teasing look in his eye. "Guess what his name is."

"Uh—"

"Jack!" Joe and Nareth said together, one with exuberance and the other with deep exhaustion. "Because he's a *Jack*alope, you get it?" Joe went on, barking out a laugh at his own cleverness. He gave the animal a quick scratch on the nape as it finished its serving of whisky, then scooped it up under the armpits like a cat and deposited it back on the floor.

"I get it," Ethan said with a nod and a slightly forced smile.

"Now I think I can see what your problem is, friend," Joe started again, undeterred. "You tell me if I'm wrong, but I got an eye for these things, you know. And I think you need to loosen up a little. Got a bit of the whatsit, don't ya—the anxiety."

"Uh—"

"Now that's all right; you don't have to talk about it if you don't want. I've got just the thing." Joe went back behind the hanging curtains and returned after a few seconds of clinking glass. He gently thunked a mason jar onto the counter, its label just an askew white sticker with "Brain" written on it in Sharpie. It was three-quarters full of a clear liquid. Joe stood for a moment as if waiting for his customer to be impressed, but Ethan just glanced uncertainly between the jar and the sun elf's smiling face.

"What...is it?"

"It's moonshine," Nareth answered for him, stepping back to the counter to peer down his nose at the jar.

"Of course it's moonshine!" Joe said with a laugh. "Treated special to aid in the remedy of all manner of anxieties, depressions, distractions, manias, and maladaptive coping methods. It'll help you feel less stressed."

"*All* moonshine does that," Nareth pointed out. "That's what alcohol does."

"Don't listen to him," Joe said, waving the dark elf away. "You take that for free this time, and you'll see. Joe knows how to get you right."

"Thanks," Ethan said before Nareth could snipe again, and he checked the lid on the jar before nestling it carefully in his messenger bag. "I'll let you know how it goes."

"Well I guarantee all my work, so if it's not to your satisfaction, you just tell ol' Joe, and I'll make it right for ya."

"I appreciate it, Joe. It was nice to meet you," Ethan added, trying to inch his way toward the door. Nareth already had a hand on it, ready to push it open, and as soon as Ethan took a step, he was out. Joe's friendly goodbye followed Ethan out onto the sidewalk, and once the door had swung shut, Ethan let out a small laugh.

"I told you," Nareth said, dusting the sleeve of his shirt as if to brush away any trace of the shop.

"He seemed nice," Ethan offered, and Nareth snorted.

"Yes, he's *nice*. He's just an idiot." Nareth looped his arm through Ethan's again, which drew their bodies alarmingly close. "Now, I think we've about exhausted Adelbury's bustling shopping district," he said. "How about dinner?"

"Oh. Sure? Isn't the diner just—"

"No, no," the elf interrupted, tutting softly at him. "Come back to my place, and I'll make sure you're well fed."

Ethan's whole body went rigid, as if someone had stuck a broomstick up the back of his shirt. "Uh. Your place? The place...where you live."

"This shyness is going to undo me," Nareth murmurs. He fingered the collar of Ethan's shirt and flattened his hand gently against his chest. "You don't find me attractive, Ethan?" he asked with a slight tilt of his head, his pendant earrings catching the light from the lamppost overhead.

"Oh," Ethan said again, way too loudly, his cheeks burning with heat. "Yeah I really do and that's uh—that's the problem here. Sorry."

"Adorable," Nareth chuckles. "But I'm in no rush. Ophelia's for now. We'll see about satiating your other desires later on, hm?"

"Yes that—that sounds good. Yes."

The elf smiled at him, and they crossed the street to the diner. Ophelia wasn't subtle about keeping an eye on them the entire time, like she expected Ethan to be abducted. What sort of reputation did Nareth have around here, anyway? He seemed quite friendly with Zoe, at least. And now that the conversation was on something other than being invited over for sex, Ethan was able to relax—a little bit, anyway. Nareth had such a calm, easy demeanor that it was hard to stay too worked up around him. He even paid for dinner, though Ethan offered.

He didn't bring up coming back to his own place again; when they left the diner, he walked Ethan back to his car at the library—a sleek silver Lexus—and drove him back to the farmhouse. Ethan was grateful, but by the time Nareth was pulling into the yard, his stomach was in knots again. The porch light flickered on as Nareth pulled in close enough to set off the sensor and put the car into park.

"Do you feel as though you've had the complete Adelbury experience?" the elf asked, leaning an elbow on the center console to smile at him.

Ethan chuckled. "Maybe not quite, but I'm getting there. Thanks for...taking me out."

Nareth's voice dropped into the soft, low tone that punctured Ethan's chest. "Thinking of one thing more you've yet to experience?" He reached out and brushed his fingertips over Ethan's cheek, urging him a little closer, and when he subtly tilted his head, Ethan responded automatically, allowing himself to be drawn into a kiss. Nareth's slender fingers pushed into the hair behind Ethan's ear, and he kissed him softly but eagerly. A sound caught in Ethan's throat as the elf's tongue brushed over his lips and entered his mouth. He gripped the bag in his lap tighter against him.

It was a good kiss. A really good kiss. Nareth teased him gently, toying with the hair at the back of his head. Ethan's breath quickened, his whole brain overwhelmed by the elf's mouth on his own, and when they broke apart after what felt like an eternity, he took a slow, deep breath and forced his hands to unlatch from his bag.

A few long beats of silence passed, and Ethan hesitated with Nareth's eyes on him and his hand still lightly on his jaw. He was clearly waiting to be invited in. He was expecting to be invited in. They were both adults, and they'd just had a fun date—it would have been normal to invite him. Ethan had met plenty of people in the city who had no problem sleeping with someone on the first date—or just sleeping with someone without even doing the date part. Nareth was clearly one of them, but Ethan never had been.

So he unbuckled his seatbelt, held tight to his bag, and opened the door. "I'm sure I'll see you tomorrow when I need the WiFi," he said, already one foot on the ground. He got all the way out of the car and had a hand on the door to close it when Nareth called his name.

"Have a good night," he said with a smile, and Ethan returned it, relief flooding his chest. He wasn't mad.

"You too," Ethan answered softly. He shut the door and backed away, watching the low car lurch its way out of the yard and down the long drive for a few seconds before turning to go up the porch steps.

Carlos was in the kitchen when Ethan stepped inside, a proud, beaming smile on his face—shirt soaked, but kitchen faucet attached. He leaned a little as Ethan came in, peering around him as if he thought there might have been someone behind him, but he relaxed as the elf's tail lights disappeared from the lane.

"Did you guys have fun? Are you going to go out again?"

"Maybe?" Ethan shrugs. "It was fun."

The centaur's expression softened. "Good. Anyway, the showerhead is back on upstairs, and this is done!" He turned the faucet on with a flourish and let it run for a few seconds, then turned it off again, smiling. "I'll get out of your hair. Night, Ethan," he added on his way past him to the door.

"Thanks, Carlos. Good night."

Ethan locked the door behind him, undressed on his way upstairs, and rolled into bed. The stairs in this place were pretty narrow—how had Carlos gotten up here?

But more importantly, how was he supposed to be brave enough to set foot in the library again tomorrow, knowing Nareth would be there waiting for him?

3

Ethan forced himself out of bed at a reasonable hour the next morning, hoping to catch Carlos before he left to start his route. It was way too early for Ethan to be up under normal circumstances; even after he'd gone to bed, he'd stayed up looking at his phone for another two hours, at least. He rubbed at his eyes with the ball of one hand while he knocked on Carlos's large barn door with the other. It opened almost immediately, and the centaur smiled at him. He was already wearing his uniform.

"Ethan! Good morning!"

"Hey," he began with a sleepy smile, "sorry to bother you, but I need to get into town, and I don't know if, like, rideshares don't exist here or what, but I haven't seen any—"

"Oh, yeah, I don't think anybody does that here. Somebody should!" He paused. "Oh—you need to go get your car, right? I'm going to work in just a little bit; do you want a ride?"

"I don't want to impose, I just thought you might know—"

"No no! It's no trouble! You hardly weigh anything anyway, and I like the company." He smiled and took a step back from the door. "You want to come in? I'll just be a minute."

"Thanks," Ethan answered as he moved inside. "You've really been way above and beyond any landlord duties."

Carlos shut the door behind him and headed deeper into the house and over to the kitchen counter. Ethan stayed close to the entryway, not wanting to intrude any more than he already was. He'd never been inside a centaur's house before. The floor was made of the same sturdy, semi-padded material as a gym or a garage—good for hooves. The whole place was very open; there were only a couple of interior walls, which he guessed hid the bathroom. Having more doorways must have just been a pain when you were built like a centaur. Even the long cushion and padded recliner that served as a centaur bed was just tucked somewhere near the far corner of the house next to a freestanding wardrobe. Something that looked vaguely like a sofa sat in front of a large television hung on the wall, but it was folded down into a weird configuration—presumably comfortable for someone who was half horse. Even the kitchen counters were adjusted. They looked normal when Carlos stood beside them, but they came all the way up to Ethan's chest.

"Well," Carlos said as he rinsed a glass in the sink, "I hope we can be friends, too. I don't think a person can ever have too many friends, especially in a new place. Don't you think?" He set the glass down on a towel laid out near the sink and turned toward Ethan and the door with a smile. He took up his sun hat from its little hook on the wall and dropped it onto his head, the ends of his black curls sticking out at his temples.

Ethan smiled. "Yeah. I think so too."

The ride into town didn't feel awkward now. Ethan just held onto the centaur's waist so he didn't have to reach behind him, and Carlos complimented him on the steadiness of his leg grip. That was a little weird—but at least they weren't holding hands.

When they approached the auto shop, two green-skinned figures standing outside the office door turned to look at them. One was Luke, and the other was an even broader orc with a noticeable belly under his coveralls and a cigarette hanging out of one side of his mouth. That must have been Rob.

Carlos waved and called a cheery hello to them, which the older one returned. Luke only gave him a nod of acknowledgment.

"You offering a shuttle service now, Carlos?" the elder orc said as Carlos twisted to give Ethan a hand down to the ground, and the centaur laughed.

"Centaur-based ridesharing?"

"We'll get you a sticker for your ass," Rob said with a grin, taking the cigarette from his mouth with his thumb and forefinger. "Who's this?"

"This is Ethan! He just moved into my house."

"Uh, the adjacent house," Ethan clarified, straightening his bag on his shoulder once he found his feet. "Not, like, roommates."

"He's the serpentine belt from yesterday," Luke said, already pulling open the office door and tilting his head toward Ethan to get him to follow. He let the door go once Ethan had a hand on it and circled the counter. He took a clipboard with Ethan's key hung on it from the rack behind the desk and dropped it with a sharp clack, then turned to wake up the ancient-looking computer. The wired mouse looked tiny under his hand.

Ethan jumped as a small, pink, four-legged animal with a long, thickly-scaled body and a narrow snout leapt up onto the counter, its toothy mouth opening to let out a small hissing screech.

"Down, Manny," Luke said, gently shooing the creature away. It gave another soft shriek, so he scooped it up under the belly and let it down onto the floor with one hand. "Sorry about him."

Ethan frowned, leaning over the counter a little to watch the animal scurry into a back room. "What is he?"

"He's a cincin. They eat oil, so they're good to have around. Spoiled, though."

"He's cute," Ethan offered, but Luke's attention was on the screen again. So he waited, peeking back and forth between the countertop and Luke's face. Luke's lips were a dark, subtly pink-tinted green. That must be what color his—

Ethan blanched and made a short, wet gurgling sound as he tried to strangle his own brain into submission. "So, uh, thanks for letting me leave it here overnight," he said, very loudly in the small office.

"No problem. I'm glad it wasn't stolen, since I left the keys in the ignition all night."

Ethan blinked and stared at him. "...What?"

Luke flicked his pale gaze over to him, stone-faced. His yellow eyes seemed to bore through Ethan's skull, but he still couldn't stop looking at one stupid, perfect little black curl brushing the orc's forehead.

"It's a hundred."

"Uh. Yeah. Yeah." Ethan fumbled his card out of his wallet and handed it over. He waited awkwardly while the computer did its work, then held out both hands like a child so Luke could drop his keys and card into them. "Thank you," he said too quickly, not even trying to put his card away before leaving. He pushed the door open and bumped into it in his hurry to escape the office.

"All good?" Carlos asked, and Ethan held up his key with a nod. "Great! I've got to get to work; I'll see you later, okay? Oh—the Internet guy said he'd come on Friday!"

"Okay. Thanks again for the ride."

"Anytime!" He offered a wave and trotted away down the sidewalk, calling a goodbye to Rob and Luke as well.

Ethan headed for his car, managing to fight the urge to look back over his shoulder at Luke, but when he dropped into the driver's seat, he was facing him anyway—and the orc was looking right at him. Ethan tried his very best to smile like a normal person, briefly lifted his hand in a wave, and pulled out of the little lot to head downtown.

Why couldn't he just be normal? Had Luke been teasing him? That hadn't looked like a teasing face. But he was also clearly lying?

Ethan sighed. Luke was too big and too hot to be playing games like that. It was bad for Ethan's heart.

He found a place to park not far from the library and walked up the path to the door, but then he paused mid-reach to the handle. Nareth was in there. Ethan didn't really *need* WiFi anyway, did he? The park was nice. Then he wouldn't have to sit next to the elf again and make a fool of himself. He'd already done that once today.

He frowned at the door. What was he doing, anyway? He had a good night with Nareth. He had an *excellent* kiss with him. Now he was going to get to hang out with him again. These were good things, Ethan. This was a good outcome. So open the door.

Open the door, Ethan. Just—just open the door. Click the thing, and pull the door. You're just standing there, Ethan. He definitely already saw you walk up, Ethan. Just—pull the door. Jesus Christ.

He whipped the door open so fast that Nareth startled at his desk, looking up at Ethan with raised eyebrows as he stood dramatically in the open door.

"Good morning—"

"Good morning!" Ethan yelled over him halfway through his greeting as he tugged the door shut behind him. He stalked past the desk in a hurry and dropped down into the same seat as yesterday, and he pulled out his tablet and earbuds with laser focus, but when he glanced up at the desk, he found Nareth watching him with an amused smile, his chin resting lightly on the back of his knuckles.

"You seem distressed."

"I'm fine," Ethan promised, "sorry; I'm just..."

"I hope I didn't do anything to upset you last night."

"No!" Ethan dropped his tablet onto the table and scrambled to pick it up again. "It was great. Really! I'm just—fucking awkward. Sorry."

The elf chuckled and rose from his seat to circle the long table, fingertips trailing on the slick surface as he drew closer to Ethan's chair. He had on a dark blue shirt today, the top buttons undone as before, and his white hair fell across his forehead as he leaned his weight on one hand and bent down close to Ethan, seeming to draw joy from the way he tensed up under the heated gaze.

"Maybe tonight you'll let me cook for you," he said. "We could put on a film, just the two of us." He reached up and brushed a light touch behind Ethan's ear and down his neck, bringing up goosebumps on his skin. "We'll pick one you've seen before."

Oh Jesus. Ethan looked up over his glasses at him and tried to swallow the lump in his throat. He really wasn't shy, was he? Ethan wasn't a *complete* idiot—if he agreed to go to this man's house and watch a movie, Nareth was going to expect sex. With Ethan. For some reason, that seemed to be something he wanted.

He must have stared a little too long without answering, because Nareth moved to lightly grip Ethan's chin and tilt him up perilously close to a kiss.

"Or I could just lock the door now."

Ethan's whole body jerked backward in a panic, and he leaned so far back in his scramble that Nareth had to grab the arm of his chair to keep him from toppling over. Ethan grabbed for the table to steady himself and caught the strap of his bag instead, sending his sketchbook and bag of markers tumbling onto the floor.

"Oh, geez," Ethan said in what he refused to call a whimper as he scooted his chair back. "Oh geez. I'm sorry." He dropped down to his knees to start gathering up his things, and Nareth crouched down beside him, holding out one of the escaped markers. When Ethan tried to take it from him, he held it fast.

"This is a library, Mr. Kwon," he said with a sly smile. "I'm going to have to ask you to settle down."

Ethan froze, locked in his eyes in a moment of heavy silence—and the next thing he knew, he was sitting on the table with Nareth's hands on either side of his hips and his lips on his own, the elf's dark shirt gripped tight in Ethan's fingers between them. Nareth pressed close to him, flattening a hand against the small of his back and placing himself brazenly between Ethan's thighs.

This was a lot. It was a lot a lot. Ethan just met this person yesterday. His stomach was in knots, and his heart hammered painfully against his ribs. But Nareth was a *very* good kisser.

When the elf's hand slipped under the bottom hem of Ethan's shirt, he jumped, and he pulled back to break the kiss and put a little distance between them.

"So skittish," Nareth chuckled, and he leaned in, casually licking a long, slow line up the side of Ethan's neck to his earlobe, making him almost levitate off the table in alarm. "It's not your first time, is it?"

"No," Ethan blurted out, sounding a lot more defensive than he intended. "I'm—" His face scrunched in shame as he spoke. "I'm just always like this."

Nareth mercifully pulled back and stroked Ethan's cheek gently with his thumb. "Poor dear. How can I put you at ease?"

"We're—in the *library*," Ethan reminded him, and the elf paused, glancing over at the door as if he'd forgotten he was at work.

"It would be just my luck for someone to come in. You're right," he said with a soft, resigned frown, and he backed up to let Ethan down from the table. "I'll behave myself. Try not to be so adorable while you're working today," he added on his way back to his desk.

Ethan didn't get a lot done for the rest of the morning with the elf so close to him, no matter what he said. Nareth didn't pay him any unusual attention; he busied himself with scanning a stack of returned books, which flapped themselves away as if their covers were wings as soon as he released them, floating like lazy butterflies back to their places on the shelves. A handful of town residents came and went, dropping off books or picking up ones Nareth had laid aside for them, and a pair of teenagers lingered at the shelf on the mezzanine for a while. They looked like dryads—both young women with brown skin and leafy, vinelike hair chatted quietly between themselves while they browsed the shelves.

Ethan tried to focus on his own business, but he was distracted by the near constant eyeballing Nareth was giving the two young patrons. It was hardly subtle, in a building this size. They noticed, too—they whispered to each other while they flipped through books, one of them flipping a few locks of green over her shoulder while she peered back at the librarian. It was starting to get a little weird, actually.

After a few minutes, they tucked their chosen books into their elbows to carry them down the steps, but when the girl at the back pushed the others they'd examined onto the shelf, Nareth's hands hit the desk, and he stood, leaning both palms on it to glare up to the mezzanine.

"Maris Aylward," he said in a calm, steady voice, "if you don't bring those here to be put back properly, I'll tell your father where you really are on Saturday evenings when he thinks you're here."

"Oh my god, Nareth," the girl groaned, already turning back to snatch the books back from the shelf. "What do you care? If they're on the shelf, what does it matter?"

"What's that?" Nareth lifted a hand to touch one of his sharp ears. "You want me to stop ordering new volumes of *Shooting Star Love Story* as they come out?"

Maris stood up straight and leaned over the railing to narrow green eyes at him. "Don't play with me."

"Or maybe you wanted to know what happens at the end of that *Summerkeep* novel in your hand?"

"Fine!" she insisted with a huff, gathering the books in her arms. She dumped them unceremoniously into the bin beside Nareth's desk, and by the time she came to face him, Nareth was blithely sitting with one elbow propped on his desk and hand extended.

The first girl placed a library card from her pocket into his hand, and then her book, and the other followed suit.

"Three weeks," he reminded them, giving the girl called Maris a sly smile as she turned from his desk and followed her friend out.

Ethan stayed quiet for a few seconds after the girls left, then took out one of his silent earbuds. "Weren't you just—using magic to sort the books anyway?"

Nareth gave a curious hum as he looked up, as if he didn't understand the question. "Well it isn't about being precious. Keeping track of what's been pulled is part of good library record-keeping, which she well knows."

"And you really cover for her sneaking around like that?"

"It's hardly covering for her if her father never *asks* me. I'm merely aware of her lie."

"I...guess," Ethan agreed.

"Don't be so wholesome at me, Ethan. You wanted to be left alone, didn't you?"

Ethan's cheeks warmed, and he stuffed his earbud back in and hunkered down into his seat to return to his sketch, but it wasn't much use. None of the ideas that ran through his head seemed worth pursuing, anyway. Maybe this was just it for him. He'd had two reasonably successful books, and now maybe his well was dry forever. He could get a job at McDonald's, maybe. Starbucks. He could move in with Maya once his bank account was empty and live under her sink.

4

When Ethan left around lunchtime, Nareth promised to text him that evening. Ethan smiled at him on his way out, but he didn't think he could take the anxiety of another date right away.

He went shopping for a few groceries before heading back home, hoping that getting away from Nareth would help to clear his head a little. The store wasn't as big as the ones he was used to—in the city, groceries had to cater to innumerable different types of people, and their diets were just as varied. Ethan had seen a wide variety of people in Adelbury, too, and there were still sections for specialized foods— just not quite as many. Ethan wondered if a new sort of person moving into town sent the whole grocery store into upheaval.

When Ethan got home, a tall box was sitting on his porch, and before he could even get his front door open, Carlos had appeared behind him. They spent the next couple of hours installing the range hood Carlos had brought. Carlos did most of the work—he was actually really handy. Ethan was able to follow instructions, at least, and he could help reach the top of the hood with one bare foot on his kitchen counter and the other on Carlos's back. They got it done in the end, and Ethan celebrated by cooking one of the frozen pizza's he'd bought.

Carlos was chatty while they ate, of course; he asked about Ethan's new sketches and said that he liked to paint but was awful at it. He liked to go to the diner when Ophelia hosted her occasional painting tutorial nights. He showed Ethan a picture he'd taken of his latest painting—it was supposed to be a lion but definitely looked more like a cow—and they laughed until Ethan's sides hurt.

Nareth texted, as promised, to ask him to dinner, but Ethan feigned illness and apologized. He shouldn't lie. Nareth hadn't done anything wrong. Ethan had been the weird one, here.

After Carlos said good night, Ethan stayed up and unpacked a little—at least enough to make the spare room that would be his office usable. He laid out his pencils and markers, turned on some music, and curled up in the desk chair with his sketchbook. He sketched out some things from around town to get warmed up—the lanterns in Piri's bar, Rob with his cigarette, the deer he saw in the park. He drew Nareth sitting at his desk, delicately supporting his chin in his hand, but when it was time to draw his expression, Ethan faltered. He'd spent too much time under that sultry gaze already—he couldn't bear to put those eyes on paper.

Why was he so enamored with Ethan, anyway? Was it just for sex? But he seemed kind, and nice to talk to, and while he was clearly...*interested* in sleeping with Ethan, he hadn't pushed. He was stupid pretty; he seemed smart; he had a stable job that he was knowledgeable about. He ticked a lot of positive boxes. So, looking at the checklist, it made sense for Ethan to go for it, right?

But if he ticked so many positive boxes, what could he possibly see in Ethan?

He put down his pencil and rubbed at his eyes. This wasn't working, either.

Downtown was pretty abandoned at night. The yellow street lights made a sheen on the asphalt after the evening's light rain, and most of the shops were closed. But the lights in the glass front of the diner were still on, and the neon "Open" sign was still lit, even this late at night. There must have been more than just Ophelia and her daughter running the restaurant—when did they rest? But when Ethan parked along the street in front of the door, there Ophelia was, right behind the counter, wiping her hands on a towel as she talked with the only other customer in the place.

Luke, looking too big for the booth he slouched in, one leg stretched out from underneath the table and his phone propped up in one hand.

A cord trailed up to his ear, but he'd turned his head to answer Ophelia. His other hand was loosely cupped around a mug, and an empty plate and fork sat at the edge of the table. He looked quiet and calm—and a little lonely. He looked up briefly when the bell above the door signaled Ethan's entrance, but then he dropped his eyes back to his phone again.

"Ethan!" Ophelia called with a smile. "Couldn't keep away, huh?"

"I didn't expect you to be open this late," he answered as he took a seat at the counter, trying not to be too obvious about glancing back at Luke.

"Oh, we're open all hours. I'm here whenever someone needs something to fill their belly or warm them up." She folded the towel and laid it aside on the bar. "What is it you need, sweetheart?"

"Can I just have some coffee, please?"

"Of course." She chose a thick yellow mug from under the counter and set it in front of him to fill from a steaming pot, then scooted over a ceramic container of sugar packets and a bowl of single-serving creamers. "You know," she said after he thanked her, "I don't want to twist your arm, but Luke over there left me *one* single piece of apple pie with no one to eat it. I'd hate to throw it out."

Ethan smiled as he tore the tops from a couple packets of sugar and cream. "I'm ready to do my part."

The satyr winked at him with a smile, and a moment later, he had his own plate and fork.

The pie was impossibly good, of course, and the coffee seemed to warm him from the bones outwards. Maybe she used some kind of magic to make everything so delicious—but of course it would be rude to ask. She left him to enjoy it on his own, her quiet humming fading as she began sweeping the floor in the kitchen.

Ethan peeked over his shoulder as he heard the soft thunk of Luke's mug on the table behind him. He was out of his mechanic's uniform; he was wearing dark jeans, his heavy boots, and a black hoodie with a logo on it that Ethan didn't recognize—the white outline of a fox head surrounded by nine tails.

The orc glanced up and locked eyes with him, so Ethan whipped back around, staring down at his half empty mug with great purpose.

Luke's quiet voice drifted across the diner, barely outdoing the drone of the fluorescent lights. "They don't have orcs where you come

46

from?"

"What?" Ethan craned his neck to look at him as much as he could without actually turning his body. "Of course they do," he mumbled, a little muffled by his own shoulder.

"Then how come you keep acting like I'm feral or something? I don't bite."

"I don't mean to!" He did turn around then, almost knocking his cup off the counter. He grabbed it with both hands and held it tight, only sloshing a little onto his hands, then paused to sigh. "I'm sorry. It's not because you're—because of what you are. I promise it's not. I don't care about that, like, at all."

"Let me guess," he drawled, "you have a friend who's an orc?"

"Well—no, not really." He turned fully on his stool and held the mug loosely in his lap with both hands. "I guess the only other orc I've ever been around a lot was one of the other artists at Wendigo, and we were never really *friends*, but she was nice. But she also wasn't so..."

One of Luke's thick eyebrows ticked up again. "So what?"

Don't say hot. Don't say hot. Say something. Anything other than hot. "Tall."

A moment of silence passed, and then Luke laughed—a sudden, gentle, half-stifled sound that put a warm pit in Ethan's stomach. "I'll try crouching down next time."

Ethan smiled, relief flooding him. "So...how come you're here so late?"

"Same reason you are, probably. Can't sleep."

"What are you watching?"

He seemed briefly hesitant to answer, then scooted up a little straighter in his booth. "It's just a stupid sci-fi movie. Hoping it'll put me to sleep."

"You like sci-fi?" Ethan perked up. "Have you seen *Battlefield Mars*?"

"With James Navolta? It was really bad," Luke said with a small snort, and Ethan laughed.

"It was *so* bad. But not as good-bad as *Infrared*."

"I didn't see that one."

"Oh, man." Ethan was up from his seat and across the diner without hesitation then, sliding into the booth next to Luke without giving him time to scoot over. "You won't believe it." He pulled his phone from his pocket and typed into the search bar to bring up the movie trailer, and in just a few seconds, he had his screen tilted toward the larger man and the volume turned up just enough for them both to hear.

For about two minutes and thirty seconds, Ethan forgot that he was supposed to be nervous around the bulky orc beside him while they both made fun of the ugly costumes and bad dialogue. Then the video ended—and he looked up to discover he was in fact almost leaning right up against Luke, who'd moved his arm to rest along the back of the booth to make more room for Ethan on the bench.

"So, yeah," Ethan said suddenly, and he awkwardly slid himself out of the booth and stood at the end of it instead, his phone in both hands. "Pretty dumb."

Luke watched him silently for a moment, then glanced down at the table and tilted his mug. "I was planning to have another cup of coffee before I go. If you were going to stick around."

Ethan paused, his face heating, and opened his mouth once or twice without getting any words out. Before he managed to answer, Ophelia reappeared from the back and called out to them.

"You boys need refills yet?"

"Yes," Ethan heard himself say, his eyes still on Luke's face. "Yes please." He hesitated just a moment more before taking the bench across from Luke, who tugged his single earbud loose to give Ethan his full attention as Ophelia crossed the room.

"So was *Pluto Descending* the absolute worst, or what?" Luke asked, and Ethan laughed and settled more comfortably into his seat.

Ophelia left them downstairs long after she'd cleaned up the rest of the diner, and the sky outside was growing brighter by the time either of them noticed.

5

Over the next couple of weeks, Ethan began to feel like he was actually settling in. He ate dinner with Carlos sometimes, and he frequently found himself inundated with fresh-baked bread and pie from Ophelia because of it. He told Carlos he didn't have to feed him as often as he did, but he was actually grateful—he regularly got caught up in his work and forgot to feed himself. Maya had seen it, too, and many times had shown up at his door with takeout. Carlos had the same caring nature, and he was fast becoming a good friend to Ethan—he was fun, easy to be around, and didn't take himself too seriously. He'd even opened up a little about a centaur woman in town named Evie, who he was perpetually too nervous to ask out.

Ethan had offered to share some of Joe's anti-anxiety moonshine with him, but Carlos had pointedly refused. When Ethan finally took a sip for himself one evening, he understood why—he felt like he'd taken a mega-combination of Xanax and Adderall that left him wandering the house and backyard in a daze for over an hour, after which he'd cleaned the entire kitchen. He put the jar in a top kitchen cabinet and tried to forget it was there.

Ethan didn't see Nareth every day, now that the Internet was up and running at his home, but they texted most days, and they'd been to the bar for drinks a handful of times. A few days ago, Nareth had driven him to the next town over to visit a vineyard for a wine tour, and they'd had dinner at a fancy restaurant of the elf's choosing. It was nice, but it probably wouldn't have been Ethan's choice of how to spend a day if he'd been on his own. All of their dates tended to go the same way, even the couple of times Nareth had come over to Ethan's house—the elf told Ethan what they were doing, and they did it. Ethan usually had fun; Nareth was quick and witty and interested in the ins-and-outs of Ethan's publishing history. They had a good time together.

But Ethan still couldn't work up the nerve to sleep with him.

He couldn't make any more excuses for not coming to the elf's apartment, though. Nareth had insisted that tonight was the night he would cook for Ethan, and he would accept no further argument.

Nareth lived in an apartment complex on the outskirts of town called Hercynia Village. It was a cute place—unsurprisingly, Ethan guessed. The furniture was dark leather and brass, and the small dining table sat just outside a well-appointed kitchen. It was tidy, but pleasantly warm and lived-in; it seemed like the home of a settled bachelor content with his own company. Ethan almost felt like he was intruding.

Ethan took a seat at the bar counter at Nareth's request, but when the elf excused himself to the bathroom, Ethan risked getting up for a quick peek into the other doors. The bedroom was tidy, with a large bed stacked with silk pillows and covered in a lush purple duvet, and the second room looked like an office—a simple wooden desk with a closed laptop on it sat under the window, and on the adjacent wall, a full bookshelf stood beside a polished black upright piano. A pair of bone conduction headphones sat in a little stand on top, and a cushioned chair had been pushed in close to the keys. He didn't know Nareth played the piano.

The toilet flushed in the next room, and Ethan scrambled back to his seat, almost toppling his stool in his hurry to get back before the bathroom door opened. If Nareth noticed, he didn't say anything; he just breezed past Ethan into the kitchen and opened the fridge.

"Do you like duck, Ethan?" he asked as he laid a package in the sink.

"Uh—yeah. But—"

"You're about to tell me that I didn't need to go to the trouble and/or the expense of duck, and I won't have it," the elf cut him off without looking up from gathering cookware. "Let yourself be spoiled now and then. It's good for the spirit."

Ethan smiled at the brief, smirking look Nareth shot him, and he waited while his date cooked for him. He didn't even offer to help—he could tell just by the quality of Nareth's pots and pans that he was far too advanced for Ethan to hope to contribute. So he just sat, watching the elf move about the kitchen and listening to the soft classical music Nareth had playing over the speaker on the bar. He was so academic, so refined—a librarian who plays the piano and cooks gourmet meals and goes to wine tastings—what did he possibly see in someone like Ethan?

Dinner was duck breast and apricot chutney on a bed of lentils and greens—a far cry from the microwave dinner Ethan would have made for himself if left to his own devices. It was so delicious that Ethan had to force himself to eat slowly, trying to match Nareth's casual pace. He didn't do very well.

"You don't have to be shy," the elf said over his glass of pinot noir. "I like a man with an appetite."

"Sorry," he said with a shy smile. "It's—really good."

"I'm glad." He set down his glass. "I've just about exhausted my repertoire for seducing you otherwise."

Ethan choked on his next mouthful of lentils and coughed into his napkin, taking a few deep breaths and clearing his throat before he tried to speak again. "Sorry?" he asked in a croak.

Nareth rose and brought him a glass of water from the kitchen, lingering at Ethan's side of the table once he'd set it beside him. He touched Ethan's hair with slender fingers and let them rest at the back of his head, curling lightly against him and prickling his scalp. "You do play hard to get," he murmured with a teasing smile.

"Do I?" Ethan squeaked out. He was glued to his chair, his eyes on the elf's dark golden gaze.

Nareth cupped the back of his head with casual ease, and Ethan suddenly realized how close he was to an indecent position, sat in his seat with Nareth standing so near to him. His body flushed hot as he tried to wipe the thought of the color of Nareth's lips from his mind. He hated Maya.

"Can I interest you in something sweet, Ethan?" Nareth asked with a slight tilt of his head.

"Sweet?" he echoed, barely audible.

The elf hummed, and he let his fingers slip from Ethan's hair as he returned to the kitchen. Ethan chugged the glass of water, but it did little to calm his nerves. Why had he agreed to come here? This was so dangerous.

The "something sweet" was, it turned out, just some lemon sorbet, which Ethan was happy to eat. Unfortunately, Nareth also suggested he stay a while after dinner, and so Ethan found himself on the leather sofa, drinking more red wine than he really cared to just so he had something to pay attention to other than how close beside him Nareth was sitting.

It didn't work.

He could taste the wine on Nareth's lips when the elf kissed him. All the air was sucked from Ethan's lungs as his back pressed into the soft leather of the couch, Nareth's tongue in his mouth and his knee settling itself between his thighs as if it naturally belonged there. Ethan gasped for breath as Nareth's body pressed against him, the elf's lips finding his jaw and earlobe and running heated bites over them. He was good at this. He was too good at this. Nareth knew exactly what he wanted from Ethan, and he was eager to take it. A normal functioning adult might have let him.

Unfortunately for probably both of them, Ethan was not a normal functioning adult—and when Nareth's fingers worked the button of Ethan's jeans undone, Ethan's heart leapt up into his throat so suddenly he choked, and he flailed so violently that they both tumbled off of the sofa. Nareth thumped to the floor with a soft "oof" as Ethan landed on top of him, but Ethan left no time for misunderstanding or charming teasing. He scrambled to his feet and stood with his arms straight at his sides, shoulders heaving with his strained breath as Nareth pushed up onto his elbows to look at him.

"I'm sorry!" Ethan shouted, and Nareth stared at him in disbelief for a few beats before he laughed.

"Good lord, Ethan." He lifted a hand, silently requesting help up. "It's a penis, not the Hope Diamond."

"Sorry," Ethan said again as he took the elf's hand to help him to his feet. "It's not—you didn't do anything wrong, I just—"

Nareth waved him away and dusted himself for a moment. "You're always like this," he finished for him. "Right?"

"Right," Ethan confirmed miserably.

Nareth gave him a long look up and down with one hand on his hip, then let out a slow sigh of regret through his nose. "Well. Perhaps let's use our words next time it comes to that, yes?"

"Sorry. Yes." Ethan's shoulders hunched a little, but he relaxed when Nareth stepped closer and lightly patted his cheek.

"Another glass?"

Ethan exhaled into a small smile. "Sure."

It wasn't as weird going to Nareth's apartment next time. He even came to Ethan's house once, and they had takeout from the diner and watched a movie about King Henry V that was outside of Ethan's usual wheelhouse, but still pretty good.

The only problem was that whenever they saw each other—especially if the date ended at one of their homes—they ended up kissing. Sometimes a lot. Ethan couldn't reasonably complain—Nareth was obviously well-practiced, and he seemed to have had the part of his brain that produced shame surgically removed. He'd tried to take things further with Ethan more than once, but every time, Ethan got too worked up and nervous. He said something stupid and made excuses. Nareth never said anything to make him feel bad, but how many times could Ethan reject him before he got pissed off? He must have been annoyed with him already.

Maya's voice rang in his head, reminding him after multiple 2 a.m. panic calls that "the right dude would never pressure you." But it was hard to believe there would be any reason to date someone like Ethan at all if he wasn't even putting out.

On top of everything, he'd made zero progress on his next book. He'd scrapped at least a dozen half-formed ideas—nothing seemed any good. It all felt like surface-level fluff, like rambling. He'd had more than one self-pitying cry about it in the wee hours of the morning, but Maya had reassured him through texts and voice messages that everything would turn out all right. He tried to believe it.

Meanwhile, Carlos had gotten into the habit of waking Ethan up very early in the morning—sometimes when Ethan had only been in bed for a couple of hours—on the pretense of "just one more thing" he wanted to fix—but to his credit, the house was steadily looking more like the photos he'd put online and less like a retirement home for spiders.

He'd gotten used to the intrusions, so when a knock at his door woke him up, he didn't think anything of answering the door in his boxer briefs and baggy t-shirt—except this time, Luke was standing on the porch. Ethan really wished he hadn't been wearing the pale green shirt with the cute cartoon bunny and strawberries on it.

"Hey," Luke said after an awkward, heavy pause. "Carlos sent me— did I wake you?"

"Uh. No. Nope." Ethan tugged down on the front of his shirt with both hands, only succeeding in hiding an inch or so more of his thighs. "Nope, um, wide awake, just uh—sorry, why did he send you?"

"He said there's drywall that needs patching in the bedroom upstairs." He lifted the heavy canvas tool bag in his hand. "He asked if I'd do it, since it would be a lot of stairs and crouching for a horse's ass."

"The bedroom," Ethan squeaked out. "Sure. Yeah. Uh. Bedroom," he repeated once more in a whisper, but he stepped back from the door to let Luke inside. "If you'd just, uh. Just give me like. Like five minutes. Two minutes. Just give me one minute," he babbled, progressively louder as he raced up the stairs.

He scooped up the clothes on his bedroom floor and spread them as flat as possible across his mattress, then covered them up with one flap of the blanket, successfully masquerading his slovenliness as a mostly-made bed. Then he ran a hand towel over the sink to mop up the globs of toothpaste and threw it into the shower, where it could be hidden behind the curtain. He pulled on a pair of jeans and a less-embarrassing t-shirt, then threw his last remaining box to be unpacked into the closet and slammed the door shut before it could fall out again.

"Okay!" he called down. "Okay uh—you can come up!"

Each step of Luke's boots on the steps put another lump of anxiety in Ethan's chest, but he stayed put until the orc was in his bedroom doorway, ducking his head slightly as he came through.

"This shouldn't take too long," Luke said as he passed the bed and bent down to touch the wall where a missing outlet had left a hole. "Not so bad." He set down his toolbag, then paused, eyeing the narrow gap between the bed and the wall, and in one movement so easy and casual it was almost sexual, he hooked one hand under the edge of the bedframe and shoved it a couple feet out of place to give himself more room.

It took him a few seconds to settle onto the floor, one leg stretched out straight and the other curled underneath him—as strong as he was, he seemed to move a little slowly when it came to getting up and down. He'd leaned against the car to get up that first day Ethan met him, too. Maybe he had some kind of injury? It definitely wasn't Ethan's business either way.

Ethan watched from across the room, standing awkwardly near the door while Luke got to work sanding the edges of the small rectangular hole.

"So, um," Ethan started, forcing himself not to fidget with the hem of his shirt, "thank you for doing this."

"It's not charity work," Luke answered. "Carlos cooks for me sometimes, and I do the stuff he can't reach. I did a lot of the fixes upstairs before you got here, and I put the showerhead back on the other day."

All the blood left Ethan's face and pooled at his feet. "You were—in here before? In my room?"

"Don't worry," Luke said dryly, "I rinsed your toothbrush after I used it."

"What—wait you—"

"Joking," he added with a brief glance over his shoulder, and Ethan slumped a little. He was never going to get used to the orc's deadpan delivery.

"Right. Sorry."

He kept quiet while Luke worked, peeling and sticking some kind of mesh over the hole, then applying a pale sort of paste from a small metal trough with a scraper. Ethan was useless at home maintenance— he'd lived in apartments most of his life, even with his parents. He tried to pay attention, maybe learn something, but he didn't even know what the goop was that Luke was spreading over his wall.

"Are you going to Carlos's for the movie night tomorrow?" Luke asked after a bit of silence, and Ethan perked up.

"Yeah. You too?"

"Mhm."

Ethan smiled, his bottom lip tucking briefly into his teeth. The three of them had had two movie nights together so far—Carlos had the biggest television and made the best snacks, so he hosted, and they'd gotten through a couple of truly terrible movies together. Nareth hadn't been joining them; he didn't get the same enjoyment out of so-bad-it's-good cinema as the others did, so he left Ethan to it.

It was fun. Ethan had even stopped being in constant panic mode whenever Luke was around—current bedroom intrusion excepted. Carlos kept insisting that the orc was actually a big softie, but Ethan found it hard to believe. He was almost completely unreadable most of the time—but when he did loosen up and smile or joke about whatever corny movie they had on, he was a lot of fun. Ethan had started to be excited instead of anxious when he heard the rumble of his motorcycle coming up the lane.

"Cool," he said. "It's Carlos's turn to pick, so I hope he delivers."

"Is it possible *not* to deliver when there's no bar for the quality of the movie?" Luke scraped his wide drywall knife onto the edge of his trough and used it to scoop the remainder into a small tub from his bag, which he sealed shut again. "Anyway, that's done." He zipped up the bag and used the edge of the mattress to ease himself to his feet again. "Don't touch it—it's got to dry. It might need another coat; I'll check it when I come by tomorrow, if that's okay by you."

"Oh, uh—yeah. Yeah that's fine."

"Cool." Luke let him lead the way downstairs again, then he stepped down from the porch and dropped the toolbag into the back of his parked pickup. "See you tomorrow."

"Yeah—yeah; see you tomorrow."

Ethan waved and shut the door with a sigh. That wasn't a total wreck of an interaction, at least. Maybe tomorrow would be easier.

Tomorrow was not easier. Ethan had already done his part for their movie night by preparing nachos and soda, and Luke had finished sanding and painting the patched drywall in the upstairs bedroom when Ethan's phone rang. Some sort of last-minute emergency favor for Evie, the girl Carlos had mentioned. He wasn't going to make it. He apologized at least a dozen times over the course of the three minute phone call, but Ethan promised him it was fine—though he felt anything but fine.

Luke stood in his kitchen, watching in silence until Ethan hung up.

"Carlos can't come," Ethan said simply. "I guess we'll have to take a rain check." He glanced over at his tray of nachos with a faint frown—there was way too much for him to eat on his own. His stomach gave a small flip. "Unless—you're already here, so—" What was he saying? Inviting Luke to stay and watch a movie? Just the two of them? "If you wanted to—" Oh my god, just shut up!

The orc paused, eyes flicking briefly between Ethan and the food. "...Do you like MST3K?"

Ethan laughed despite himself. "Uh, yeah I do."

It didn't take long to get the movie chosen and set up, but this was an entirely different vibe than getting together at Carlos's house. Carlos's couch was large, so it was easy to sit all three of them at a casual distance, but Ethan's sofa was more like a loveseat. That was fine when it was just him—but now that Luke was at one end of it, Ethan found himself crushed into the far arm of the couch, legs crossed away from him. He wasn't going to risk accidentally leaning on him again like he had that night in the diner. Luke didn't seem exceptionally comfortable, either—he ate some of the nachos Ethan had made and chuckled at a few of the movie critics' jokes, but he didn't look over at Ethan once during the whole thing. When it was over, he thanked Ethan for having him, said a quick good night, and left.

He probably just wasn't as interested in spending time with Ethan on his own. That was pretty understandable, honestly. Ethan wouldn't want to spend time with himself, either.

He went to bed with his face buried under his pillow.

Carlos brought him some lunch the next day as an apology for ditching movie night, and Ethan kept the awkwardness of the evening to himself. He sat on the railing of his porch with Carlos in the yard nearby, sharing some black bean burgers and corn on the cob the centaur had made and trying to think about anything but the tall orc on his couch the night before.

He jumped when his phone buzzed against the wood where he'd laid it aside, and when he checked the screen, he grimaced and turned it upside down again, pressing it into the railing. It was Dee—he'd already dodged one of her calls a couple of days ago, so he really should pick up. But he didn't have anything to tell her, so he didn't. He needed something new—something that would really make him feel something. And he didn't have it yet.

Carlos swallowed a bite of his burger. "The editor lady again? Isn't she going to be mad if you don't answer?"

"Yeah," Ethan admitted, "but if I never answer, she can never yell at me."

"Does she yell?"

He hunched into his shoulders a little. "She really does. It's not good. She's a harpy."

The centaur frowned. "I'm sure she's not that bad."

"What? Oh no—she's an *actual* harpy."

"Oh! Oh no!" Carlos shuffled nervously on his front hooves. "I didn't mean that harpies are all bad! I'm not like that! Please don't tell her— she sounds great!"

Ethan laughed. "I won't tell her. She is great, really; I don't deserve her. I will talk to her—just...not yet, you know? I feel like I moved all the way out here and don't have anything to show for it."

"It hasn't been that long," Carlos reassured him. "Creativity takes time, right? I'm sure you'll come up with something." He crumpled up the paper he'd been holding his burger with and took Ethan's from him to tuck into a small bag of other trash. "Are you going into town today?"

"Maybe," Ethan shrugged. "I should probably get groceries. Why? You need something?"

"I thought maybe you could take this extra food to Luke for me," Carlos said, his tail gently swishing as he packed up a little paper bag of burger and corn cob. "He doesn't always eat the healthiest when he's working, and I owe him for the drywall work."

"Oh," Ethan breathed. "Uh. Sure, I can—I can do that, I guess."

"You don't still think he's mean, do you?" Carlos handed Ethan the bag as he dropped down from the porch railing.

"I just...think I irritate him. But maybe he can be bought with food."

"Definitely," Carlos agreed with a smile. "Thanks."

Ethan grabbed his keys from the house and carried the lunch bag to the car to drive into town. He could just say hello, drop off the food, and go do his shopping. Easy, quick, friendly encounter. That would be it. Maybe, if he was lucky, he'd be able to get away before he said anything stupid.

He spotted Luke walking into the garage as he pulled into the parking lot, but by the time he got out of the car and over to the open door with his bag, the orc was already rolling underneath the car jacked up inside.

"Hey, Luke? Sorry," he said preemptively.

The cart wheels ground on the concrete again as Luke crept out enough to look up at him. "Hey. Car making more weird noises?"

"No, uh—" He held up the bag in both hands. "Carlos made lunch."

Luke paused, watching him for a moment. Then he snorted softly. "Sure. Sounds good." He scooted a little farther out from under the car and put a hand on it to stand up, but his right foot caught on the nearby tool cart as he started to stand, and when he tried to tug it free, he seemed to get stuck and stumble. Luke dropped back onto the floor, his hand catching the rolling creeper on his way down and sending it sharply out from under him. His shoulder hit the side of the car, and Ethan dropped the paper bag and rushed to him to try to help catch him before he fell fully to the floor. When they came to a stop, Luke was holding himself up on one elbow, and Ethan knelt beside him, cradling his head with his hand latched like a barrier between the orc's skull and the side of the car.

A moment of tense silence passed between them, their eyes locked on each other, Ethan's heart pounding in his chest.

"Are you okay?" he asked softly, and Luke gave a faint wince as he pushed himself up into a proper seat. Ethan frowned at him, but when he realized he still had a hand on his face, he whipped it back close to his chest and backed up a few inches.

"Yeah," Luke grumbled, "just this goddamn thing." He situated himself with his back against the side of the car and reached down toward the leg that had tripped him—and Ethan noticed for the first time that the leg seemed a lot longer than it should have, and an odd dip had appeared in the stretched pant leg in the middle of his thigh.

Ethan sat frozen as Luke doubled over and grabbed his calf. He tugged up the pant leg of his coveralls and shimmied his boot downward, slowly revealing a black artificial knee and a pale grey metal brace. Once the whole thing was free, he passed the limb over to a motionless, staring Ethan, and he braced himself against the car as he scooted and hopped his way to standing.

Ethan looked up at him from where he sat crouched on the ground, mouth hanging fully open as he cradled the leg in both hands.

"Can you drag that chair over here?" Luke asked, gesturing over to a folded metal chair leaning against the wall, and Ethan snapped back to life, stammering out his agreement as he scrambled to his feet.

He hugged the leg in one arm and pulled the chair with the other, but he jerked to a stop again as he saw Luke unzipping his coveralls.

What exactly was happening right now?

Luke stripped the jumpsuit from his shoulders, revealing a white v-neck t-shirt that clung ridiculously to his thick, rounded pectorals and sleeves that bunched as they struggled with the size of his biceps. The bottom hem was rumpled, showing a strip of green skin at his hip above the waistband of what looked like a pair of black athletic shorts. His entire torso was meaty and thickly muscled—more so than Ethan had ever been able to notice when he had on his usual dark hoodies. Luke paused with the coveralls hanging around his waist and looked over at Ethan, clearly waiting for him to finish bringing the chair.

Ethan startled himself into movement again and shoved the chair closer, allowing Luke to push his jumpsuit down into a puddle on the floor and ease himself into the seat. He settled on the chair in just his shorts and t-shirt, supporting himself on his left leg as he dropped. Where the right leg would normally have been, there was only a strap of ragged Velcro hanging from the end of some kind of sleeve—covering the end of what looked like about half a thigh.

He probably should have been concerned with the fact that he was holding what was clearly Luke's prosthetic leg—that Luke *had* a prosthetic leg—but instead, he was staring at the curls of black chest hair peeking from the orc's collar, the soft tuck of fabric against the undershelf of pectoral muscle, and the solid thickness of his remaining thigh. This was too much. How did he look even bulkier than he did in his coveralls?

"Can I have that back?" Luke asked.

Ethan jumped, almost dropping the leg he still clutched tight to his chest. He rushed forward, then hesitated, shifting the limb in his arms a moment before inching it awkwardly toward the other man. Was he supposed to help put it on? Should he kneel? Did he need to—what exactly was the positioning here?

"Just—" Luke started, and when Ethan started to bend down, he leaned forward. "No, just—here." He took the prosthetic from him, then scooted to the edge of the chair and slid the sleeve-covered half limb into the opening at the top of the artificial leg. He fiddled with the Velcro strap for a few seconds, then spat out a curse and pulled the limb away again. "The damn thing's been getting finicky for weeks, and I guess the strap finally went." He sighed and gave the Velcro one more little pull, tearing it free from its small tab completely.

"I—I'm sorry, I—" Ethan wrung his hands in front of him. "I didn't know you were—that you had a—I mean, that you didn't—I didn't know," he finished, standing awkwardly to the side as Luke leaned his prosthetic against the side of the car.

"Yeah, well, here it is," he muttered, frowning over at the offending limb.

Ethan's heart hurt. This explained why he had trouble getting up and down from the floor, at least.

Luke looked up at him with an expression on his face that Ethan hadn't seen before—hesitant? "Listen, do you think you could...take me to the store? I'll have to make an appointment to get this fixed properly, but in the meantime, I'm going to need a new strap. And I can't ride like this."

"Oh! Of course!" Ethan rushed past him, pausing to pick up the bag of food he'd dropped. He held it in both hands and stood silent for a moment, frowning. "Should I—do you still want this? Or—"

"Maybe after," Luke said evenly, and Ethan gave an awkward laugh.

"Right. Of course. Let me just—" He wavered for a few seconds, trying to decide how to empty his hands, then set the bag on the nearby cart. He rushed out of the garage, got halfway across the parking lot, then let out a sound not unlike a startled parrot and whipped around so fast he skidded on the concrete. "You need help getting to the car! Right? Of course you need help getting to the car."

"There's a crutch in the office, under the counter," Luke said, his calm doing little to douse Ethan's adrenaline.

"Right. Got it."

He took off again, quietly excusing himself to the empty room as he circled around behind the counter, and he found a single metal crutch tucked onto the shelf. He hurried back and offered it to Luke, who hefted himself up to standing and started toward Ethan's car on his own, seemingly without much difficulty.

Ethan hesitated by the garage door. "Do you uh—do you need the, uh—"

"My leg? If you don't mind."

"Yeah—yeah I mean—of course." Ethan stared down at the limb for just a second before scooping it up and trotting after Luke. He opened the passenger door for him and traded him the leg for the crutch, which he slid into the back seat before hurrying around to climb behind the wheel. He gripped it tight until Luke's seatbelt was buckled, then started down the road toward downtown without taking his eyes off of the street in front of him.

Luke had never been in his car before, he'd never been this undressed around him before, and he'd definitely never been *missing a leg* around him before. Well, he had, technically, Ethan guessed—but this was different. This was, like...*missing* missing.

Ethan tried really, really hard not to look, but once or twice before they reached the general store, his gaze had drifted to the empty space where the majority of Luke's right leg should have been.

"Sorry if it weirds you out," Luke said, his deep voice sounding even softer than usual.

"No!" Ethan blurted out immediately. "I'm just surprised. I had no idea."

"Yeah, well." He looked out the window as he answered, "Never came up. And it's not exactly small talk."

Ethan frowned, tucking his lips between his teeth to keep from letting out anything else stupid. He kept quiet until he was able to park on the side of the street in front of the general store, then he switched off the car and turned in his seat to look at Luke more directly. "Tell me what you need me to get."

"I can go in," Luke protested, "I just—"

"But it's harder for you on crutches, right?" Ethan gave him the most stern look he could muster. "So just tell me what you need."

He seemed hesitant to accept the help, his brow knit into a pensive crease, but after a moment, he described the measurements he would need and handed Ethan the ruined strap to take with him.

Ethan left the car with a quick promise to hurry, and he jogged into the store, immediately asking the older woman at the counter where he could find Velcro. He rushed past bins of cheap candy and aisles of t-shirts and socks, candles, spell scroll parchment and ink, batteries, herbs separated by poisonous and non-poisonous, hoof buffer kits, and prepaid cell phones on his way to the hardware section. He bought a few different kinds of Velcro that all looked approximately correct and rushed back to the car, mildly out of breath by the time he got back in his seat and offered Luke the bag.

The orc looked down at the bag, then at Ethan's face, and as he accepted the offering and set it in his lap, he let out a soft laugh. "You know I lost my leg a while ago, right? You don't have to rush to get this one back on. It's not on ice."

"What?" Ethan paused, and then heat washed up his neck and face all the way up to his hairline. He was being an idiot. He let his head drop to the steering wheel. "I'm sorry!" he said in a half laugh. "I just panicked!"

Luke's low chuckle prickled the skin at the back of Ethan's neck. "Don't worry about it. It's cute."

Ethan peeked over at him with a sudden tension in his chest. Cute?

Luke didn't elaborate; he was already looking through the bag and choosing a package to open. Ethan watched him fasten the new strap onto the small tab at the end of his half-thigh and string it through the metal loop in the top of the artificial one, testing the fit.

"Is that...gonna work?"

"Yeah," he answered with a nod. "For now, anyway."

"It's—do they normally break like this?"

Luke shrugged. "It's six years old. They wear out. The prosthetist said I need to replace it. Just haven't yet."

"Oh." Ethan's brow furrowed as he tried to remember if he'd ever heard how old Luke was exactly. How old was he six years ago? How had he lost it? He stared silently for a while, somewhere in the vicinity of Luke's shoulder, until the other man tilted his head to catch his eye.

"Mind taking me back to the shop?"

"Yes!" Ethan snapped up straighter in his seat and started the car again. "Sorry. Sorry."

Soon he was parked next to the garage again, and he hurried around the car to offer Luke his crutch from the back seat. He carried the prosthetic into the garage for him and watched from a polite distance while he sat in the folding chair. Luke tucked his coverall pant over the leg, then situated himself and fastened the prosthetic onto his thigh. From there, he was able to quite handily re-dress himself and zip up his coveralls, which was a relief to Ethan on more than one level. He didn't know how much more of the orc in that snug white t-shirt he could have handled.

Luke folded the chair up and laid it against the far wall again, then moved back to the cart to open his abandoned bag lunch. "You can ask what happened," he said quietly. "I know you're curious."

Ethan put his hands in his jacket pockets and moved a half step back out of his way. "I didn't know if it was...something you wanted to talk about."

"It's not a big sad story. I was in a motorcycle accident."

"Oh," Ethan answered in a soft breath. He frowned, standing awkwardly aside while Luke unwrapped his bean burger. He got why Luke never brought it up on his own—how weird would that have been? *Hey, just so you know before we watch a movie together, I have a prosthetic leg.* Weird. And in a town this size, he was probably used to everyone already knowing, anyway.

A pickup truck rolled into the parking lot, and a door slam later, Rob appeared in the garage.

"Hey there, Ethan," he said, giving him a too-hard clap on the shoulder that lurched him forward. "Something wrong with your car?"

"Oh—not today." He smiled. "Just dropping off some food from Carlos."

The older orc gave a lamenting groan. "Man, how come I never get any home-cooked—" He stopped, frowning as he took a step forward and put a hand on Luke's crutch. "What is this doing out? Did something happen?" He moved closer to take Luke by the arm, and the younger man hesitated, glancing briefly at Ethan before shaking his head.

"Just the strap. I fixed it."

"I told you, you ought to have Daniel re-fit you properly when you go in next. You're gonna wear that thing out from underneath you, and what happens if you're alone? Or on your bike?"

"I will when I need to," Luke muttered, not meeting his uncle's eyes.

Rob gave a heavy sigh, and Ethan got the feeling it was time for him to go. This seemed like a family conversation.

"Hey," he said to draw Luke's attention, "I'll, uh...I'll see you later, okay?"

Luke smiled faintly at him. "Sure. Thanks, Ethan."

"Of course." He said a quick goodbye to Rob and excused himself, hurrying back to his car so he didn't overhear anymore of Luke's uncle scolding him.

He couldn't remember what he'd meant to get from the grocery store.

6

The weather was getting colder—Halloween was close now. Ethan found himself looking at the banners advertising the Big Bad Pumpkin Patch whenever he was in town—he'd never been to something like that before. He'd made the choice to come to Adelbury for the sake of having new experiences, hadn't he?

The next time he was at the library, he spent some time pretending to draw at the conference table while working up the nerve to say what was really on his mind. On his way out, he forced himself to stop, but then couldn't make the words come out, so he stood lingering by Nareth's desk in silence.

"If you keep staring like that, dear, I'll think you need attention," the elf said, looking up at him over the rims of his glasses and giving his body a brief flick of his eyes.

"I—was going to ask if you wanted to go to the pumpkin patch tonight," Ethan forced out in a rush. "I've never been to one."

Nareth tilted his head at him. "Like a date?"

"Well—yeah, I guess," he muttered with heat in his cheeks.

"To the pumpkin patch."

"...Yeah?"

"Hm." Nareth considered him for approximately one second, then shook his head and returned his attention to his computer screen. "No thanks. Sounds boring."

"Oh." Ethan gripped the strap of his bag a little tighter, a knot forming in his stomach. "Right—I didn't think so. It looks lame, right? I only said it as a joke," he added, forcing himself to give a small laugh as he moved quickly toward the door. "I'll talk to you later."

He escaped the library before Nareth could answer him and rushed to shut himself in his car. Stupid. He leaned his head on the steering wheel and sat without moving for a few minutes, sniffling and trying to settle his queasy stomach. He took a few slow, deep breaths, until he felt the tension in his chest ease ever so slightly, and he wiped at his damp eyes with the sleeve of his jacket.

He didn't need a date to go to the pumpkin patch. Even if it was boring and lame. He'd never been—he wanted to go. That was that. If Nareth texted him later, he would just say that he was working.

It was a bit of a long drive out to the farm hosting the pumpkin patch, but Ethan's GPS was able to get him there. All sorts of people wandered around the field expanding from the entrance—magic and human alike—and kids raced across the grass and clambered over a jungle gym in nebulous gangs of adventurers that always formed when you got enough loose children in one place. Far across the field, a tractor pulled a trailer full of people sat on hay bales, and in the distance, Ethan could see the pumpkin patch, sprawling next to a barn and a fenced yard. Endless rows of sunflowers grew beyond the wall of corn making up one edge of the maze, and a pair of trucks nearby sold hot cider and caramel apples.

It looked amazing.

Ethan paid for his entry and tucked his pumpkin ticket carefully away in his jeans pocket, then stood for a while just inside the gate. There was a lot to take in, so he tried—he ambled with his hands in his jacket pockets and his shoulders a little hunched to keep his scarf snug up around his chin, exploring what the farm had to offer.

The barnyard turned out to be a petting zoo, so he spent some time crouched by the fence, trying to earn the love of a pair of goats and laughing when they slobbered on him.

Someone called his name, and he turned to see Carlos approaching him, hitched into the lead of a small wooden wagon and waving excitedly at him.

"Hey!" the centaur said. "I didn't know you were coming!"

"It was sort of a last minute decision," Ethan answered with a shrug as he straightened and wiped a bit of goat spit onto the thighs of his jeans.

"Is Nareth with you?"

"Uh." Ethan hesitated just a moment. "No. He...wasn't into it."

"Oh." Carlos's brow furrowed faintly, but if he wanted to press for more, he kept it to himself. "Well, I wish I could hang out with you, but I'm on volunteer duty." He threw a thumb over his shoulder at the wagon. "I'm helping bring pumpkins in from the field once people pick them out."

"Oh, cool." Ethan smiled at him. "Don't worry about it—I probably won't stay long. I just wanted to check it out."

"Well catch me before you leave; I'll help you find a good pumpkin!"

"Sure," he chuckled, but before Carlos could orchestrate backing his wagon up in the right direction, another centaur trotted up to him.

She was young and pale-skinned, with sturdy-looking black legs and a slate grey flank. A dark stripe ran down her spine, disappearing into a black tail with threads of white. Her long hair was tied back from her face in a black-and-silver braid that trailed down over her shoulder, and a splotchy grey birthmark spread unevenly over the left side of her neck and jaw. Large pumpkin earrings dangled from her ears, and her dark blue flannel shirt was unbuttoned enough to show a plastic pumpkin pendant around her neck.

"You slacking off again?" she asked with a bright smile, and Carlos's whole face instantly went pink.

"Evie! No Hi!" He pointed at Ethan without taking his eyes from her. "This is Ethan! Ethan this is Evie!"

"Oh, so you're Ethan!" She turned her smile on him. "I've heard about you; nice to put a nace to the fame. A fame to the—a *face* to the *name*," she finished carefully, laughing at herself as she offered her hand.

Ethan smiled and accepted the handshake. "You too."

"I'd like to chat, but I've gotta get back to work. So does this layabout."

"I'm working!" Carlos insisted weakly.

He frowned and twisted his torso to check his wagon, but when he tried to back up, it turned the wrong direction, so Evie trotted over to stand behind him and began to direct him as if she was waving him back on a runway, making loud "beep-beep" noises until he was turned the right direction again. Then she smiled at him, gave him a thumbs up, and took off across the field.

Carlos gave a long, loud sigh. "Gosh, she's so cool."

Ethan ticked an eyebrow at him, doing his best to hold back his smile. "So ask her out."

"Oh, I can't!" He scuffed one front hoof in the dirt. "She'd never go out with a weirdo like me."

Ethan shrugged. "You never know. I think she likes you."

"Oh!" Carlos flushed even deeper than before. "Hush. You're—teasing me. I'm not going to pick you a good pumpkin."

Ethan laughed, returning Carlos's wave as the centaur pulled his little cart back into the pumpkin patch. He took a deep breath, stuffed his cold hands back into his pockets, and took another look around the bustling farm yard. What now? The sun was starting to set, and the air was getting chillier—it was time for some sweets.

When he approached the trucks, he spotted a station he hadn't noticed on the way in—a deep blue lifted pickup truck had been backed into the field, its tailgate down and the bed filled with open coolers. Joe sat on one of the hay bales stacked up to make steps to the truck bed, wearing a denim jacket over his red flannel shirt. He smiled at Ethan as he noticed him and waved him over.

"Hey there! Interest you in a bottle? It's just soda. Make it myself out of fruit from Marcus's orchard. This one's gooseberry."

"What's a gooseberry?" Ethan asked, already taking the offered bottle of pale green liquid. The label had a leaping jackalope on it.

"Ah, little guy 'bout so big," Joe said, making a grape-sized ring with his thumb and forefinger. "Little sweet, little sour." He took a bottle opener from his jacket chest pocket and popped the lid for him. "Go on and give her a try."

Ethan took a small swig and paused with the soda in his mouth before swallowing. He was right—it was a little sweet, and a little sour. "That's really good! You make this?"

Joe gave a modest shrug. "Well, I've already got the setup. Passes the time." He smiled at a pair of purple-skinned children as they climbed the lowest bale. He handed them each a glass soda bottle from the nearest cooler and took the tops while they held them.

"Joe, do it!" the little girl said, and the boy with her bounced on his heels.

"Do it!"

The elf's long ears perked just slightly, and he pursed his lips in thought. "Do what, now?"

"Do it!" the girl repeated, extending both words while she shook Joe's knee by his jeans.

He laughed, lifting a hand in surrender, and he opened a bottle of his own, holding it up for them. "Y'all ready?"

"Ready!" they both shouted, already laughing.

Ethan watched while Joe touched the narrow mouth of the bottle to his bottom lip, then gave it a swift, vigorous spin as he knocked his head back, creating a soda tornado inside the bottle that sent the liquid pouring down his throat at an impressive speed.

The children cheered as Joe thunked the empty bottle down onto the tailgate, and the little boy tried to copy the maneuver but ended up with a shirt front covered in gooseberry soda. Joe laughed, told him to keep practicing, and handed him a freshly opened bottle from the cooler before sending them on their way.

"I get the feeling you don't normally do that with soda," Ethan said, and the elf grinned at him and winked.

"So—where's Nareth at?" he asked. "He ain't come with you?"

"Oh—no. Not today."

"Heard y'all were an item now," Joe went on, looking away from Ethan to better organize the bottles left in the cooler beside him.

"Uh. Yeah. I guess," Ethan answered. He took another long drink so he didn't carry on rambling.

"Well good for y'all." Joe's faint smile crinkled the corners of his eyes, and he held out his hand again. "I'll take the bottle back if you're gonna empty it. Recycling."

"Oh—sure." Ethan finished the bottle in a couple more big gulps, then handed it back. "Thanks, Joe."

"You have fun, now. Get you a good pumpkin."

"I will," Ethan laughed, returning the elf's wave as he moved on.

He crossed over to get in the line up to the cider truck and watched some kids laughing and hanging upside-down on the jungle gym while he waited. It wasn't so bad, being alone—but it would have been better if the person he was pretty much dating had wanted to come with him. Nareth didn't seem like the type who'd want to sink his hands into pumpkin guts to carve one, either, so Ethan guessed he'd be doing that on his own, too.

A looming shadow appeared at his shoulder, and when he turned, he found Luke standing startlingly close to him, holding a caramel apple in each hand. They looked tiny in his large grip. He wore his usual dark jeans and boots, and he had a black leather jacket over the top of his grey hoodie—effortlessly looking fundamentally cooler than Ethan himself could ever have hoped to be.

He has to be handsome *and* fashionable? *And* tall?

"Geez," Ethan sighed as he moved back a step and took a moment to adjust his scarf around his neck as an excuse for not looking Luke in the face. "How did *you* sneak up on me?"

"Are you here by yourself?"

"Yeah." Ethan fidgeted with his scarf fringe, his eyes on the ground. Was literally everyone going to ask him that? "I just thought I'd come see what it was all about, you know? I've never been to something like this."

Luke was frowning faintly when Ethan looked up at him, but he didn't say anything for a few seconds. Then he offered Ethan one of his caramel apples. "Been in the corn maze yet?"

Ethan hesitated, but he smiled as he took the offered treat, warmth prickling up the back of his neck. "I haven't."

"Great. You want to help me babysit?"

"...Babysit?"

As if summoned, three orc children seemed to appear from a pile of hay bales, each of them covered in bits of straw and grass, tumbling into each other as they raced over to Luke.

"Are you done yet?" the smallest one asked. She only had one tiny tusk showing; Ethan could see a gap where the other ought to have been when she talked.

"I want to go in the maze!" one of the bigger boys said, and the other nodded along enthusiastically.

"Just hold your horses," Luke said. "Act like people for a second. This is my friend Ethan," he said, gesturing toward him with his remaining apple. "We're going to wait for him to get some cider, and *then* we'll go in the maze." He glanced sidelong at Ethan and tilted his head toward the children. "These are my cousins—Riley, Joel, and Ezra." He pointed them out from youngest to oldest, starting with the little girl. "They look like kids, but they're actually cave creatures, so don't mind them."

"I am not a cave creature!" little Riley objected, but her pout faded when Luke reached down to ruffle her hair.

Ethan smiled. He could have guessed they were related without being told—they all had the same wavy black hair as Luke and Rob, and the same pale golden eyes. "Well, it's nice to meet you, cave creatures or not."

He jumped when he glanced behind him and realized the line had moved without him. Soon he'd paid for his cup of cider, and he walked back to meet Luke feeling exceptionally autumnal. Half of Luke's apple was already gone, and he wiped a drop of caramel from one blunt tusk and licked it from his thumb as Ethan approached. Was it rude to look at someone's tusks? The way they parted his lips just subtly and looked bigger when he smiled? They suited him. Did they get in the way when he—

Ethan forced his gaze away and took a pointed bite of his apple as he followed the orc family toward the maze of corn plants. What was he thinking about? He held his cup of cider close to his face after he sipped and hoped Luke would think it was the steam making his cheeks red.

The kids scampered ahead of them, disappearing around corners of tall corn stalks, but Luke didn't seem concerned. He walked beside Ethan, munching on his apple and seeming to enjoy the relative quiet.

Ethan peeked over at him now and then, watching the orc's gait, trying to decide if he could tell the difference now that he knew there was metal under one of his pant legs. Would he be okay walking such a long distance through a maze? Ethan opened his mouth to ask, but then clamped it shut again. That would be rude, right? Luke wouldn't have done it if it was going to be a problem—and Ethan didn't want him to feel like he was worrying about him unnecessarily again.

"How's the strap working?" he asked instead, hoping it was an appropriate middle ground of concern.

"It's fine for now. Thanks again for your help."

"Oh no, of course. No problem." They walked in silence for a few more steps, but Ethan couldn't stand it for long. "It's nice of you to take your cousins out."

Luke shrugged one shoulder. "Yeah, well. My parents died when I was just a kid, and Rob raised me, so these rascals are more like siblings, really. Really annoying siblings," he added as he took another bite of apple, and Ethan laughed.

"They seem like a handful."

"When I used to live with Rob," he said before swallowing, "they'd steal my leg while I was sleeping. I'd come into the living room and they'd be using it like an oar to sail a cardboard box across the carpet."

Ethan snorted and tried to hide it with the hand holding his apple. "I'm sorry. It's not funny."

"It's a little funny," Luke admitted with a sidelong smile at him. He paused, and he reached up like he meant to touch Ethan's cheek—then he stopped short, his expression turning subtly more stern as he cleared his throat and tapped his own cheek with one finger. "You've got a little, uh..."

"Oh." Ethan wiped at his cheek and found a smudge of caramel there, which he licked quickly off his finger with a smile. "Thanks."

Luke nodded and returned his gaze to the path ahead of them. Joel reappeared with a flap of cornstalk leaves and handed his older cousin an empty, gooey apple stick, which Luke dutifully tucked into a small plastic bag from his jeans pocket, along with his own and Ethan's empty cider cup. The boy was gone again before the bag was closed, his cackling laughter echoing in the dark.

"So how come you came alone?" Luke asked after some brief quiet. "Nareth's too cool for the pumpkin patch?"

"Yeah," Ethan answered softly. "I guess he is." He frowned at the trampled corn lane ahead of them. "You know, I—I've done everything he asked ever since I got here. Even stuff I didn't really want to do, just because he asked. Because he wanted to do it."

Luke stopped walking then, and Ethan paused to look back at him. "What stuff you didn't want to do?"

"Oh—oh not like that!" He raised his hands and shook his head as he realized the implications of what he'd said. "Just like—date stuff! Activities!"

The orc visibly relaxed. "Right."

"I just—you know, he didn't want to watch movies with us either, and now when I told him I wanted to come here, he just said no. He didn't even try to make an excuse or anything. Just said 'no thanks.'"

Luke gave a quiet hum. "I'm...not sure his boundary is the problem here."

"What does that mean?"

He looked over at Ethan with a soft furrow in his brow. "You know you don't have to do something just because someone asks, right?"

Before Ethan could answer, a long, high-pitched howl pierced the darkening sky around them, and he froze, hand clenched tight around his apple stick. "Uh—what the hell was that?"

"You didn't know? This is a haunted corn maze."

Ethan stared at him with wide eyes. "What is a haunted corn maze?"

Luke chuckled as the kids flocked around his legs again, and he handed each of them a small plastic flashlight from his jacket pockets, then produced another and flicked it on while the children's beams of light danced away beyond the corn along with their laughter.

"It's a maze," he said, "where sometimes things chase you."

"Oh," Ethan whispered. "Great. Cool. Definitely knew that. Just uh. Things like what?"

"You know," Luke answered in a drawl. "Things."

Something rustled the cornstalks very near to Ethan's side, and he tensed, his hand latching onto Luke's jacket sleeve at his wrist. Another howl echoed in the distance, and when a growl and snap of teeth sounded directly behind him, he fully jumped, dropping what was left of his apple.

"Uh oh," Luke murmured, bending down close to Ethan's ear. "Might have to run."

"Okay but like, fake things right, like somebody in a mask, or a fake chainsaw or something, right?"

"Sure."

A barrage of yelps and growls burst from the stalks, and Ethan took off, holding onto Luke's sleeve as he bolted down the path. Screams of various intensity reverberated through the corn. Luke trailed behind him a little, and for the first time, Ethan noticed him moving unevenly. Of course he shouldn't be running.

Ethan scolded himself, reminded himself that this had to all be fake—that a corn maze at a family-friendly pumpkin patch would not have any real threats in it—but that didn't help him when something very real seemed to be breathing heavily behind him and nipping at his heels. When he looked back, a mass of black fur was on the path behind them, with too many eyes reflecting in the moonlight.

"My leg," Luke said when Ethan tried to pull him even faster. "I can't keep up—go without me."

The animal—or whatever it was—leapt onto him from behind, and he fell to the ground with a startled shout, overrun by snarling black. Ethan backed up in surprise, and when he turned to check the path ahead, his heel caught on a fallen cornstalk, and as he tried to catch himself, his ankle failed him, and he fell to the ground.

Something heavy thumped into the dirt ahead of him, and as Ethan pushed himself up on his hands, he came face to face with two massive, black-furred paws. He scrambled back onto his ass and looked up at the towering figure above him—a werewolf, at least eight feet tall, with long, hairy ears and a fearsome, snarling mouth full of sharp teeth. It took a deep breath and howled toward the sky, so loud that Ethan slapped his hands over his ears.

This was it. This was how he died. In a corn maze.

The werewolf looked down at him, and it paused. Then its ears perked forward, and it dropped onto long, clawed hands to peer more closely at him. When it sniffed, Ethan scooted backward in alarm, and it rose again—but then it began to shrink. In a few seconds, it was just a man, standing in front of him in a pair of black shorts.

"Hey, you all right?" the man asked, bending down with one hand on his knee to offer Ethan the other. He smiled at Ethan from behind a trim salt and pepper beard, his mussed dark hair falling over his forehead.

Ethan took the hand hesitantly and was lifted to his feet by a strong, tanned arm, but when he tried to put weight on his left foot, he stumbled—directly into the thick bare chest of the man in front of him.

"Woah, easy," he said, putting a hand on Ethan's shoulder to steady him. He looked up as Luke approached with a small flock of furry creatures at his feet. "Ah, geez, kids," the half-naked man said with a weary sigh. "Luke, did they knock you over?"

"Only a little."

In the light of Luke's flashlight, Ethan finally realized what he was seeing—four werewolf children, looking more like puppies as they growled and rolled over the top of each other. They all had little black shorts on, too.

"Let's not get too carried away, huh?" the man says. "This gentleman hurt himself."

The children hardly seemed to be listening, so he sighed and shooed them away down the path, sending them off in a flurry of howls.

"It's really not a big deal," Ethan insisted, but he winced as he tried to take another step.

Luke took him gently by the arm to hold him up. "I'll take him back. I can carry him."

Ethan's heart skipped several beats at the suggestion, but the werewolf shook his head.

"Not gonna happen on that leg, bud. Besides, I'm pretty sure I spotted your three a ways over terrorizing one of the scarecrows. Might want to gather them up. I'll take care of him; don't worry."

Luke frowned a little, but he nodded, looking down into Ethan's face. "I'll meet you back by the entrance."

"Okay," Ethan whispered, and he let out a startled yelp as he was lifted effortlessly from the ground and cradled against the stranger's naked chest. He heard Luke calling for the kids as he was carried away down the path.

"I'm Glen, by the way," the man holding him said. "Sorry about this—but thanks for acting so scared. The kids really are trying their best."

"Ethan," he answered. He tried to keep his hands tucked tight against his own chest so he didn't accidentally touch the dark hair his face was perilously close to being pressed into. "And yeah—no problem. Acting scared." He scrunched his eyes shut, hoping the werewolf couldn't see his face in the dark. The man's body was hot against him, and he seemed to be having zero trouble carrying Ethan's weight. This was humiliating on so many levels. How was this how the night had ended up? Who ever heard of a haunted corn maze?

Glen dropped him off at one of the picnic tables near the entrance, and once Ethan promised him that he was okay to stand on his own, the werewolf gave a toothy grin and took off back into the corn, already furry again before Ethan lost sight of him.

He should just go home. He'd made an idiot of himself in front of Luke—again—who'd clearly gotten great joy out of teasing him. Ethan was destined to be the butt of the joke wherever he went, he guessed.

He waited a little while, testing his weight on his ankle, then started to limp his way back to his car. He stopped when a voice called his name, and he looked over his shoulder to see Luke walking toward him with his cousins in tow, all three of them cackling with glee.

"Hey," he said. "You leaving without a pumpkin?"

"I'm—" Ethan stopped himself and swallowed, hoping to stop the waver in his voice before it developed into actual tears. "I'm fine to get home, but I don't know if I'm up for tramping through a pumpkin patch just now."

Luke frowned and glanced down at his injured ankle. "...Wait here, okay?"

Ethan started to call after him, but he was already walking away, so Ethan waited, lips tucked between his teeth. Before long, Luke returned with Carlos beside him, hauling his wagon behind.

"Ethan!" he called. "Are you okay? Luke said you got hurt!"

"It's fine—it's not that bad. Just fell on it wrong."

The centaur beamed at him and trotted a few more steps, turning the cart around until it stopped in front of Ethan like a hay-lined carriage. "Come on! I said I'd help you find a good pumpkin. So hop in."

"Hop—really?" Ethan laughed.

"Of course!"

He hesitated, but Luke tilted his head toward the cart, so he nodded with a little heat in his cheeks. The orc stepped closer and put gentle hands on Ethan's waist, hefting him up and over the side of the wagon while Ethan grabbed at his shoulders in a panic. Luke chuckled and patted his arm once he was settled, and together, they headed off into the patch.

The field was a little picked-over this close to Halloween, but Carlos did manage to find him a nice round one—and even three smaller ones for the kids. Ethan felt a little bad being carted around in a wagon pulled by his landlord, but the centaur didn't seem to mind—he was all smiles.

"So you met Glen?" he asked on the way back. "You know, this is the only place in the state that has a haunted corn maze with a *real* werewolf. People come from all over!"

"He seems nice," Ethan said. "Scary, but nice."

"Oh, all the howling and growling's for show," Carlos promised. "Glen's the sweetest. You should see this place all done up for Christmas! He has, like, literally half a million lights. You can probably see us from space."

Ethan laughed. "I'll have to check it out."

When they got back to Ethan's car, Luke had gone missing—only the kids trailed behind them now. Carlos gave him a hand out of the cart as best he could, and he set Ethan's chosen pumpkin in the passenger seat.

"I'll see you tomorrow, Ethan!"

"Thanks, Carlos." He smiles. "It's a great pumpkin."

The centaur waved at him, and he called to the kids to keep up as he headed back across the field toward the patch.

Ethan hesitated, a frown on his lips as he watched them go. Why did Luke leave? Had Ethan said something wrong? He got into the driver's seat, but when he reached for the door, he jumped as he realized Luke was standing in the way.

"You've got to stop doing that," Ethan says with a laugh.

Luke leaned an elbow on the roof of the car and bent down. He held out a sunflower, rich and yellow and bigger than Ethan's hand. "Sorry about what happened in there," he said in a voice so gentle it churned Ethan's stomach. "I didn't mean for you to get hurt."

Ethan faltered for a few seconds before he remembered to move his hands, and he took the flower carefully. He didn't know what to say—his heart was beating so loudly he couldn't hear himself think, and it seemed to be lodged somewhere in his throat. He looked up at Luke with a nervous furrow in his brow.

The orc watched him in silence for a moment, looking almost like he wanted to say more—but after a pause, he straightened and lightly tapped the roof of the car. "Take care of that ankle, okay?"

"Uh—yeah," Ethan managed, though it came out pretty weak.

"Good night, Ethan."

He got out a timid "good night" in response before Luke shut the door for him. Ethan watched him walk back into the field, Luke's shoulders hunching a little against the wind as he put his hands in his jacket pockets, then looked down at the flower in his lap.

It wasn't such a disaster of a night, after all.

7

Ethan spent a chunk of the next afternoon carving his pumpkin. Carlos complimented him on the spookiness of the face once it was set out on the porch, and Ethan was pretty pleased with it himself. He'd never done stuff like this back home. Even if he'd had a porch to put a pumpkin on, his holiday spirit during his adult years had thus far only extended to watching the scary movies Maya brought over. He didn't even like scary movies—but she insisted, saying it was an important tradition, and she didn't make fun of him when he hid his face.

He sat on the porch for a while after he'd cleaned up, leaned against the railing and doing some sketching. He found himself trying to get down the shape of Luke's prosthetic from memory and searching for reference pictures online when he couldn't quite get it right. He tried to capture the way Luke stood, the way he looked bent over himself as he tightened and fastened the false limb to the remnants of his real one.

The part that hooked over the leg was called the socket, apparently, and the part underneath that stayed on the leg was the liner—it was made of silicone, and it stuck to the skin to help keep the limb in place. Ethan found himself down a rabbit hole of information—about the different types of prosthetics, different sockets, how they worked and fit and stayed on. Luke's would be considered a transfemoral, or above-knee, amputation.

Ethan also came across a lot of casual references to the remaining limb as a "stump," which seemed way too offensive to ever use. Residual limb sounded much more polite–overly medical, maybe, but more polite.

It wasn't until his phone rang on the deck beside him, jolting him out of his flow, that he realized his sketches had shifted from pose and limb shape studies to Luke's face.

Ethan's stomach crumpled as he looked over at his phone screen. Nareth.

Who called instead of texting, anyway? Ethan sighed as he reached for the phone, but then he paused.

You know you don't have to do things just because someone asks, right?

He frowned at the phone until it stopped, and he waited, but instead of a voicemail, a text message popped up on the screen.

Busy?

Ethan exhaled slowly through his nose. It wasn't fair to avoid him. He didn't *want* to avoid him—he liked Nareth. He was dating Nareth, sort of. They hadn't said anything specifically about labels or exclusivity or anything, but they were as dating as Ethan had been with a lot of people.

But Nareth did kind of boss him around. Ethan didn't think he really meant to, and Ethan had never complained, but...

He shook his head. What if Nareth needed something, and Ethan was ignoring him? He put down his sketchbook and picked up his phone instead.

Not really; what's up? Sorry I missed your call.

How about a drink?

Ethan checked his watch. It was close to evening, he guessed. That was enough for Nareth. And maybe with a drink in him, Ethan could actually tell him how he felt about being refused.

As if Ethan had any right to be upset when he'd been refusing Nareth physically for weeks.

Ugh. Just go.

Sure, he texted back. *I'll meet you.*

Piri greeted Ethan when he entered the bar, pale eyes crinkling with his smile. Only a few of the tables had anyone at them this early in the evening, but a familiar face was at the one nearest the door.

"Hey! Ethan, right?" Glen, the werewolf with the muscular chest and the salt and pepper beard, leaned on his elbow to catch Ethan's attention as he drew close. A half-drunk beer sat on the table in front of him, and he wore a soft, green flannel shirt, the top couple of buttons undone to show a hint of the thick chest hair Ethan had been casually cradled against just the night before. In the daylight, he could see a sprinkling of dark freckles across the werewolf's nose and cheekbones that he hadn't noticed yesterday.

"Hey," he answered, pausing near the table. "Yeah."

"Really sorry about what happened. How's that ankle?"

"Oh—yeah, it's fine. Just a little sore. No big deal. Thanks for, uh...carrying me."

Glen beamed a toothy grin up at him, showing subtly pronounced canines. "No problem. Hope you had a good time at the farm anyway."

Ethan returned his smile. "It was great," he promised.

"Good." Glen flattened his hands on the table and gave a decisive grunt. "Well. I'd better get back before it gets dark—kids to wrangle and corn to haunt." He pushed back from the table and stood, then took up his beer and tilted his head back to drain it.

Ethan's eyes were focused on the bob of his Adam's apple and the tan skin at his collarbone so hard that he jolted a little when Glen looked down at him again.

"Have a good one," the werewolf said, and he tapped Ethan genially on the shoulder as he went by. He gave a nod to Nareth in the doorway and stepped past him onto the street.

"Making friends everywhere you go," the elf said, stepping close to Ethan with his usual casual boldness and pecking a kiss to the corner of his mouth.

"I met him last night at the pumpkin patch," Ethan said, fighting the blush he knew was on his face anyway.

"Oh, you went?" Nareth approached the bar and took a seat, trusting Ethan to follow—which he did, of course.

"Yeah, you know—just to see." He sat on the stool beside the elf and leaned on his elbows, staring down at the bartop. Why was he like this? He should have been able to tell Nareth what he was really thinking, right?

He opened his mouth to speak and was interrupted by Piri taking their drink orders.

"How are we tonight, boys?" the fairy asked as he poured their requests. "Ready for Halloween?"

Nareth ticked an eyebrow at him. "Are you doing that thing again this year where you say you're dressed as a cowboy, but really you're only wearing boots and a leather harness?"

"Are you going to break out the maid costume again?"

Ethan glanced between them with a crease in his brow. "...Maid costume?"

"It looks really good on him, actually," Piri admits. "Maybe he'll show you the garter belt this year." The fairy winked at him, then scooted his glass toward him and turned to carry on with other business farther down the bar.

Ethan pressed his palms against his hot cheeks while Nareth chuckled. The elf rested an elbow on the bar and leaned his chin into his hand to look at him.

"I did want to discuss something with you," he said, completely unfazed by any talk about his undergarments. "Well—ask something, I suppose."

"Uh—yeah?" Ethan looked over at him without moving his hands from his face, his blood pressure spiking. Had he done something wrong?

"I had a wonder," he started evenly, tracing one slender finger around the rim of his glass. "I know you've been uncomfortable about the...physicality of our relationship to this point."

Oh no. Ethan's fingers curled slightly against his cheeks, stretching his bottom eyelids downward.

"I thought perhaps you'd gotten the wrong idea; I know I do tend to be rather assertive, and I hadn't considered that it might be putting you off. I admit I made an assumption about your preference."

Ethan swallowed. "My...preference?"

"Well, yes. I expected you would want to be more on the receptive end. You just seem like the type who likes to be thrown around a bit, you know?"

Ethan sat up straighter, his hands slowly dropping as he stared directly ahead at the back of the bar, and he took a long drink instead of replying. They were not having this conversation. Not right here in the bar where anyone could hear them. Not anywhere.

"So I thought I'd make it clear that if you'd rather top, I'm totally fine with that."

Scotch and soda dribbled from Ethan's suddenly open mouth onto the bartop. He put his glass down and slapped his napkin to his mouth, wiping first at his chin and then at the bar until the cocktail napkin was little more than a soaked wad in his fingertips. He pushed the puddle remainders around the slick wood surface with pathetic determination until Nareth reached close to him and laid his own napkin over the rest of the liquid, wiping it smoothly away.

Nareth held out his hand once the table was clear, allowing Ethan to put his own wet napkin in it, then he leaned over the bar to drop them both in the bin underneath the countertop and calmly took his seat again.

"So I'm going to assume that's a *no*," the elf said evenly.

"Uh. I, uh." Ethan cleared his throat and coughed and gripped the edge of the bar, shifting on his stool and looking anywhere but Nareth's face.

"It's all right, dear," he assured him. "I understand. I can be patient."

Ethan's shoulders crumpled, and he put his face in his hands. "I'm sorry. I'm so weird about this."

"Nonsense. Everyone has different comfort levels." He took a sip of his drink. "Don't let my sluttiness think I expect the same of everyone else."

"But it would be nice, right?" Ethan muttered, still muffled by his hands.

"Well—I won't lie," he answered with a chuckle. "But it's not my place to determine what other people do with their bodies, is it?"

Ethan's chest hurt. Nareth had been so nice to him. So understanding. He was never upset by how fucking weird Ethan was. He never complained. Ethan let his hands drop and looked over at the elf beside him, and Nareth was just watching him with a faint smile, his head tilted and his soft white hair falling alluringly over his brow. The thin gold chain attached to his glasses glinted until it disappeared behind his neck, the same warm color as his eyes.

After all this, he deserved honesty, didn't he?

Ethan took a deep breath. "I did actually want to go, you know."

Nareth paused with his glass in his hand, as if he needed a second to catch up to where Ethan's brain had taken the conversation, then he chuckled softly into his drink and took a sip. "To the farm? I take it you did, since you ended up going anyway. Did you have a good time?"

"I did. But I—" He hesitated, turning his glass on the bar in front of him. "You know, I—we've been going on whatever dates you wanted these last few weeks, and I asked you to go to the pumpkin patch with me, and I never ask you to do anything because we're always doing what you want to do? But then when I asked you, you still said no."

The elf listened with a steady expression while Ethan ranted, then set his glass back on the bar. "Well, I didn't want to go," he said simply. "Ethan, I do hope you know that all of my invitations were just that— invitations. You could always have said no; my feelings wouldn't have been hurt."

Ethan pressed his lips together, his brow knitting as his gaze fell back to the bar.

"I hope that if I asked you to do something you actually didn't want to do, you would have said no."

"I definitely would not have," Ethan answered with a dry laugh.

Nareth leaned closer to catch his eye. "Well, dearest, perhaps you ought. What's the point of spending time with someone if you're not comfortable with them?"

Ethan paused, frowning. Why did the image of Luke with caramel on his tusk flash through his head?

"At any rate," the elf continued, "why don't you finish your drink, and you can be the guinea pig for a new recipe I found."

"Uh. Yeah," Ethan forced out. "Yeah that—sounds good."

"Actually good, or am I twisting your arm again?" Nareth asked with a teasing smile, and Ethan nodded—but his mind was distracted by the memory of quietly walking side by side in a corn maze.

8

Over the next few days, Ethan fell into his work. He started planning characters and ideas for a story about a young boy who had to get a prosthetic leg—and his noisy but caring little sisters. He sent a few concept pages to Dee, who said she liked them—and to send more.

Nareth invited him to a Halloween party hosted by Piri, but he worked up the nerve to decline—and, true to his word, Nareth didn't seem to mind. Ethan didn't plan to make a big deal out of the holiday—but he made sure he had some candy on hand and kept his porch light on just in case.

Carlos, on the other hand, had filled the entire yard with pumpkins and light-up skeletons, and he'd hung sheets with eye holes cut in them from every low tree branch available to him. There was even a fog machine. He stood in the yard with a giant bucket of full-sized candy bars beside him, wearing the costume he had been working on for weeks—an inflatable horse head was attached around his waist, a pair of black pants filled with sand and hung over his forelegs like a rider, and on his torso, a frilled shirt and long black frock coat. He'd fitted a plastic pumpkin mask over his head and come over to Ethan's porch to show off his work, and he'd been thrilled when Ethan had correctly guessed that he was the headless horseman.

Every kid in town seemed to know that Carlos's was one of the good houses—they showed up in droves. Ethan's paltry offerings of Nerds and Sweet Tarts didn't get nearly the same reception. The flow of children was so near-constant that Ethan ended up sitting on his porch rather than continuing to interrupt himself to answer the door. He could still sketch on the porch in between kids, at least, and Carlos seemed to enjoy the company.

Ethan looked up when a pickup truck he recognized pulled into the drive, and his heart rate ticked up. It was Luke's truck, and three small orc children spilled from the bed as soon as it came to a stop.

Luke stepped out wearing a pair of tropical swim trunks, one flip flop, and an unbuttoned Hawaiian shirt—but instead of his prosthetic leg, he had a stuffed shark attached to his thigh, its felt-toothed mouth latched around what remained of his leg.

Ethan snorted a little and covered his mouth to hide it, but Carlos was cackling as Luke crossed the yard on his crutch.

"That's great!" the centaur said between breaths of laughter, and he bent down to get a better look as the kids gathered around him. They'd dressed as more traditional Halloween creatures—a cat, a mummy, and a skeleton. Carlos laughed while they shouted their trick or treats, muffled by the pumpkin on his head. "Excellent choice this year. And you guys look amazing!"

Luke moved himself closer to Ethan's porch so that he could lean against the railing up the steps while his cousins helped themselves to Carlos's candy. This close, his open shirt was like psychological warfare—he had nothing on underneath it, and Ethan's eyes ran disrespectfully over the orc's thick torso, as if he could count the number of black hairs spread across his chest and trailing down to his belly-button. And below, disappearing into the waistband of his shorts, Ethan realized with a sudden flush that reached all the way to his ears.

"Trick or treat," he said with a glance toward Ethan, who snapped his gaze back to Luke's face and forced a smile.

"You—you want candy?"

Luke snorted softly and shook his head. "I'm good. Just here for the kids."

Ethan chuckled. "You look thrilled to be here."

He shrugged. "I'll keep taking them until they're too old to want me to. They always like to pick what stupid thing I wear, and it's just one night. Small price to pay."

"Well, this," Ethan said, gesturing to all of Luke, "is hilarious. But how did you drive here without your leg?"

"I don't drive with my leg anyway. There's no real fine control with it, you know? And learning to drive with my left foot was way too much of a pain in the ass. So the truck's got hand controls."

"Huh," Ethan murmured, a slight crease in his brow. "I guess I never thought about that."

"Why would you?"

Before Ethan could say more, the kids trotted up to accept candy from him, too.

"What's your costume?" Riley asked, giving Ethan a pointed look up and down in his jeans and baggy sweater.

"I'm a starving artist," Ethan answered with a dry chuckle.

"That's lame," Ezra, the oldest, muttered, and Luke cuffed him lightly on the back of the head. "Sorry," he said like a reflex, and Ethan smiled.

"It's okay. It's a little lame."

A pair of centaurs appeared at the drive, and Carlos seemed to come to attention. One of them was Evie, and the other was smaller, her body a darker grey with large patches of black freckles on her flanks. She wore a black and white striped shirt, and as they got closer, Ethan could make out her cat ear headband and drawn-on whiskers. Evie had plastered white spots to her side, and she wore a white bathrobe, a rubber cow nose, and a gold tinsel halo that bobbled on its headband. She screamed with delight when she saw Carlos, and she trotted up to him to inspect his costume, both of them laughing as he struggled to pull off his pumpkin head.

The younger centaur beside her seemed less enthusiastic, but he still answered Carlos when he greeted her.

"Ethan!" Evie called, smiling as she came closer to the porch—but she stopped and barked out a laugh that turned into a snort when she spotted Luke. "Oh my gosh, look at you! Aren't you freezing?"

He shrugged. "A little bit."

Ethan's eyes shot like laser beams to Luke's bare chest and the single dark green nipple visible where his shirt hung open. His stomach clenched, and he coughed into his sleeve to hide the redness in his face. What was wrong with him?

"Well you look great." She turned her smile on Ethan. "Oh—this is my sister, Kate."

Ethan smiled at her and said hello, but she only nodded at him—she had the air of a teenager far too cool for trick-or-treating. Her black hair was cut into a neat bob just at her chin, and she had her hands tucked into the long sleeves of her shirt, her gaze wandering across Ethan's porch with ennui only a high schooler could muster.

Evie, however, was staring at him, hands on her waist and a bright smile on her face, clearly waiting for him to say something.

"Uh. You look great," he offered, and she took a step closer.

"Do you get it?"

"Uh," he started, but she cut him off before he had the chance to admit his ignorance.

"I'm a *holy cow*!" she said, almost laughing too hard at herself to get it out. She reached over and shook her sister's shoulders with both hands. "A *cat* burglar!"

Ethan shared a brief glance with Luke, and they both gave a polite chuckle, but Carlos was wheezing.

"That's so great!" he half choked out. "You're so clever, Evie."

She snorted and pushed him lightly by the arm. "Oh, go on."

Luke threw a quick sidelong smirk at Ethan, then called to his cousins. "Come on, creatures. Let's go bother the next house." As the children thundered across the yard back to the truck, Luke spared one more quick look back as he pushed away from the porch railing. "I'll see you later, Ethan. Happy Halloween."

Ethan didn't answer right away, momentarily stunned by the softness in Luke's eyes and the way his thick lips curled away from his large lower teeth when he smiled. He was halfway across the yard before Ethan managed to yell, "H-Happy Halloween!"

Kate was staring at him with one eyebrow arched, and the familiar knot of being judged uncool by a teenager grew in Ethan's stomach, so when she opened her mouth to say something, he shoved a handful of candy at her and wished her a happy Halloween also, then rushed back to his seat on the porch and picked up his sketchbook again with great purpose.

Why did Luke have to look at him like that? He was going to give Ethan the wrong idea.

Ethan spent the next week doing his best to focus on his work and little else—designing characters, planning out story beats—but something kept nagging him. Luke was obviously his inspiration for the story. Ethan had never considered the difficulties and minutiae of having a prosthetic limb of any kind, and reading up on it had been more interesting than he'd thought it would be. He would never include anything too personal or close to Luke's lived experience, of course, but it still felt...weird not to ask him for permission.

He should at least bring it up to him and see how he felt. Maybe he could even ask him some particulars—see if he was willing to answer some questions that were harder to solve with a web search. Things that would help give the story a more real, personal touch.

But that was a very personal thing to ask.

Still—it would be the right thing to do to at least run it by him. It would be far worse if Luke found out about it later and felt exploited. Ethan would hate to think he'd just been trying to use him for a story. Then again, there was still a chance that Luke would feel that way anyway if Ethan just showed up and asked to use him for information.

It was two more days before he worked up the nerve to go down to the garage. When he got there, he saw Luke's motorcycle parked near the front of the office, but there was no sign of him. Rob waved from inside, and Ethan returned it. He was headed toward the office door to ask after Luke when he paused—Luke's voice was coming from the back of the building.

Ethan circled around the garage and found a small clear patch of grass between the building and the treeline of the nearby woods, and it was there that Luke sat—on the ground with his back on the exterior wall, his legs stretched out in front of him, and a little calico cat curled up on his lap. Two other cats lounged nearby in the sunny grass, including the small tabby Ethan had seen the first time he came to the garage. A couple of water bowls and plates with leftover kibble on them sat on the concrete not far from where Luke was resting.

The cat on Luke's lap hopped away when Ethan rounded the corner, and it sat down near the other two to join them in keeping wary eyes on him as Luke looked up.

"Hey."

"Hey," Ethan answered. "Sorry—didn't mean to interrupt."

"You're fine. I'm just getting some air."

"You feed these guys?" Ethan crouched down and held an open palm out toward the cats to offer a soft pspsps. The tabby took a few cautious steps toward him and gave his fingers a sniff.

"Yeah. They've hung around for years now."

Ethan smiled and scratched the tabby behind the ears when she bumped into his hand to allow it. "Do they have names?"

"Do they have names," Luke repeated dryly. "That one is Noodle, the calico is Frog, and the fat grey one is Special Agent Dan Cooper. We just call him Dan. There are a couple more I see sometimes, but they're more skittish. One is still mad at me for catching him to have him fixed, I think."

Ethan laughed softly. "Great names."

They sat in silence for a few seconds, Ethan happy to just distract himself with petting the cat, and then Luke spoke.

"So what's up? Did you need something?"

"Oh!" Ethan startled himself and in turn startled the cat, who distanced herself again. "Sorry. Not really. Just um—wanted to see if you wanted to get some lunch. If you're free. And wanted to."

"What's the occasion?"

"No—no occasion. Just lunch."

Luke watched him for just a second, seeming to hesitate, but then he nodded. "Sure."

Ethan wanted to offer him a hand while he pulled himself up, leaning himself carefully against the wall so he didn't lose his balance on his prosthetic, but he didn't want to overstep. He didn't have much chance of catching someone Luke's size if he fell, anyway.

A brief vision flashed through Ethan's mind of Luke stumbling and falling—Ethan would try to help and find himself pinned underneath the orc, their faces scant inches apart, Luke holding himself up on one elbow near Ethan's shoulder. They would have to take a second to catch their breath, and maybe Luke would hesitate to pull away, and then—

"You coming?"

Ethan blinked and whipped around as he realized that Luke was already around the corner of the building, leaned back a little to look around the edge of the wall at him.

"Yes!" Oh god, that was too loud. Why was that so loud? Ethan cringed as he hurried over and headed toward his car to unlock it.

He drove down the road to Ophelia's in tense silence, bringing up yellowy white on his knuckles from gripping the steering wheel so tight. Why was he thinking about things like being fallen on, like he was the heroine in a romantic comedy? It was...rude didn't quite seem to cover it. Didn't Ethan have a boyfriend anyway? Sort of.

They settled into one of the booths at the diner so that Luke could stretch out his leg comfortably, and Zoe greeted them with as much cheer as she ever greeted anyone—Ethan still hadn't talked to her very much, but she seemed like a quiet, moody young woman who would rather live anywhere on earth than in Adelbury. Ethan liked her.

Both he and Luke ordered the special of the day—a vegetable stew with fresh-baked bread for dipping—and they drank cups of hot cider Ophelia sent them without asking. It was a welcome warmth after the chill of the coming winter outside.

The table was quiet while they waited—awkward quiet. Ethan's palms went clammy around his cup of cider, his heart beat fast, and he bounced his heel under the table. This was awful. He would almost rather just not write the book at all than try to talk to Luke about this.

"So how'd Nareth do after Halloween?" Luke spoke up, and Ethan actually jumped a little in his seat. "I heard Piri's party was a bit of a rager."

"Uh. He seemed fine. He holds his liquor really well. Practice, I guess," he added with a small chuckle.

Luke snorted. "You don't strike me as a big drinker."

"Not usually. But I like a drink sometimes. How about you?"

He shrugged one shoulder. "I'm not really a party guy. But I don't mind a beer."

"Cool. Yeah. Same." Ethan tapped his fingers on the tabletop, pulling his lips between his teeth and nodding way too much. This was so weird. Why couldn't he just talk to him?

Zoe brought their food before he had to endure too much awkward silence, and Ethan immediately started shoveling stew into his mouth to avoid talking. This was a terrible idea. Just eat and take him back to the garage, then go home and smother yourself.

"I have to go see the prosthetist next week," Luke said softly, his eyes on his bowl of stew.

Ethan's brain screeched to a halt at the low rumble of the orc's voice, and he frowned. "Is there something wrong?"

He shook his head. "Rob griped at me until I agreed to have my leg replaced. But it's such a pain in the ass. It's half a dozen appointments, thousands of dollars, weeks of waiting. I've been saving up money, but...I've heard some horror stories. Sometimes the new leg isn't as good as your old one. What if I hate it?" His brow furrowed, and he pushed some vegetables around in his bowl. "I already lost one leg, and now that I'm used to this one, they want me to give it up, too."

Ethan paused, watching the orc's soft frown with a growing knot in his belly. He looked different from the usual calm, cool person Luke usually was—the person he showed to everyone else. Was he...nervous? Luke got nervous? And he was talking to Ethan about it?

He was talking to Ethan about it.

And when Ethan was upset about Nareth, he didn't tell Nareth about it—he told Luke. He'd been telling Luke everything. He'd been thinking about him and wanting to see him.

Oh no. Oh no oh no oh no.

He liked him.

He liked Luke. *Actually* liked him.

This was terrible. The worst possible outcome. How had it taken him this long to notice?

Luke shifted a little in his seat and shook his head. "Sorry. I wasn't trying to unload on you. Don't mind me."

"No!" Ethan sat up a little straighter, his whole face and neck growing warm. He'd been quiet for too long again. "I'm sorry! I'm listening! I just—I don't know what to say. I don't know a lot about the...process, I guess. Does it...hurt?"

"No. It's just...a whole thing, you know?"

"Do you want me to come with you?" The words were out before he even realized he was about to say them, and his whole body tensed once he heard his own voice. Why would he ask that? Why would Luke want Ethan to go to what was essentially a doctor's appointment with him? They'd known each other for a little over a month, and every single interaction they'd had had been awkward and weird—because Ethan was awkward and weird. Luke was probably only at this lunch at all out of pity. There was no way he would actually want to—

"...You'd do that?"

Ethan's head filled with a buzz of static for a solid few seconds before he processed Luke's quiet words. "Well uh. If you...if you want company. If it'll...help? I don't know how it would help."

Luke's expression changed subtly. Was he uncomfortable? He looked upset now. Was he upset? What a stupid thing to offer. "I appreciate it," he said after another pause. "Maybe if I say you're coming with me, Rob won't. I love him, but the guy tends to take over every room he's in, you know?"

"Oh. Yeah I'm not—I don't do that."

"Right," Luke said with a soft, snorting chuckle. "Thanks, Ethan. I'll let you know."

"Sure. Sure." Ethan tried to smile at him but was positive he came off more manic than supportive, so he kept his eyes on his stew instead while his racing heart tried to creep upward and strangle his brain.

When they'd finished eating, Ethan drove Luke back to the garage with minimal chatting—he didn't trust himself to say anything else today. He thought about getting out of the car when Luke did, but that would just lead to more conversation, and more weirdness, and he absolutely did not need any more of that. So he just waved—Jesus Christ, who *waves?* Then, as soon as Luke was out of the way, he pulled out of the parking lot and sped back down the road. He hadn't even mentioned his project, which had been the entire point of inviting Luke to lunch in the first place.

He needed to call Maya.

9

"I'm really not seeing what the problem is."

Maya's voice over the video call would normally have made Ethan happy to hear—but today he was too keyed-up to be relieved. He sat cross-legged on the couch and held his phone in both hands to watch her while she watered the plants in her sunny living room, her ghostly familiar slouched over her shoulder—a pale white, mostly translucent spirit in the shape of a cat. Her name was Gertie. Maya's long hair was dark today, but the bottom half was a rainbow of neon pink, yellow, green, blue, and purple, like she'd done it with highlighters. She changed it frequently with magic, so it wasn't uncommon to see it drastically different from day to day. She'd offered to do Ethan's before—one of the perks of being best friends with a witch, she said— but he felt silly no matter what color she tried, so in the end, he'd kept it black.

"I just told you the problem!" he countered, all too aware of the whimper in his voice.

"So let me just recap a second," she said, tucking her finger into the soil in one of her pots to check it before adding some water. "You met this orc. You've hung out with him a few times, and you've realized you like him. Like, romantically. He's hot, he's soft-spoken, he's beefy as hell, he's good with children and animals, and he walked through a corn maze with you and gave you a flower when he realized you were alone. And he trusts you enough to open up about a pretty personal source of anxiety."

"Exactly," Ethan confirmed. "Yes."

Maya turned her attention from her plant to stare into her phone screen. "So, like...date him."

Ethan sputtered noisily for a few seconds, as that idea was patently ridiculous, but Maya was just staring at him. He shook his phone a little for effect. "It's not as easy as *just date him*!"

She shrugged. "Why not?"

"Because we're just now to the point where we're even kind of a little bit friends! What if I fuck it up?"

"People say no to dates all the time, Ethan," she said with a sigh as she turned her attention back to her next potted plant. "Just don't make it weird."

Ethan flopped sideways onto the couch. "You want *me* to be the one to not make it weird."

Maya's laugh echoed through her apartment. "I believe in you, buddy. Before you know it, you'll be all, *ah, hyung*," she said in a singsong voice.

"He's younger than me," Ethan grumbled, cheek squished into the cushion.

"Even better. A virile young man. You're the sugar daddy."

"But I don't even know if he likes guys!"

"So ask him."

"Just—just *ask him*?"

"Yeah, dude." She moved another step away to touch the fat leaves of another plant. "Does he seem like the type who would get pissed about it even if the answer's no?"

"Well—no," Ethan admitted. "He knows I'm dating Nareth and he seems fine with it."

"Nareth, who you *don't* like, by the way."

"I don't *not* like him, I just—"

"But he didn't make you do the thing," she cut him off.

"What? What thing? I don't have a thing."

"Oh, you've got things, friend. I mean the thing you do when you actually like someone. The thing where you make up reasons not to go out with them because you've decided in advance that they're not going to like you back. Even when they clearly do like you back. Like you're doing right now."

"Maya," Ethan said in a long whine, lightly banging the phone against his forehead. "That's not fair! Please, I need help!"

"I'm giving you help, you dweeb!" She set down her small brass watering can, and her image on the screen shook as she dropped down onto her throw-blanket covered sofa, her little ghost cat oozing into her lap. "This guy at least likes you enough to hang out with you, so what's the worst that can happen?"

"Uh," Ethan began, chuckling without humor, "I tell him I like him and ask him out, and he's disgusted by the idea of someone like me having the audacity to feel romantic feelings for him, and he avoids me forever, and I have to get my oil changed in the next town over an hour away?"

"Hell's bells, Ethan," the young witch sighed. "If you think this guy is so horrible that he'd do that, why do you like him anyway?"

"I don't think he's horrible!" Ethan shot back immediately.

"Then *ask him out*!" Maya shouted, her head falling back onto her couch cushion in exasperation.

Ethan turned his head face-down into his own sofa and gave a long half-scream of frustration.

"Give me his number," she said, and he whipped his head back to look at her. "I'll do it."

"No!"

"At least send me a picture of him in his little mechanic's onesie."

"Maya," Ethan begged, but she was already moving on.

"Okay, so, second issue—didn't you just say you're already dating someone?"

Oh god. Oh god—he hadn't considered that he would have to break up with someone. He sat still and stared somewhere past his phone and across his living room, a thousand thoughts racing through his mind. He'd never broken up with someone before—he'd always been the break up-ee. How was he supposed to do it? What was he supposed to say? What would Nareth say?

"Ethan," Maya called, sounding like she was underwater. "Ethan! Wake up, buddy. Stay with me."

Ethan's brow knit into a tight crease. "But what—"

"From what you've said, this guy seems very casual anyway, right?

So he'll probably be fine."

"But—what if he's not?" Ethan sat up again, holding his phone tight in both hands to stare down at her. "I went out with him all this time, and he took me to these nice places, and he cooked for me, and we never even slept together, and now I have to tell him I like someone else?"

"Uh, if he has a problem with you not sleeping with him because he took you places, then you should never speak to him again anyway. Has he said that?" she added, sitting up a little straighter and scowling. "Give me *his* number. I'll fight him."

"No, no!" Ethan promised in a rush. "He hasn't. He's really nice about it. That's why it's even worse!"

"Oh my god." Maya gave a soft huff. "Okay. Worst case scenario time, friend. You tell Nareth you don't want to date him anymore. He asks why. You tell him you have feelings for someone else. He cries. Do you think he'll cry?"

Ethan paused. "I...would actually be very surprised if he's ever cried in his life."

"Okay. Do you think he'll get mad? Yell? Call you names?"

"Well...no; I've never seen him get mad, either."

"Okay," she said again. "So. What's the worst case scenario, then?"

"He's...disappointed?"

"Uh-huh. And so what?"

"...What if I can't go to the library anymore?"

"Ethan, he is not going to ban you from the library for not wanting to date him anymore!"

"You don't know!" he yelled back, and she clicked her tongue at him.

"I'm hanging up on you. Go break up with the hot elf who wants to date you so you can go confess your love to the hot orc who also likes you. You fuck."

"Maya," he tried, but she shook her head.

"Nope. Goodbye. Go. Text me when it's done."

"Maya!"

Ethan's phone gave a small chime as she ended the call, and Ethan rolled face down onto his couch again and pulled one of the pillows over his head. He ought to just go live in a hole in a tree in the middle of the woods, where his only worry would be baking a nice pie for Mrs.

Rabbit down the lane. He could be a little mouse, and he'd wear a handkerchief as a shawl and eat berries the size of his head. Instead, he had to break up with someone. Impossible.

But *not* breaking up with Nareth when he knew he was having feelings for someone else was wrong—whether Luke would ever return his interest or not.

He met Nareth at the bar that evening, but he insisted they got a table for themselves instead of sitting at the bar like normal—he didn't need Piri to hear everything he had to say. Nareth kissed his cheek to greet him, as usual, and smiled across the table at him once they'd settled with their drinks.

"You see?" the elf said, "If you ask me to go somewhere I was going to go anyway, I do say yes."

Ethan forced out a weak laugh. "Yeah."

"Something wrong, dear?" Nareth tilted his head to get a better look at Ethan's lowered face. "You look peaked."

Ethan didn't answer for a few seconds—he took a long gulp of his drink instead in the hope of making the words come out easier.

"Oh," the elf said with a soft hum. "This is going to be a serious conversation, is it?"

He thunked down his glass and frowned at it, trying to hype himself up to speak and more and more aware as the seconds went by that Nareth was just patiently staring at him, leaning his chin in one hand.

"I—" Ethan tried to begin, but he was interrupted by a loud thump from across the room, followed by a man's voice.

"Piri! I dropped my phone behind the booth again! Can you get it?"

The fairy behind the bar stared across at the offending patron, running his tongue over his teeth in irritation, then threw open the flip-up bar door and stalked across to the table. "If you do this one more time, Steven, I'm going to ban you."

"Aw, come on," the man said with a laugh. "It's the only way to see you so cute."

Piri held him in a long glare, and then in a puff of faint, glittering light, he was gone. Actually—not gone. Ethan squinted across the room and realized that Piri had shrunk. He was only as tall as Ethan's hand, maybe, and he slipped between the booth and the wall and reappeared a second later, shoving a phone ahead of him with both hands and the weight of his entire little body. With another soft burst of light, he returned to his usual size, holding the phone in one hand while his mothlike wings fluttered in irritation.

"You can have this back when you pay your tab," he said, ignoring the man's called arguments as he carried the phone back behind the bar with him. He'd sounded annoyed, but by the time he tucked the phone away and returned to wiping down the bar, he had a hint of a smirk on his face.

"I don't know when they're going to stop dancing around each other," Nareth said in a light, weary sigh. "They've been flirting like this for *literal* years. It's disgusting."

A frown pulled at Ethan's lips as he glanced between the two men across the room. "Maybe they just...don't know how?"

The elf scoffed and waved a hand in the fairy's direction. "He enjoys the attention, I'm sure. I wouldn't have the patience for it. I much prefer to be direct and honest, don't you? Waste of time, otherwise."

Ethan felt like rocks were piling up inside his chest. He took another long drink, almost emptying his glass, but he still hesitated after setting it down.

Nareth gave him a few more seconds before speaking again. "You're either about to tell me something very good or very bad, aren't you?"

"I can't go out with you anymore," he blurted out, and Nareth leaned back ever so slightly.

"Pardon?"

"I can't be your boyfriend. Anymore. Did you think we were boyfriends? Are boyfriends. Should have asked that first. I kind of thought we were boyfriends."

"You're getting a touch out of breath, dear," the elf said, reaching out to lightly pat Ethan's hand. "Settle down. Did something happen?"

"Are you my boyfriend?" Ethan asked instead of a reply that made sense.

Nareth's fingers moved to cover his mouth in a poor attempt to hide his laugh. "I suppose I am if you want me to be. Do you need me to be your boyfriend before you stop dating me?"

"What?" Ethan paused, the conversation catching up to him inside his head, and he whimpered and dropped his forehead heavily onto the table. "I'm sorry. I'd say this went better in my head, but it really didn't."

"Why don't you start again?" Nareth asked, an amused smile on his face as Ethan slowly raised his head. "Assume I'm your boyfriend."

"I just—" Ethan took a quick breath. "You're really great, and I've had fun hanging out with you, and you haven't done anything wrong."

Nareth waited a few beats, but Ethan didn't say anything else. "So...how does this lead to the part about *not* being your boyfriend?"

"Well, I...I think it wouldn't be fair. Because I like you, like as a person I like you, but I don't..." He hesitated, struggling to keep his eyes on the elf's face. "I don't feel..."

"Butterflies?" Nareth said softly, and Ethan's face flushed hot.

"Right."

He smiled and took a sip of his drink. "I understand."

"...You do?"

"Of course. I'm not in love with you either, Ethan; sorry if you were expecting heartbreak. I thought we were just having a good time. But I suppose I should have expected you would be more attached than I am to the idea of attachment."

"I—yes?" Ethan paused. "Wait. What? Really?"

"Well, that's the reason you get so skittish when things get heated, isn't it? You don't want to sleep with someone you don't have feelings for."

Ethan didn't answer—all the blood in his body was rushing to his face.

"It's understandable," Nareth went on. "Lots of people are that way, aren't they? It's not a fault." He shrugged and adjusted his glasses.

"You're...actually being much cooler about this than I imagined," Ethan managed to get out.

"First of all, excuse yourself, as I'm cool about everything. And it isn't as if you're saying you never want to see me again. Are you?" he asked with a slight arch in one pale brow.

"No! Not at all! We can still like—hang out," Ethan promised. "Just, uh—just not—"

"Just no more pinning you to my sofa," the elf finished for him in a low, purring voice. He chuckled as Ethan took his time making sure all the liquor was fully drained from his glass. "A shame."

"Well anyway," Ethan blurted out, grabbing onto his glass like he thought it might get away, "thanks for...understanding."

"So who is it then?"

Ethan's eyes whipped back to Nareth's face. "Who's what? Where?"

He smiled. "Who is it you've got feelings for?"

"What? Why would—"

"Oh, come on," he chuckled. "I at least know you well enough to guess that you would have continued to go along with this half-dating situation forever if there wasn't anyone else."

Ethan slouched a little closer to the table, shoulders hunching. "There...is someone."

"So, tell me. Maybe I've had them and can give an honest review. If I can't be your boyfriend, I can at least be your gossipy confidant."

"Had—*had* them?" Ethan choked out.

"Well it's a small town, dear." He paused and leaned in a little. "It isn't Carlos, is it? He's very sweet, but even I wouldn't dare."

"What? Dare what?"

"Well, you know." Nareth's head tipped briefly back and forth as though weighing options. "It's a simple matter of ratios, isn't it? Elasticity."

"Oh my god," Ethan murmured, his whole body feeling like it was about to cave in on itself in embarrassment. "No. It's not Carlos."

"So who is it then?" the elf pressed, leaning both elbows on the table in interest now.

Ethan took a few deep breaths. "It's...it's Luke," he said, barely audible above the general murmur of the bar.

"Ah," Nareth said, nodding as if this was somehow the answer he suspected.

"But you can't say anything!" Ethan added in a rush. "To anybody!"

"Oh, I won't. I was just thinking that you're likely to have a similar problem with him. Ratios."

"Oh my god, Nareth!" Ethan reached out and put both hands over the elf's mouth, but Nareth brushed them away with a teasing smile, and Ethan found himself laughing.

"I can't give you any true sexual review of him, unfortunately."

"I'm actually really glad about that?" Ethan said, still smiling as Nareth turned his warm honey-colored eyes on him.

"Luke is a good man," he said, real sincerity in his voice. "Better than me, certainly. You should give it a shot."

Ethan softened a little. "...You think?"

"Why not?" He shrugged. "The worst he can say is no, and he seems polite enough to at least say 'no thank you.' Then you can rush back into my arms and let me heal your heartbreak."

Ethan chuckled and shook his head. "You're a better guy than you act like. I hope you find someone to date who does get butterflies when they're with you."

"Bite your tongue," he said with a sneer as if Ethan had suggested he drink gasoline. "Who has time for such nonsense?" He tapped Ethan's glass with one fingertip. "Another?"

He smiled. "Sure."

10

When the dreaded day came—the day Ethan had promised to accompany Luke to his prosthetist appointment—he parked his car at the garage and found the orc in the office, sitting on a stool and reading something in his lap. As Ethan pulled the door open, Luke seemed to startle for a moment, and he pushed his reading material underneath an old motocross magazine resting on the countertop.

"You're early," he said as he rose. "Give me a second to change."

"No problem! I just—never mind. Go ahead." He smiled until Luke was out of the office, then sighed, grateful he was at least able to avoid admitting how nervous he'd been about the possibility of being late.

His eyes drifted to the open magazine while he waited. Luke suddenly hiding what he was reading was suspicious. Was it something he was embarrassed about? Something he didn't want Ethan to see? What could someone like Luke possibly get embarrassed about?

He shouldn't look. If Luke didn't want Ethan to know what he was reading, he should respect that. Privacy was important.

...But if he *really* didn't want Ethan to see, he would have taken it with him, right?

He leaned forward as far as he could without actually taking a step, and he carefully, silently lifted the corner of the magazine to peek underneath it—then froze.

It was his book. Ethan's book. *Wildlight*, the first graphic novel he'd published three years ago. Ethan's heart jumped into his throat, and he forced himself to drop the magazine and stand up straight again at the first sound of Luke's steps from the back. He'd taken off his coverall, and now he wore his usual black hoodie and a pair of simple grey sweatpants.

Ethan forced himself to look at the ceiling, the floor, his own hands—literally anything except the spot where he knew his eyes would go if he even glanced in Luke's direction while he was wearing *grey sweatpants*.

"Good to go?" he asked with his gaze already on the office door, and when he saw movement that he assumed was Luke nodding, he walked purposefully out and across the concrete to his parked car. He kept his face front while Luke locked up the office, and once Ethan's SUV shifted with the other man's weight and the passenger door was shut, he started down the road. This would be fine. Luke had a small bag with him that he'd laid in his lap once he settled, so the danger had passed for now. Just drive and act like a normal person, Ethan. No problem.

Did that mean talking? Should Ethan talk? Should he wait until Luke talked? He'd seemed anxious about the appointment when he'd mentioned it before; maybe he just wanted to ride in silence. Ethan definitely couldn't be sure he wouldn't make an immediate idiot of himself if he opened his own mouth—so maybe it was best to wait.

They drove quietly for a while, the only noise in the car the voice of Ethan's GPS through his car speakers. It was a lengthy drive—the prosthetist was in Marburn, the larger town an hour or so away from Adelbury. It was going to feel even longer if nobody said anything.

Sitting here next to Luke, just quietly driving, with both Maya and Nareth's voices in his head urging him to "just ask" was miserable. Was this the way liking someone was supposed to feel? Like your stomach was crinkling into a ball of plutonium, and the rest of you couldn't decide if it was going to melt or freeze to death? It had been so long since Ethan had been around anyone he had any kind of real romantic feelings for—probably since high school, when literally any emotion had sent him into a death spiral like this. He'd later chalked that reaction up to being a hormonal teenager, but what was his excuse now?

"How's Nareth?" Luke asked just as Ethan was about to lose his grip on the steering wheel from palm sweat.

"He's, uh. He's fine. Seemed fine. I haven't seen him in a few days."

Luke nodded, and another few beats of silence passed. Say something else, Ethan! Provide some information to base a conversation on, Ethan! Please just be normal, Ethan!

"Fine is good," Luke answered, but then the car went quiet again.

Ethan would have considered running the SUV into a tree if Luke hadn't been in it with him. This was the worst. Just say something. Say anything. Tell him what you want to tell him. Just tell him.

"We broke up," Ethan said suddenly, and he felt more than saw Luke's eyes on the side of his head. "Me and...and Nareth. We broke up."

Tense silence filled the space inside the car until Ethan felt like he was trying to breathe in gelatin.

"Oh," Luke said softly.

"Just a couple days ago. Nothing bad or angry or anything, just, uh...I think—I think maybe we're looking for different things."

"Sorry to hear it."

Ethan waved him away and tried to make his laugh sound genuine. "It's fine. I wasn't sad because he wasn't sad. He's probably got a whole line of people waiting now that I'm gone, anyway," he added with a quiet chuckle.

Luke didn't answer, but when Ethan glanced over at him, he had tilted back to lean against the headrest, a faint furrow in his brow. That wasn't an upset face—at least, Ethan didn't think so. He almost looked...relieved? Why would that be? Maybe Nareth had a worse reputation than Ethan had realized.

Ethan turned on the radio rather than endure any more silence, and they made it the rest of the way to the prosthetist office with minimal awkwardness. He waited in one of the cushioned chairs in the lobby while Luke went to the desk, and he sat beside him while he filled out forms on a clipboard.

"Lukash?" Ethan asked, unable to keep his eyes from the paperwork. "Is that your real name?"

"Yeah," he grumbled as he filled out his address. "It's a family name, I guess. But I've never gone by it."

"It is kind of..."

"Old-fashioned? Orcish?" Luke finished for him, a faint smirk on his lips as he looked sidelong at Ethan. "Yeah. It is."

"Luke suits you better," he said, and Luke seemed to pause a moment before continuing to write.

Soon they were brought into a back room, where Ethan sat on a chair to one side while Luke situated himself on the paper-covered examination table. A set of parallel bars stood across the room next to a rolling stool and a small desk and computer. It looked mostly like any other doctor's office—which made Ethan suddenly acutely aware of what a personal thing this was to accompany someone to. Maybe he shouldn't have come. But Luke hadn't turned him down—he must have been okay with it. If Luke was okay with it, Ethan had a duty to also be okay with it. He wasn't going to be the one to make this weird. For once.

The prosthetist, a middle-aged Black man with short-cropped hair and two extra arms underneath the first set at his shoulders, greeted Luke with a smile when he came in.

"You didn't bring Rob with you?" he asked, and Luke shook his head.

"This is Ethan. He's a friend."

Ethan smiled as he shook the prosthetist's offered hand, hoping it hid the uptick in his heart rate from showing on his face. Luke did think of Ethan as a friend.

"Nice to meet you, Ethan. I'm Daniel; I'm the one who's going to get all up in your friend's business today." He smiled and jerked his head at Luke. "Go on and get that leg off, and let's see about getting you a new one," he said as he pulled over his rolling stool. "It's about time."

Luke stood, and Ethan did his best to avoid staring as he pulled down his sweatpants. He couldn't help but look—but at least Luke's back was to him as Ethan took in the thick curve that filled his black boxer briefs. If he'd known this appointment was to involve Luke taking his pants off, Ethan might never have offered to come, but now that he was here, it was hard to argue with the view.

Luke passed his prosthetic over to Daniel, who gave it a brief check-over before laying it aside, then traded out his liner for the one the prosthetist offered him. Once that was done, he moved over to the parallel bars and waited for Daniel to scoot over to him. Luke didn't look at Ethan much, and he soon understood why—this was not a glamorous process.

Daniel made a few marks on the liner Luke wore with a black marker, then took at least a dozen different measurements, both with tape and with a weird slide-rule caliper amalgamation that Ethan couldn't guess the name of. He gave Luke a pair of beige-colored, thin fabric shorts to pull on that were less than flattering, even after the orc had pulled them up more snugly than looked comfortable, and Luke waited, holding himself up on the bars while Daniel stretched the pant leg taut, tied it off at the base of his thigh, and trimmed off the edges. He made a few more marks, then began to wrap strips of plaster around Luke's residual limb.

He hadn't been kidding about getting in Luke's business—the strips came just as close to Luke's groin and ass as his socket did, and they had to be smoothed with firm swipes of the prosthetist's many palms. Having more hands must have made him efficient at it, at least. Ethan had done some reading about this process while he sketched out ideas for his story, but seeing it was entirely different. And seeing it happen to Luke felt...very intimate.

Daniel chatted with Luke while the first layer of plaster dried, asking him about Rob and the kids, and Luke answered politely, but he didn't seem to want to get into any deep conversation. He just waited patiently while Daniel wrapped his second layer of plaster, and once it had been given a few minutes to dry, Daniel cut him out of his sad little shorts and helped him step out of the newly-made cast.

"Looks good," he said after a brief inspection. "You all good?"

"Yeah," Luke answered, already leaning against the examination table to pull the remnants of shorts and plaster from his good leg.

"Well all right then," Daniel said. "I think we're done. You know how to get out, right?"

"Yeah," Luke said again without looking up.

"Great. I'll give you a call next week." He shook Luke's hand, nodded to Ethan with a smile, and left with the cast cradled in one arm.

Ethan stayed silent while Luke got his prosthetic secured again and his pants pulled up. Luke didn't seem to have much to say, either, so when he gathered up his bag and walked out of the room, Ethan followed without a word. It wasn't until they were back in the car and pulling out of the parking lot that Luke spoke again.

"Thanks for coming," he said, sounding subdued. His eyes were on the bag in his lap. "There are going to be lots more appointments after this; you don't have to come next time."

"I want to," Ethan shot back before his brain had even calculated that it was true. "It's—it's really interesting. I don't know very much about all this at all. I want to."

Luke watched him for a few silent moments, one eyebrow ticked just slightly. "Really?"

"Yeah! I mean, if you—want the company."

"I do," he answered in a soft voice. He looked back down at his bag and worried the zipper pull between his fingers. "You know, when I went the first time, it was...a lot. I'd been in the hospital for a long time after my accident. It was almost four months before I was even healed up enough to see the prosthetist. They made a cast for me, just like today, and when I went back to test the first socket they made, that was—it was the first time I was able to actually...*stand up* since the accident."

Ethan frowned, his heart aching, but he stayed silent.

"I almost lost it," Luke went on with a faint, dry chuckle. "I wanted to cry. It was like...that was the first time I realized what had really happened, you know? That my life had totally changed. This was what it was going to be from then on, and some of the things I'd wanted, things I'd taken as a given were just...not going to happen anymore."

"That sounds hard," Ethan said softly, and Luke gave a small nod.

"It was. It is, I guess. I felt really self-conscious for a long time. Everybody in town knew about my accident, pretty much, and the people that didn't, I was always wondering if they could tell. It was hard to learn to walk without feeling stupid. Like I was out of sync with a whole part of me. I practiced a lot—recorded myself a lot so I could watch it back," he added with a quiet laugh. "But I had to learn to trust the new leg, you know? I was actually...really happy when you seemed so shocked in the garage that day. Like it meant I'd finally passed with a new person."

"Well I'm glad one of us was happy about it," Ethan said with a smile. "Scared the crap out of me."

"Sorry if I snapped at you about it. Rob had been griping at me a lot the last few days, and..."

"It's fine," Ethan cut in. "I'm glad I could help. With the strap."

"Right. Thanks for that, too."

"Yeah, of course; no problem." Ethan shifted his grip on the steering wheel, a knot growing in his stomach. He needed to say something about the story he intended to write—if ever there was a moment laid out for him, this was it. "Hey so actually—this is going to sound weird," he started, as if any conversation with him was ever not weird, "but I've been working on ideas for this book, and I thought maybe I would do one about this kid who loses his leg because after I found out about yours, I looked into it a lot, and it was all really interesting and I feel like it's not represented as much, and I thought it would be good if I could—but I don't want you to feel like I'm just, like, pumping you for ideas or information or anything, and I—I guess I felt like I should ask for your permission? Since you were the...the inspiration."

Luke didn't answer right away. Ethan risked a glance over at him, and he was staring, eyebrows lifted. It was a weird thing to say. Ethan knew it. He shouldn't have said anything. He should have just—

"I think...that would be great," the orc said. "I mean, I was an adult when I lost my leg, and it was tough, but for a kid...I think if you can make a story that would help..."

"That's what I was thinking," Ethan agreed. "Something that if—if a kid felt like he was alone, maybe this would make him feel...not," he finished simply, and Luke's smile was so warm that Ethan's insides almost melted.

"Yeah," he said. "You can ask me anything you want about it."

Ethan nodded and thanked him, and the silence that fell between them after that felt just a little bit more comfortable. He couldn't keep the smile off his face.

Luke asked to be dropped off at his house, rather than the garage. It was the first time Ethan had been there—but the place seemed to suit Luke perfectly. A small, cozy cabin sat at the end of a long dirt driveway, separated from the road by trees that steadily thickened into forest beyond the back of the house. It was a single story of dark wood with a pale blue porch and front door, a chimney, and wide front windows. The garage at one end looked like it had been added on, but though it was plenty large, Luke's pickup sat in the yard instead of behind the door.

It looked like a really nice little place—but so much more isolated than Ethan's little farmhouse right next to Carlos's barn. After the things Luke had said on the drive home, Ethan wondered if maybe the solitude was on purpose.

Luke climbed out of the car, but when he turned to close the door, he hesitated with one hand on it. For a second, Ethan thought Luke was going to invite him in, and his stomach clenched—but then Luke just quietly thanked him for the ride, shut the door, and started up the yard.

Ethan watched him go for probably longer than would be considered normal, frowning as he started to back out of the drive. Had he done something to upset him somehow? Just when he'd thought they'd made a little progress. Luke had been so open with him, and then he'd seemed to shut down again.

Maybe friends was the best Ethan could hope for—no matter how the soft, gentle look on the orc's face had made his heart pound.

11

The next time Ethan saw Luke was at Carlos's for a movie night the centaur had planned to make up for missing the last one—and he had gone so all out on snacks that both Ethan and Luke ended up taking boxes home. It didn't feel so awkward sitting next to Luke with Carlos on the couch with them, but Ethan still had trouble focusing on the movie. When they both said good night to Carlos and started across the yard—Ethan to his house and Luke to his truck—Ethan hesitated. He wanted to say something, but he didn't know what. Well—he knew what he *really* wanted to say. But it felt impossible. He should just enjoy the time he got to spend with Luke anyway, right? Luke was handsome, and kind, and funny, and so cool—there was no way he'd take someone like Ethan seriously. He ought to be happy for what they had.

"I think we maybe shouldn't let Carlos pick the movie anymore," Luke said, startling him back to the present. "I don't know how many more of these sappy rom-coms I can take. At least now you're here to add into the rotation."

"Glad to hear you think I have better taste," Ethan laughed.

"You definitely do." Luke's smile, even in the dim yellow of the porchlight, put a knot in Ethan's chest. Having feelings for someone was the worst.

Ethan fidgeted with the box of leftovers he held, his eyes on the dirt. Just say good night. The evening had gone as well as he had any right to expect—best to end it here before he ruined it.

"Well," Luke said, "I guess it's pretty late."

"Yeah. I guess so."

Luke nodded at him, said good night, and turned to get into his truck, so Ethan started back toward his porch with his box clutched tight in his hands.

"Ethan?" Luke's voice called, and he turned to see the orc with one hand on the open pickup door and a hesitant crease in his brow. "Are you going to be free tomorrow night?"

"Uh." Ethan swallowed the sudden lump in his throat. "Yeah. I don't have anything planned."

"Good," Luke said softly. "Keep it open for me, will you?"

"Wh—yeah. I will. Sure."

"Okay." Luke smiled at him, just faintly, and then climbed into his truck, leaving Ethan on the porch with his heart threatening to break his ribs.

He raced into the house, throwing his box into the fridge on his way to the sofa, and dropped down onto his back, his phone held a few inches above his face as he frantically texted Maya. He tried to form coherent sentences as he explained what had just happened in the yard, and he waited with anxious tension in his shoulders as typing dots blinked on his screen.

I don't have time for you until you tell me you've at least kissed him.

Ethan shoved his phone under the couch pillow and flailed his feet in a brief tantrum, then huffed and stared up at the ceiling. He definitely wasn't going to get anything done until tomorrow night.

Ethan was in the middle of attempting to force some food into his stomach in the late afternoon the next day when he heard the rough, high-pitched drone of Luke's motorcycle coming up the lane. He plastered himself to the front window, holding the curtain tight so only his eyes could be seen through the glass. Luke pulled the bike into the grass not far from Ethan's car, reached down to adjust something near the engine, and switched it off.

He looked, as always, impossibly cool as he swung his leg over the bike and stood straight. Ethan didn't know anything about motorcycles, but he liked the look of Luke's blue-and-white bike with its rugged, narrow wheels and arching front mud guard. He liked the way Luke looked even better—his black leather jacket was snug against his broad shoulders, the low sport collar buttoned close to his neck and the bottom hem hugging close to his hips. His dark jeans, smooth leather gloves, and heavy boots suited him well. Too well. Ethan's eyes locked onto the solid line of the orc's jaw as he lifted his black helmet from his head and tucked it under one arm with a long exhale.

When he turned toward the porch, Ethan backed away from the window in a panic, knocking over one of his kitchen stools on the way. He scrambled to pick it up, and he even managed to straighten his hair before Luke knocked on the door—but when Ethan opened it, Luke still peered past his shoulder into the house.

"You okay? I thought I heard a noise."

"Oh, just uh—just an old house, you know—settling. They settle."

"Sure," Luke said with a faint smirk. "So. I thought, if you wanted, we could go for a ride."

"A ride?"

Luke gestured back over his shoulder toward his bike—where, Ethan noticed, a second helmet had been strapped to the rear of the seat.

A loud, disbelieving laugh fell out of Ethan's mouth. "A *motorcycle* ride? Me? You're serious?"

"Yeah. If you want to go." Luke seemed to waver a little, like he was questioning whether he should have asked. "If you don't, I..."

"I'll go," Ethan interrupted. He couldn't bear to see that uncertainty on the other man's face. "I've just—I've never been."

Luke smiled then. "Don't worry. I'll do all the work." He moved back down the porch steps, and Ethan followed, pausing only to tug on his jacket and lock his door on his way out. Luke unfastened the helmet from the seat and offered it to Ethan, who hesitated at the weight of it.

"Is this like your truck?" he asked as Luke laid a hand on the bike and carefully got his leg over the seat. "Like, don't you have to do something with your feet on motorcycles normally?"

"Yeah. I had to switch up some things to hand controls. And I have this lever here," he said, gesturing down to a metal handle near the gas tank, "so I can put down the kickstand. Had to make some other adjustments too, but it works as well as it's going to work."

"Lucky you're a mechanic, huh?" Ethan said with a smile.

"Could have done worse," Luke agreed, and he held out a hand to help Ethan climb on.

Ethan hesitated, his heart giving a few preemptive thumps, but then he accepted the hand, balancing on Luke's immovably strong arm as he settled on the back of the bike. He tugged the helmet down onto his head and snapped the buckle snug under his chin, then was faced with a chilling reality as Luke fired up the engine—he was going to have to hold on.

He would almost rather fall off the back of the bike and die.

Luke turned to look over his shoulder at him. "You ready?"

"Uh. Sure. Yes. Ready," he said, not feeling ready at all. He tried a ginger grip on the sides of Luke's jacket, but it was too fitted for him to get much of a hold on. He would just have to do his best.

He flinched a little as the bike started to move, but Luke drove smoothly even down the dirt lane away from the house. Turns were a bit trickier—Ethan fidgeted and adjusted and tried to sit as far back on the seat as possible while still maintaining balance, which wasn't working half as well as he hoped it would. When they stopped at a light on the outskirts of town, Luke flexed his wrist and revved the engine, so loud that Ethan yelped and gripped the orc tight around the waist. Luke's low, rumbling chuckle vibrated through Ethan's chest with more force than the engine ever could.

"Better," Luke called back to him, muffled by his helmet.

Oh, this was so, so dangerous.

Luke drove them past the main street through downtown Adelbury and out into the long, winding roads that led up toward the mountains. The longer they went, the more Ethan relaxed—and Luke's body was a welcome warmth in the brisk wind. The landscape was beautiful; rich green scrub brush dotted the low fields surrounding the mountains until they were overtaken by tall fir trees, thick through the valleys and foothills. The mountain road wove through the forest, the whine of the motorcycle engine echoing through the otherwise empty wood. It was clear and cold and abandoned—like it had been built just for them. Ethan's fingers curled a little tighter into the front of Luke's jacket.

They went until they reached a gap in the trees along the road where Luke pulled off, guiding the bike through to a small, dusty outcrop at the end of a steep hill. He turned off the engine, dropped the kickstand,

and pulled off his helmet, so Ethan did the same—and his breath left him.

The view was perfect. They were just high enough to see the dip of the valley below them, dense with dark green needles, and the steep ascent of the rocky mountains in the distance, craggy and sharp and splashed white with snow. The whole sky and low strips of clouds were stained pink and orange as the sun crept closer to the horizon, half of it already hidden by the peak of a mountain. Ethan's breath fogged ahead of him as he exhaled.

"Beautiful," he whispered, and Luke's expression softened as he shifted on the seat to look at him.

"I thought you'd like it. It's nice this time of day."

Ethan looked out over the valley, fingers tight on the helmet in his lap and stomach churning. This was it. If there was going to be a perfect setup for him to tell Luke how he felt, this was it. He would never have a more perfect moment than this—a motorcycle ride on a cold day, alone in the mountains, a stunning sunset. This was when he should confess to Luke that he'd been doing nothing but thinking of him for weeks. That he liked being around him so much it made him want to throw up. That he wanted to go to every prosthetist appointment with him if it made him even a fraction more comfortable. That he wanted to sit in Ophelia's diner in the middle of the night with him and talk about the worst movies they'd ever seen. This was it.

But he didn't say any of those things. He just sat, quietly hugging Luke's spare helmet to his aching stomach. He felt the other man's eyes on him and peeked over, hoping the red on his face would be mistaken for cold.

"Hey," Luke said, his deep voice seeming close despite the space between them.

"Hm?" Ethan answered. He tried to smile, but he didn't trust himself to speak.

The orc watched him for a few silent, drawn moments, and he took a breath in—then wet his lips and tilted his head back toward the road. "You ready to go?"

"Oh." Ethan breathed out a puff of steam. "Yeah. Yeah I'm—I'm good."

Luke waited until Ethan had refastened his helmet, then buckled his own under his chin and revved up the engine again. Ethan let his head rest gently between the other man's shoulder blades, arms around his thick middle as they rode.

He was such an idiot.

12

Ethan didn't leave his house for three days. Luke sent him a few casual texts, and Ethan answered them, but he didn't dare go into town and risk actually seeing him. He would just stay in here until he died, and then he'd never have to see anyone else ever again. That would be best.

On the third day, Carlos knocked on his door with a foil-covered casserole dish in his hands and a green wool blanket over his back, hunkered on the porch so he could see into the front door. Ethan stood in front of him in a pair of yellow shorts and a two-sizes-too-large Keroppi shirt, his hair unbrushed and a blue blanket over his shoulders like a cloak.

"Hey," Carlos said, scanning him with a wary frown. He lifted the casserole. "Just wanted to make sure you were eating more than crackers. Haven't seen you in a couple days."

Ethan wanted to wave away his worry on instinct, but the smell of cheese and potatoes won him over. He took a spoon from the kitchen and he came out to sit on his porch with the blanket still wrapped around him so Carlos wouldn't have to navigate his house. He thanked Carlos, rested the casserole dish in his lap, and peeled back the foil, revealing a layer of tater tots drizzled with cheese and hiding a delicious blend of lentils and onions underneath. It was amazing.

"Are you sick?" Carlos asked, and Ethan shook his head with a mouth full of tater tots. "You look...not great. Are you doing okay? Did something happen?"

Ethan paused. He swallowed his mouthful, took a deep breath—and everything spilled out of him like a flood. "I broke up with Nareth because I started having feeling-feelings for Luke, but now I'm afraid to say anything because Luke and I finally seem like friends now, but he's been acting weird ever since he found out Nareth and I broke up, or maybe I'm just imagining it—but what if I say something and make it even weirder, and I don't even know if Luke *likes* guys, and the other day he took me out on his *motorcycle* and it was the perfect opportunity and I *blew it*, and maybe I should just go be a monk somewhere. I just want to bake pies for Mrs. Rabbit," he finished, a pitiful whimper marking the end of a fast-deteriorating explanation. He let his chin hit his chest, and his spoon gave a pathetic clink against the casserole dish as his arms went slack.

"What?" Carlos stared at him for a second or two with teeth bared in a confused grimace, then shook his head and lifted his hands. "Listen, slow down." He took a small step closer and bent down a little so Ethan would raise his head to look at him. "First, you should have just asked—Luke definitely likes boys. He dated this fairy named Tariq for a while a few years ago, but he moved away. He was nice. But I think Luke didn't want to move?" He stopped, the gears seeming to turn in his head as he caught up to himself. "But you mean you like him! You like Luke! Like him like him! Oh, wow!" He laughed. "That's great!"

"Is it?" Ethan asked miserably, pushing tater tots around the dish. "Now I have to tell him!"

Carlos perked up. "Do you want me to tell him?"

"No!" he shot back instantly. "Why does everyone keep offering that?"

"But if you don't tell him, you won't get to date him!" Carlos said as if it was obvious. "And you want to date him, right?"

"Okay, but—" Ethan snugged his blanket a little tighter around his shoulders. "Knowing that you like someone and actually *telling them that you like them* are very, very different things, and one of them is pretty easy and one of them is really hard."

The centaur's shoulders slumped a little, and he scuffed one hoof in the dirt. "Yeah, I guess it is. But...I think you're lucky, Ethan. Luke obviously likes you, too."

Ethan looked up at him with obvious disbelief. "Is it obvious?"

He shrugged. "It is to me."

Ethan sighed. He set aside the casserole dish so he could fold his knees up close to his chest and enclose them fully in his blanket, then laid his chin on them with an air of dejection. "But what if he doesn't? What if he thinks we're just friends, and that's how he wants it, and I tell him I like him and then it's weird?"

"Ethan, you're going in circles. The truth is there's no way to know for sure without asking, right? And it's always going to be a risk, but...even if he doesn't feel the same way, don't you want him to know that he's special to you?"

Ethan puffed his cheeks in a pout and stared up at his friend for a few petulant seconds. "I'll tell him if you tell Evie."

"Evie!" Carlos repeated, fidgeting on his hooves. "What does this have to do with Evie? Evie is totally different!"

"How?" Ethan laughed. "You guys so obviously like each other."

"But she's so—she's so perfect," Carlos said with a long sigh. "What would she want with a dork like me?"

"Carlos. I don't know how to tell you this, but I've only met Evie, like, twice, and I can tell she's a *huge* dork. Besides—don't you want her to know she's special to you?"

Carlos opened his mouth to protest, then gave a very horselike huff as his own words were thrown back at him. "Fine," he said, and he held a hand out to Ethan. "By the end of the week. Both of us."

Ethan hesitated, then snaked his hand out of the blanket to accept the agreement. "By the end of the week."

A week could go by surprisingly quickly.

Ethan tried to keep his promise—he really did. But now that he'd decided for sure to tell Luke how he felt, he had to decide on the moment. The perfect one had already passed him by, of course, which was his own fault. But it would be weird to set something up just for the purpose of confessing, wouldn't it? Super cheesy.

A date would have made sense, but wasn't asking someone on a date kind of telling them that you liked them anyway? And what kind of date could Ethan even ask him on that wouldn't be super lame? He could invite him to something normal and non date-like—maybe just lunch, or a movie—but then it felt too much like tricking him into going on a date.

This was the absolute worst. He ended up avoiding Luke over the next few days, giving the briefest possible answer to his texts and staying far away from both the garage and Ophelia's. Being away from him was the opposite of what Ethan wanted. Luke had even answered some of the questions Ethan asked about his leg earlier in the week. He was still being so nice, and Ethan was being awful.

On day five, just when Ethan was face-down on the sofa considering burying himself in the backyard, he heard a car approaching the house and darted to the window—but it wasn't Luke. He didn't recognize this car. He watched while it pulled cautiously into the yard and came to a stop. The back door opened, and a petite female figure in black jeans, a wide-brim felt hat, and a cropped sweatshirt appeared, trailed by a translucent white cat.

Maya.

Ethan practically exploded out of the door, racing across the yard without even bothering to put on his shoes. He latched his arms around her neck, almost tumbling her back into the car, and she laughed and shoved at him so they could both move out of the way. She hauled her suitcase and broom from the trunk and thanked the driver as she shut the door.

"What are you doing here?" Ethan asked, finding it suddenly hard to breathe.

"Well, I was going to surprise you for Thanksgiving, but I got permission to work remotely until then, so here I am! Ready to crash on your couch!"

Ethan smiled, but his next breath came in a hiccup. It was such a relief to see her.

"Oh," she chuckled in a warm scolding, wiping the burgeoning tears from his face with one long sleeve. "You idiot."

Ethan sniffled and laughed, and he took her suitcase to carry it up the porch and into the house for her. He left it next to the sofa while she hung her hat up and leaned her broom on the wall near the door. "Do you want something to eat?"

"Please," she said, but when Ethan crossed the room to open his fridge, all he found inside was a few cans of Red Bull and a half-eaten packet of string cheese.

Maya leaned over his shoulder and sighed. "Yeah, this is about what I expected." She shut the fridge for him and went right back to the door to pick up her hat. "How do you expect to land a hot, beefy orc when you have such a skinny ass?"

"Oh my god, Maya, you actually cannot be like this," Ethan begged. "If you say something in front of him—"

"Ethan," she scolded, "you know that I always look at a man's heart first. It's not my fault they keep them behind their tits. Now come on," she carried on over the top of his attempted protest. "Put some pants on and take me somewhere nice in this podunk town. I had to ride for an hour from the airport to get here; I'm starving."

"I'm serious!" he called back to her, already heading upstairs to obey. He didn't have it in him to get too upset—he was just happy she was there.

On the way into town, she talked about some of their mutual friends he'd left behind, a concert she'd been to, and some general gripes about work—he'd missed the way she chatted away. Video calls weren't the same as seeing her wild gesticulations in his passenger seat. Maybe this was why he'd taken to Carlos so much—similar energy.

When they arrived at Ophelia's, she and Maya were instant friends. This was how it usually went—Maya was gregarious and warm, and she could find something to talk about with just about anyone. With someone like Ophelia, it was a guaranteed match. Maya wanted to know about every plant Ophelia had in her garden, and Ophelia complimented Maya's chunky silver jewelry and highlighter-colored hair. Maya also wanted to taste every single flavor of pie Ophelia had in the diner, and she was more than happy to oblige. Ethan didn't argue with the pieces pushed in front of him, but he did feel like he might burst after the third sample.

A large body moving fast outside the window caught Ethan's attention, and he looked over to find Carlos with his whole torso and face plastered against the glass, still in his USPS-branded button-down, puffy jacket, and earflap hat. He burst inside so fast that the bell above the door gave a startled jangle.

"Ethan, who is this?" he demanded, but before Ethan could even answer, realization came over his face, and a grin spread across his face. "This is Maya! Are you Maya? I've heard a lot about you!"

She laughed as he stood to greet him. "I am! And you're Carlos!" She shook his hand with just as much excitement as he offered it. "God, you are even cuter than I imagined! Look at you! Can I wear your hat?"

Carlos blushed visibly even through his tan skin, but he smiled as he freed his curls from the fur hat and offered it to her. Maya cackled with glee as she pulled it onto her head so low it almost covered her eyes, and she fastened the ear flaps under her chin and turned back to face Ethan.

"How do I look?"

"Ready to deliver packages like a queen," he said, and she laughed.

Carlos was happy to join them in some pie tasting, and he and Maya bonded right away over Ethan's poor eating and self-care habits. Maya thanked him for helping keep Ethan fed, as if he were a particularly sensitive pet rabbit. He didn't mind—he knew his hermit-like tendencies and appreciated that he had friends willing to put up with him.

"How long are you staying, Maya?" Carlos asked over his fourth piece of pie.

"'Til after Thanksgiving."

Carlos's long tail flicked once against the floor, and he glanced between Ethan and Maya's faces before speaking. "Are you guys...planning on doing anything?"

Ethan shrugged. "It'll just be the two of us, so—"

"Please come over!" Carlos interrupted, half-yelling. He winced at his own outburst and cleared his throat. "I mean, I've always wanted to cook a big meal, and I never have anybody to cook for, but if you guys are going to be here..."

"Uh, yes," Maya answered for both of them, "please have us over for dinner, adorable postman."

Carlos positively beamed. "You won't regret it. I'm gonna—it's gonna be great." He drew a clean napkin close to him and plucked a pen from his shirt pocket with a click so he could start making a list of planned dishes, but then he paused. "Oh!" He leaned on the counter to look up at Ethan. "I saw Luke earlier and asked him over for a movie tomorrow night, if you guys want to come to that? I was going to make popcorn in the fireplace."

Ethan's heart lurched upward into his mouth. He didn't even have time to think of an excuse before Maya agreed for him.

Carlos peered pointedly at him. "I just thought that it's been *almost a week* since we've done anything together."

Ethan's lips pursed into a glaring frown. "It sure has been *almost a week*, hasn't it. How's Evie, by the way?"

"Who's Evie?" Maya cut in as she leaned around Ethan to insert herself more fully into the conversation.

Carlos tucked his arms a little closer to his body, heat washing his cheeks pink. "She's fine," he said. "Last I heard, she was fine. I was—I was going to call her tonight, actually," he insisted.

"Were you?" Ethan narrowed his eyes at him. "Why don't you do it now? It's getting kind of late."

"Ethan, I can't do it now!" he shot back, tail whipping briskly back and forth.

Maya waved a hand between them to draw their attention. "Hello; what's happening? Who's Evie?"

"Evie is a girl Carlos likes," Ethan explained, "that he promised he'd actually ask out."

She stared flatly at him. "And *you're* giving him shit about this."

"Anyway," Ethan said loudly over the top of her, but Ophelia's clicking hooves approaching rescued him from further explanation.

"Carlos," the satyr said, her hands laced in front of her chest, "are you finally going to say something?"

"What—what do you mean *finally*," Carlos said, his voice dropping to a murmur of dread.

"Oh, honey." Ophelia reached out to lay a hand on his arm. "Everybody knows."

"Everybody?"

"Everybody," she promised, eyes closing briefly in a sage nod. "Give her a call."

Carlos hesitated, then gave a short huff of determination and took his phone from his jacket pocket. He held it in both hands and stared at the screen for a long while without doing anything—so everyone else just stared at him, too. He seemed to be scrolling through his apps at the slowest possible pace, his breathing slow and almost distressingly steady—then he squeezed his eyes shut, tapped the screen, and lifted the phone to his ear. A hush fell over the entire diner.

"Hey," he said, face still scrunched tight, "Evie, it's Carlos. Yeah—hi. Yeah it was good! How about you? Great. That's great." He peeked open one eye, and he slapped at Ethan's hand when he made a rolling gesture at him to keep going. "So listen, um—I called because I wanted to ask you something. Tell you something. And then ask. Um. So I know this sounds weird, but I've actually—I've really liked you for a long time, so I was wondering if maybe you would let me, um—I don't know. Take you somewhere. Or—or cook for you. I'd love to cook for you."

A brief moment of silence went by, and the whole diner seemed to hold its breath along with Carlos.

"Really? I mean—yeah! Yeah that would be great!" Carlos's whole face had gone red, and his freckled cheeks were almost split by his grin. "Okay—yeah. Yeah I'll text you. Great. Thank—thank you. Yeah. Bye."

As soon as he hung up, everyone around them broke into a laughing cheer, and Ophelia reached across the counter to grab him by the face and pull him forward to kiss his cheek.

"You did so good, honey!"

Carlos couldn't stop laughing. "Why did I say thank you?"

"Don't worry about it," Ethan said. "I hear she likes dorks."

Carlos folded his arms on the table and hid his face in them, but his shoulders still shook with relieved laughter.

Maya nudged Ethan gently with her elbow. "That means it's your turn."

Ethan slumped a little and ate another bite of pie, and he nodded.

It was his turn.

13

Ethan's phone woke him up at 9 a.m. sharp the next morning, and he rolled over in his blanket burrito to fumble it off his nightstand. When he saw the name on the screen, he almost turned it off.

Dee.

He hadn't sent her any pages for days. She was going to yell at him. Maybe he deserved to be yelled at. He mushed his face into his pillow and answered the call on speakerphone.

"Hello?"

"Ah. There you are," his editor said curtly. "I assumed you were dead. I can't think of any other reason to explain not having anything new for me this week."

"I'm not dead," he mumbled, tucking the blanket up close to his face. "I'm sorry. I know I should have been working, and I know you were waiting for me, but it's been a really hard week actually, and I know you have deadlines just like I do, and this always happens, and—I'm sorry," he said again, trying to hide the soft hiccup in his voice.

She let out one of her feather-ruffling sighs. "Why has it been a rough week?"

"Oh, well—you know. Stuff," he murmured as he wiped at his face with the ball of his hand.

"Stuff."

"Yeah."

She let a beat of silence pass before speaking again. "I'm going to come to your house."

"What?" He sat up so fast he stayed tangled in his blanket and flopped sideways on the bed again. "No!"

"Then you'd better tell me what the issue is."

"I just—" He sighed and inchwormed his way back toward the phone. "There's—there's this guy I like, and I don't know if he likes me back."

"Oh good lord, Ethan," Dee huffed. "Write him a letter on some nice stationary, mail it away with a dash of your cologne, and wait for your reply like a good Austenian protagonist, you tearful idiot."

"Dee!" he whined. "Even if I wanted to do that, my landlord is the mailman! It would be too embarrassing!"

"Are you serious? What kind of Hallmark holiday special have you found yourself in!"

"A bad one!"

"You literally moved from the city and fell in love with a small town boy. Why don't you write a comic about that?"

"Dee, please," he said in a long sigh, muffled by the blanket he buried himself in.

"You're almost 30, Ethan. Just ask him out. Maybe things will get really steamy, and you can hold hands. But whatever you need to do, do it, and get back to work."

He whimpered. "Yes ma'am."

She paused. "And do let me know how it goes."

She hung up, and Ethan rolled over onto his back. It had gone well for Carlos, hadn't it? So there was a possibility. But the possibility that the whole thing would go very poorly for Ethan seemed so much more likely.

A loud banging clang of spoon on pot echoed from downstairs, and Maya yelled up at him.

"Get up, loser, it's confess your love day!"

Ethan pressed the balls of his hands into his eyes and sighed.

Maya and Carlos were an unstoppable force, now that their powers were combined—Ethan was expertly bustled between the kitchen and living room and made to help tend the popcorn in the fireplace while they prepared the rest of the unnecessarily broad assortment of snacks.

He'd already filled two large bowls with fresh-popped kernels when the front door opened—Luke, letting himself in.

"Hel-lo," Maya said, one hand moving up to cover her heart as Luke stepped into the room.

He glanced between the girl and Ethan with a faint frown, like he hadn't expected her to be there. "Hey," he offered anyway, and she walked up to him with hand already out.

"I'm Maya, Ethan's big city bad influence," she said with a grin. "You have to be Luke. I've heard *so much* about you."

"Maya, please be normal," Ethan muttered at her, but she ignored him, just shaking Luke's hand as he accepted her offer.

"Ooh, goodness, these hands. You never need to ask for help with a pickle jar, do you? And look at your arms! Bet you put *together* some IKEA furniture."

"Uh—"

"That's so funny," Ethan said way too loudly, crossing the room with a forced laugh and shoving a full popcorn bowl into her arms. "We're all here now so we can start the movie! Yay!" he added in a weaker voice, cringing to himself as he turned away from them. He planted himself at one end of the couch and sat up straight, hands resting on his thighs. He jumped when Maya bent over the back of the couch to wrap her arms around his shoulders in a quick hug.

"Don't be weird," she murmured into his ear, and she kissed his cheek before pulling away.

"You—" he started as he whipped around to glare at her, but he stopped when he saw the frown on Luke's face.

"Sorry," the orc said, gesturing briefly between them, "I might have missed it, but are you guys..."

Maya's peal of laughter was a little too incredulous for Ethan's liking. "Oh, now *that's* funny." She put a hand on Luke's chest as she started to carry on reassuring him, but then she paused, eyebrows lifting as she gave him a quick, experimental squeeze through his shirt. "Jesus." She laughed and moved a step back from him, shaking her hand as if she'd burned it. "Anyway—me and Ethan? Get real. This queer probably thinks labia majora is a Pokémon."

Luke snorted, but he held it in remarkably well.

"All done!" Carlos called, carrying a tray of cheese and crackers over to the coffee table.

He settled himself on his folded-down part of the sofa made just for centaur bodies, and Luke moved to take his place at the other end of the couch—but Maya plopped down beside Carlos and sprawled into a casual lounge, leaving only the patch of cushion right beside Ethan. Luke hesitated, but he sat, shifting subtly like he couldn't decide how to arrange himself.

Ethan shot Maya a quick glare, but she only shrugged and leaned against Carlos's haunches.

"Sorry," she said as she stretched out further, "I have to be careful how I sit. Sciatica, you know."

Luke edged an inch closer to Ethan to avoid having the girl's feet in his lap, but that pressed his shoulder against Ethan's, so, with a soft clearing of his throat, he resettled with his arm over the back of the couch.

This was the worst. But it was also...kind of the best? As Carlos started the movie and flicked off the lamp beside the sofa, Ethan couldn't stop his mind from focusing on the mass of the body beside him. He barely even registered what movie they were watching. All he could think about was how big Luke seemed next to him—how warm—and how perfectly Ethan would have fit into the nook underneath his arm, if only he'd had the nerve to lean in. It felt nice to be even this close to him, no matter how his heart raced. It was a good sort of anxiety, somehow. It was so nice that Ethan felt a little guilty for enjoying it while he'd been too much of a wimp to communicate any of his thoughts. Luke seemed stiff beside him, like he was trying to keep that small gap between them, too. That didn't mean he was nervous too, did it? There was no way.

Ethan definitely had no chance of paying attention to the movie when he kept catching Maya peeking at him out of the corner of his eye, either. She was not making this any easier.

He couldn't even stuff his face with popcorn to drown his sorrows— the first time he reached into the bowl, Luke went too, and their fingers brushed, so Ethan jerked his hand back and pressed them both underneath his thighs so he wouldn't be tempted to move them again. None of this was doing anything to build his nerve for actually mentioning his feelings to Luke today. Was it even the right day? It didn't feel like it. Stars were definitely out of alignment for this. He still had one more day before a week was up, anyway. Technically.

Ethan set his jaw and tried to take a silent, steeling breath. No. Carlos had held up his end. Ethan could do it. He needed to do it.

He wanted to. He wanted to be able to settle into the crook of the orc's arm without feeling like his soul was going to leave his body. He wanted to ride on the back of his motorcycle again and not be weird about holding onto him. He wanted to not be weird about *him*.

It had to be today.

When the movie ended, Ethan stayed quiet while the others chatted and laughed about the worst parts. After a while, Luke rose to leave, and Maya shot Ethan a pointed, urging look—but she didn't have to. Before Luke was fully out the door, Ethan was following him, and he called to him as he shut the door and stepped into the yard behind him.

Luke turned, hands in the kangaroo pocket of his hoodie. "Hey. Your friend seems nice."

"She is nice. Sorry she groped you."

Luke chuckled. "It's fine. So what's up?" he asked with a slight tilt of his head.

Ethan inhaled slowly, then took a few steps closer, until he had to crane his neck a little to look the orc in the face. "I...need to tell you something."

"Everything okay?"

"Yeah—yeah, not like that. The thing is...I didn't break up with Nareth for no reason."

A faint crease formed in Luke's brow, and his lips pressed into a thin line.

"It wasn't—not because of anything bad!" Ethan said. He pressed his hands to his cheeks and sighed. "This isn't coming out right." With a shake of his head, he let his hands drop back to his sides. "I'm saying I broke up with Nareth because it didn't feel right to keep seeing him when I was...when I was having feelings for someone else." He looked up at Luke again, trying to judge the look on his face, but he seemed to just be patiently listening. "I'm trying to say that I...like you. More than—more than a friend, and I had to—"

Before Ethan could get another word out, Luke's hands were on his face, and he was being crushed into a kiss. Ethan's heart stopped dead in his chest, but his hands moved on their own, clenching tight into the front of Luke's hoodie as he was leaned backwards by the eagerness of the other man's kiss. Luke was warm and overwhelming, and Ethan's breath hitched at the faint brush of the orc's long bottom teeth against the corners of his mouth.

Just when Ethan thought he might run out of breath entirely, Luke slowly pulled back, his gentle hands still cupping Ethan's face as he looked down into his eyes.

"Sorry," he whispered. "I've been wanting to do that for weeks."

Ethan's legs almost gave out from under him, so he held on tighter to Luke's sweater. "Really?"

Luke gave a low chuckle, one thumb lightly brushing Ethan's cheek. "Really."

"Oh," Ethan barely breathed. "Well you can—you can do it again, like, whenever," he added with a faintly dreamy smile.

The soft hum from Luke's throat sounded promisingly like temptation, but instead of taking Ethan up on the offer, he moved a step back and glanced over Ethan's shoulder at the house as he reluctantly released him. It was hard to tell on his green skin in only the porchlight, but he might have been...blushing?

"I'll text you tomorrow," Luke said, a warm smile on his lips as he retreated toward his truck. "Have a good night, Ethan."

"Good—good night," he called back, one arm holding onto his elbow as he watched Luke pull out of the yard. He smiled with his bottom lip tucked between his teeth and turned to head back into the house—then froze.

Carlos and Maya were both pressed to the front window, not even trying to pretend they hadn't been watching—they were waving and laughing at him, and Maya gave him an enthusiastic double thumbs up.

Ethan hid his face in his hands as he trudged back to the door—but he couldn't stop smiling.

14

Ethan didn't sleep well—Maya kept him up with endless questions about Luke until the early morning, and even after he'd gone to bed, it was hard for him to settle. His mind was full of the memory of Luke's lips on his, the gentle touch of his hands, the softness in his voice when he said he'd been waiting to kiss Ethan all this time. He'd more than once flailed and kicked his blanket around, hiding his face in his pillow to muffle his laughter. It was impossible to believe.

When Luke texted him the next day, Maya was slung over his shoulder to make sure he didn't say anything stupid, which he was grateful for. They'd already had plans even before Ethan's awkward confession—Luke's next prosthetist appointment was soon.

That drive was even more awkward than the first, somehow. What were you supposed to say to someone you'd already told you had a crush on but hadn't been on a date with yet? Was this a date? Did anything count as a date once two people had admitted they were attracted to each other? Was their first date a trip to the prosthetist?

"So this is early to ask," Luke said, interrupting Ethan's rambling thoughts, "but do you want to come back to the house when we're done? I thought we could spend some time just...the two of us. Not at a doctor's appointment."

"Uh—yeah," Ethan answered right away. "I mean yes. Yes please. Sorry."

Luke chuckled and shifted in his seat a little, his eyes lowered.

"Great."

At the prosthetist, Luke sat on the paper-covered cushion of the exam table again while they waited for the prosthetist, and Ethan had to bite the inside of his cheek hard when the orc stripped down to remove his leg. This felt different now. He watched while Luke slid on the test socket the prosthetist had made, leaned his weight on it, and tried crossing the room on it with a borrowed leg and the assistance of a walker.

Daniel eyed him from every angle while he stood and moved, asked him questions about the fit, then held him still to make a few more marks on the new socket. He thanked Luke for coming in and took the socket with him when he left.

Ethan looked at the closed exam room door, then at Luke, who was fitting his leg back on to get dressed. "Is that it?"

Luke paused and glanced at him, then finished pulling up his sweatpants. "Oh, yeah. This was just the first one."

"First one?" Ethan rose to follow him as he approached the door. "I thought because they did all that last time, they'd just...do it."

"It took a lot of appointments when I got my first leg, too. For something you have to wear a lot, the fit needs to be just right." He opened the door and let Ethan out ahead of him. "I might have to come back another three times before the socket is the way both Daniel and I want it. That's why I said it's such a pain."

"Oh. Yeah, I guess that makes sense."

Luke paused at the desk to check out with the receptionist, then walked with Ethan back to the car. "You really don't have to come every time. It's just going to be this again for the next couple weeks, at least."

"I want to!" Ethan promised. "I really don't mind." He climbed in and started the car for their drive back, and when he reached down to adjust the air conditioner, he jumped slightly when Luke took him by the hand.

"Thanks," the orc said, his thumb brushing over Ethan's knuckles with such softness that his whole body prickled up goosebumps. "I don't mind these annoying appointments so much when it means I get to ride there with you."

Ethan laughed loud against his will, his face flushing hot, and he tried to focus on the drive without much success—especially since Luke didn't seem willing to let go of his hand.

This was going to kill him.

He parked in the yard outside Luke's house and followed him inside, fidgeting with the hem of his jacket as he stepped through the doorway. It was cozy and comfortable inside—the floors and walls were warm, dark wood, just like the outside, with exposed beams at the ceiling and an iron fireplace sat to one side of the room near the sofa. A metal crutch like the one at the garage leaned against the wall nearby. The kitchen was small, but cute, with a wide window above the sink hung with a pale plaid curtain. It was tidy but lived in, and the whole place felt like a cabin in the woods—quiet and homey.

This was Luke's house. Ethan was inside Luke's house. Alone. With Luke. In his house.

He took a deep breath and tugged at his jacket with a soft, nervous hum.

Luke paused near the coat rack by the door, yellow eyes flicking up and down Ethan's tense body. "...Is this okay? You seem nervous."

"I'm just—always nervous," Ethan admitted. "Sorry. I'm fine."

Luke turned to face him, his large hands settling on Ethan's shoulders. "So here's what I'd like to happen today. I want to cook you dinner, hang out with you a while, maybe watch a movie. Does that sound like something you want to do?"

Ethan relaxed under Luke's touch, and he smiled and nodded with his eyes on the ground. "Yeah. It does. Sorry."

"Stop apologizing," Luke murmured, leaning in to press a warm, soft kiss to Ethan's hair before releasing him. He stripped off his hoodie and hung it on one of the rack hooks, then held his hand out for Ethan's jacket.

What had Ethan been so scared of a minute ago? He'd forgotten.

Ethan sat on the edge of the kitchen counter while Luke cooked—he didn't want any help, since Ethan was his guest. It wasn't the same kind of multi-pot, expensive ingredient recipe Nareth had made—he cooked some chicken and pasta in a simple, creamy sauce, and they ate it together on the sofa while they chatted about the next movie they might force on Carlos, Ethan's ideas and thoughts for his book, and Thanksgiving plans—Luke would be at his uncle's house, obviously, taking on the bulk of the cooking himself.

Ethan insisted on helping with the dishes, so they stood at the sink together and washed and dried—so domestic that it made Ethan queasy. He excused himself to the bathroom to take a few deep breaths and paused in the hallway as he passed the open door of Luke's bedroom. A collapsible wheelchair had been folded and pushed up to the wall at the corner of he room—it hurt Ethan's heart a little to see it, especially after the way Luke had talked about feeling so dejected after his accident. How he'd been forced to give things up.

What exactly had he given up? Maybe someday Ethan would be able to ask him.

He washed his face in the bathroom and tried to breathe out all his nerves. Luke still made him nervous, despite all the orc's efforts to be calm and quiet and warm to him. But this was an entirely different kind of nervous. Now that they'd admitted they liked each other, Ethan had to pretend he believed he was someone who deserved to be liked by a man like Luke. Even worse, he had to get *Luke* to continue to believe it.

Despite this knowledge, he still snooped through Luke's medicine cabinet and peeked into his shower while he was in the bathroom. A plastic and metal chair with rubber feet sat in the basin of the bathtub, and a small small variety of soaps and hair products sat in a wire shelf, suctioned low on the shower wall where they could be reached from the chair. The medicine cabinet held the standards—floss, a box of Band-Aids, some headache medicine—and a half-empty bottle of cologne that Ethan recognized when he brought it to his nose to sniff.

He smiled as he quietly clicked the sink mirror back into place. He was wasting time in here.

By the time he got back to the living room, Luke had finished up the dishes and settled himself on the couch to wait, so Ethan went to join him. Luke laid his arm on the back of the sofa as if to invite him into the space beside him, and Ethan sat with his heart racing. He couldn't bring himself to actually lean on Luke on purpose, but he could at least sit next to him like he knew he wouldn't bite.

"Thanks for cooking," Ethan said, and Luke smiled. Why was he so handsome when he smiled? Maybe that was why he was usually so stone-faced—he knew the power he wielded.

"Of course. I'm not great at it, but I like to cook. I had enough hospital food and takeout in the months after my accident to last me forever."

"It was good!"

Luke chuckled and let his fingers drift up from the sofa to brush the back of Ethan's neck, bringing up a shiver in him. "You'll have to come over again soon, then."

"Yeah, I—I can't return that favor. I've burned box macaroni and cheese before."

"That's just fine. You make me want to take care of you." He hesitated, as if what he'd just said hit his brain a beat after it had left his mouth, and for a few seconds, he and Ethan just looked at each other, both with breath caught in their chests. "Sorry," he said at last. "That was too intense, wasn't it?"

"It's fine," Ethan promised, though his face was hot. He curled his fingers on the thighs of his jeans and chewed his bottom lip, avoiding Luke's gaze until the orc lightly touched his jaw to turn his head.

"If I seem...farther along in this than you, I'm sorry. I actually...liked you as soon as I saw you. Not like—a love at first sight thing, I mean, I didn't know you, so it's not like I *liked* you-"

Ethan pulled his lips between his teeth to restrain his smile. Was Luke *nervous?* Was this *nervous* behavior? Who knew he was capable?

Luke paused. "Sorry," he said again, his head dropping briefly as he laughed. "I'm rambling." He shook his head and looked across at Ethan again. "What I'm trying to say is, even when I first met you, I *wanted* to get to know you. But you seemed kind of scared of me, or intimidated, or whatever, so I didn't say anything. It wouldn't be the first time someone's reacted to me that way. Then the next thing I heard, you were dating Nareth, who's...very pretty, and small, and basically my total opposite. So I guess I figured I just wasn't your type."

Ethan laughed. "I was intimidated *because* you're my type!"

Luke smiled and slid his fingers through the hair at the back of Ethan's head, his thumb brushing over the sensitive skin just behind his ear. He was so easy, so casual with his affection, that it seemed strange to Ethan now to think of him as the aloof, distant person he'd given the impression of at first. This almost didn't even feel like flirting—Ethan was just there, so Luke wanted to touch him.

He didn't hate it.

"I wanted to ask you out that day we went to my first appointment," Luke admitted. "But I thought it would be too weird since you'd only just told me about the breakup, you know?"

"I was already trying to figure out how to tell you I liked you by then," Ethan answered with a chuckle.

"I even asked you on that motorcycle ride because I wanted to tell you the truth. But then when we were up there, I guess I...chickened out."

"Oh my god," Ethan said, a laughing smile on his face, "I chickened out, too! I was hyping myself up to say something the whole time! It would have been so romantic, right?"

"That's what I'd hoped. Maybe next time," he added in a softer voice, and Ethan paused to look up at him. How was it possible that they'd both been idiots this whole time and never managed to see each other until now?

A soft pressure at the back of Ethan's neck pulled him forward just slightly, and then Luke leaned in close to him, covering his lips in a warm kiss. Ethan's hands curled into the front of the orc's shirt like they belonged there, and he found himself pliant in the other man's gentle grip. Luke was such a large person, much bigger in general than Ethan himself especially, but he never seemed overwhelming. He was eager but gentle, as if Ethan was always free to break away at a moment's notice—but when his lips parted, and he felt the heat of Luke's tongue on his upper lip, escape was the last thing on his mind. His heart rate still would have set off alarms at the hospital, but it was different from the panic that had always washed over him with Nareth and the other men he'd known—this was excitement, not nerves.

Luke's free hand held onto Ethan's waist, keeping him close as their breath quickened in the kiss, and Ethan flattened his hand on Luke's thigh to balance himself. It wasn't flesh under his palm, but the hard metal exterior of the prosthetic socket. It felt strange to touch. More personal, somehow, than if it had just been the usual sort of leg. Ethan let himself be drawn nearer by the hand at his waist, his next breath hitching in his throat as Luke's fingertips brushed hot against the skin just under the hem of his shirt. Ethan's skin prickled, and he gripped Luke's shirt tighter to stop the growing trembling in his fingers, but he couldn't help the soft gasp he took when Luke kissed across his cheek and down to his neck. His teeth were a delightful scrape on Ethan's skin, and Ethan arched subtly towards him, hands pressing into the muscle of his chest and the metal at his knee.

He smelled good. Why did he smell so good? There was a trace of the subtle, earthy scent of his cologne, but the smell of his skin was stronger. It was unfair. His hand found its way into Luke's hair, soft under his fingertips.

Ethan's stomach clenched, and a jolt fired through his groin as Luke's hand pressed into the small of his back and his lips found Ethan's collarbone. He slid a little on the couch cushion, his hips inching closer to Luke's at the other man's gentle pull—and then he glanced down. Through the narrowing gap between their bodies, startlingly close to where Ethan's hand had found itself on Luke's thigh, his eyes focused on the crease of jeans where Luke's leg met his hip.

That was just a weird crease in his jeans, right? That wasn't—it couldn't be his—

A simple matter of ratios, Nareth's voice echoed in his head, and his heart dropped into his gut.

Oh no.

Ethan's whole body tensed in preemptive alarm, and Luke pulled back immediately, looking him in the face with a soft furrow in his brow. "You okay?" he murmured. "Sorry if I—"

"No!" Ethan blurted, then shook his head and wet his lips to try again. "No, I mean—yes. I'm okay. I'm just, uh." He hesitated. There was no way he could tell him what had actually startled him. "I don't know if you've noticed this about me, but I get nervous pretty easily."

Luke's smile was so warm Ethan felt ashamed. "I may have noticed." He stroked his cheek with one large hand. "We don't have to do anything you don't want to do. I'm just glad you're here."

"There's, uh..." He gave a quiet, dry laugh. "There's a certain amount of just powering through that's inevitable for me, but...thanks. I think for tonight, I'm just gonna...go." His shoulders shot up closer to his ears, and he tried to lift his hands between them. "I mean not—you didn't do anything wrong. That was probably the hottest kiss I've ever had in my life. Is that weird to say?"

Luke kissed him again, slowly, seeming to calm him in a wave of warmth, and he pulled back with a small, reluctant exhale. "It's not weird."

Ethan looked at him, his heart thudding painfully. They were still so close—Luke's eyes were such a beautiful, pale yellow, and his hair was a little mussed. How did it still look so wavy and perfect? What could possibly make a person like this want to kiss Ethan?

And why the hell had Ethan said he wanted to go home?

Luke waited patiently while Ethan stared at him, seeming hesitant to break the silence himself. "So...you're going?" he said, his voice soft and deep.

Ethan's jaw seemed to fit perfectly into his hand, and he had no trouble supporting the smaller man even now that he'd leaned back from their kiss. The top of Luke's shirt was just low enough to show a hint of his thick collarbone, and it was frightening how much Ethan wanted to put his mouth on it. But he couldn't make his body move, and his voice didn't seem to be working.

"Ethan," Luke murmured. "Come back to me."

"Sorry," he whispered, offering a weak smile. "Sorry. I'm gonna...I'm gonna go."

Luke pulled back from him, slow to remove his hands from Ethan's body. "Can I see you later? I know it's Thanksgiving in a couple days, but—"

"Oh, yeah," Ethan assured him in a rush as he stood, smoothing out the front of his shirt in an attempt to make his arousal less obvious. "Yeah, for sure. I'll, um. I'll text you?"

"Sure." Luke stood and followed him across the room, offering him his jacket and unlocking the front door for him. "Hey," he said when Ethan had finished zipping up.

Ethan looked up at him, his stomach giving a small flop at the orc's gentle expression.

"Don't stress, okay?"

"That's like saying don't breathe," Ethan laughed, and Luke smiled.

"I get that. But with me, you don't have to. Stress, I mean—please continue to breathe."

Ethan smiled and nodded with his eyes on the floor. "Yeah. I'll try. On both counts," he added, jumping a little when he felt Luke's hand heavy at the back of his neck and a soft kiss planted on his hair. The door creaked open as Luke stepped back.

"Good night, Ethan. Drive safe."

"You too." He cringed and ran a hand over his face. "I—for good night. You're not—you know what I mean. Good night," he said again, and he scooted through the door and tried not to run to his car. He slumped into the driver's seat and took a slow, agonizing breath as he started the car.

Christ, he was an idiot.

15

Thanksgiving at Carlos's was much noisier than it should have been with only three people in the house. Unfortunately, two of those people were Carlos and Maya. Carlos had reluctantly accepted Maya's offer of cooking help only after she'd promised him she would only do the boring stuff like chopping vegetables, and he was thrilled that she was able to do it by magic. Ethan was used to seeing the kitchen like this at Maya's apartment—knives working on their own, spoons stirring stew with no hand to guide them, a little ghost cat wandering between ankles—but Carlos laughed every time he caught the movement out of the corner of his eye. Ethan was banished from the kitchen entirely once he'd been settled with his drink like a child, but he didn't mind. He just sat with one arm draped across the back of the sofa to watch them. It warmed him inside to see the two of them getting along so well. He texted Luke while they cooked and hid his laugh in his elbow when the orc sent him a picture of all three cousins holding up handprint paintings of primary-colored turkeys, just as much paint on their faces as on the paper.

He really was great to them. Ethan had never been very good with kids; he tended to treat them like little adults, which, he'd been told, was incorrect. He would have to make more of an effort with these ones.

Early in the evening, after much labor, Carlos offered his guests a full spread of delicious-looking dishes—cornbread dressing, green beans, sweet potatoes, cranberry sauce, roasted pumpkin, mashed potatoes, sweet potato and pumpkin pies from Ophelia, and even a turkey. Carlos presented it with great fanfare, and Maya helped by shooting up small sparks of orange light around him from her fingertips.

"I thought you didn't eat meat, Carlos?" Ethan asked as the centaur set down the tray at the head of the table.

"Oh—it's not meat! It's seitan!" With a large knife definitely meant for carving an actual turkey, he sliced into the turkey-shaped soy product, the knife passing directly through where bones should have been in a real bird. He cackled as he looked across the table at Ethan. "Do you want white or dark meat?"

Ethan laughed. "Dark, please."

Once they'd all settled at the table with their plates, Carlos fidgeted a little with his napkin and hesitated to begin. Ethan could have guessed that he would want to say something, so he waited, too.

"I want to thank you guys for coming," Carlos said, his eyes on the table before they lifted to look Ethan and Maya in the eyes in turn. "I don't know if I ever mentioned this, but I grew up in a foster home. So we had dinners like this, but a lot of times it was...different people year to year, you know? And ever since I aged out, I haven't really had a place to go back to, or anyone to invite, since most people already have a family," he said, glancing down briefly to nudge his fork with one finger. "So this means a lot to me. I know you guys aren't really my *family*, but it still feels nice to have people to spend today with. So...thanks."

They both stared at him for a few seconds, and then Maya was out of her chair, circling the table with tears in her eyes, and she took Carlos's face in both hands and planted kiss after kiss on his cheeks and forehead. His tail flicked on his cushion, and his face turned as red as the cranberry sauce, but he was laughing.

"I am your family now," Maya said as she leaned back to look him in the eyes, his cheeks mushed between her palms. "Do you understand? You belong to me now. From this moment. I'm your mom."

Carlos dropped his gaze with a bright smile, nodding as he gave one of her hands a gentle squeeze. "Thanks, Maya."

"So you'd better send me a Christmas card!" she added as she retreated to her chair again.

"Me too," Ethan added. "And you'd better put a real stamp on it and everything and not just sneak it in the mailbox."

The centaur laughed, wiping at his eyes with the ball of his hand. "I will." He gave a single sniffle, then cleared his throat and smiled at them. "Well, don't let it get cold."

Maya pressed him for information about Evie and their first date while they ate—with all the interest and inappropriate questions of a self-appointed mother. Ethan wasn't immune, either; she asked him at least a hundred more questions about Luke, some of which Carlos was happy to answer for him. They chatted about Maya's accounting job in the city, some of the more comedy-of-errors dates she'd been on herself in the past few weeks, and Ethan's book in progress. Carlos told them the story of how he'd bought the land he lived on years ago for cheap because both the barn and the farmhouse had been run-down, and he'd been working to fix it up properly ever since.

It felt more like a family dinner than any one Ethan had ever been to with his actual parents. He wished Luke had been there, too.

After they'd all stuffed themselves, Maya insisted Carlos relax on the couch, and she recruited Ethan to help her with the dishes. He washed while she dried—which seemed mildly disproportionate, since she was able to do it by magic, but he didn't complain.

With a quick glance over his shoulder, Ethan verified that Carlos seemed to be dozing on the sofa, but he still lowered his voice so he wouldn't be heard over the sound of the running water.

"So what I *didn't* say about Luke is that I left his house in a fit the other day. Fled, is more like it."

"Why? Something go wrong?"

"It was going right," he clarified, "until I—I saw his—"

Her mouth dropped open into an O. "Ethan, tell me you're not about to say what I think you're about to say."

"He still had his pants on!" he hissed. "Everybody still had pants on. But it was—I mean, I've seen some things on the Internet in my day, but—when I thought about where he'd want it to *go*, I lost it."

She narrowed her eyes at him while she laid a dry plate on top of the stack. "How startling are we talking, here? I need a frame of reference."

"I don't—I don't know," Ethan sighed. He set down his scrub sponge and tried to hold out his hands in an approximation of what he'd seen, then shrugged.

"The kinds of things you gay dudes complain about," Maya said with a shake of her head.

"Well it's also—it's been a while, you know?" He picked up one end of a long casserole dish and squirted some soap into it. "I've never been exactly Mr. Promiscuous, and this would be like...going straight from little league to the Olympics."

"Do they play baseball at the Olympics?"

"What? I don't know. Who cares?"

"I'm just saying," she muttered with a shrug. "Anyway, it's just a dick, Ethan. If you're worried about it, get some practice in first. We can find you a big green dildo."

"Maya," he whined, "I'm serious."

"So am I! Don't act like you own zero dildos. I helped you pack. Just get yourself warmed up before you go see him next; it'll be fine. And tell him he's so big you got scared. He'll probably like that."

"I am absolutely not telling him that," Ethan grumbled as he scrubbed, frowning down into the sink.

But she wasn't wrong.

Maya left on Sunday evening after one last dinner at Ophelia's, which she insisted Carlos, Evie, and Luke also attend. It was noisy, and Ethan ate entirely too much food, but he didn't mind at all. How could he, sat beside Luke with the orc's arm across the back of the booth?

He walked on the side of the road while Carlos gave her a lift to the house on his back, and Ethan drove her to the airport and hugged her goodbye amid promises to visit soon. She called him an idiot for crying as she pulled away, but she stroked his hair and kissed his cheek before drawing up the handle on her suitcase and waving on her way through the broad automatic doors.

Ethan kept wiping at his face during the long drive home, but after some deep breaths and loud music, he actually felt relieved as he pulled into the yard in front of his house. He would have the chance to be alone now—and Maya had been right about practicing.

16

The next couple of weeks began to feel almost like a routine. Ethan would work during the day, sometimes have lunch with Carlos or Luke or both, and most evenings, he would find himself at Luke's little cabin house. When he had prosthetic-related book questions, Luke would answer them; he seemed to enjoy sitting on the couch beside Ethan and watching him sketch. When Ethan went home, Luke would kiss him, but it never felt the way a good-night from Nareth had—there was nothing pushing or expectant about it. And he hadn't laid a hand on more than Ethan's cheek since that night on the sofa. Ethan was certain he wanted more—Ethan did too, if he was honest. And he hadn't been practicing at home for nothing. It was still just a matter of nerves, and with Luke seeming to be waiting for Ethan to make the first move, the heat death of the universe was likely to come before either of them.

Ethan had been to two more brief prosthetic-fitting appointments now. It didn't even seem awkward anymore for Luke to strip down in front of him. He'd become more used to seeing Luke without his leg on at all, in fact. He frequently took it off once he was settled in at home for the evening. Even as well-fitted as his socket was, not wearing it still had to be much more comfortable. Luke used his single crutch to get around the house, or, if he didn't have far to go, he just held himself up on the wall or the kitchen counter. Ethan had worried after him at first, but seeing how well he handled himself made Ethan embarrassed he'd ever doubted him.

His favorite pastime, though, was the one he was currently enjoying—sitting in Luke's garage, music playing, while the orc made use of his gym equipment. He'd offered, precisely once, to help Ethan do a workout too, and it had gone exceptionally poorly. Ethan was just going to have to accept that he was always going to need help opening jars and be at peace with that.

Luke, on the other hand, never seemed to need help with anything. He had a whole gym in his garage, with a bench, a squat rack, and a tower of heavy plates that took him no effort to move. Luke was ridiculously strong, even without the benefit of two natural legs— when he filled the barbell with so many plates it looked like a cartoon and the bar bent when he started to lift it, it came up off the floor just the same as if Ethan had tried to lift the empty bar. Probably easier, actually.

Ethan used it as an excuse to ogle, but also to practice sketching muscular figures while he watched. He knew the names of most of a human body's muscles, since he'd taken more than one anatomy study in college—but he'd rarely had the chance to see such pronounced ones in person. So he sat, watching Luke's arms and shoulders as they pressed pounds in the triple-digits up from his chest over and over, trying to capture the stretch and flex in the sketch on his tablet.

His fingers were getting a little numb; the garage had only a small heater in it to keep away the frost, and while Luke was kept warm by his activities, Ethan sat on an unused bench in the corner, puffy coat zipped up to his chin and knit beanie pulled down around his ears. He looked over at Luke as he heard the clang of the bar dropping back onto its safety catch and smiled as the orc slowly sat up, shoulders slumped slightly from exertion. A drip of sweat rolled down his temple, which he wiped away with the back of one wrist as he let out a long, slow breath.

It was worth the cold.

"How many of me do you think are on that bar?" Ethan asked, and Luke chuckled. He never got tired of that sound—quiet and low, almost like an engine himself.

"You want me to try to bench you, is that what you're saying?"

Ethan's heart gave a sudden thump. "...Could you?"

Luke paused, considering for a moment, then waved him over. "Take your coat off."

"Wait, seriously?"

"Mhm. I've never tried a person before."

Ethan laughed as he set aside his tablet and unzipped his jacket, leaving it on the bench as he stepped close. Luke examined him for a few seconds, then nodded.

"Okay. On your back, I think." He laid down on the bench again and patted his own chest.

Ethan inched closer, then turned around, awkwardly budging up against him. "I'm not gonna hurt you?"

Luke stared up at him. "You think you weigh enough to hurt?"

"I don't know!" He stretched himself so that his back arched over Luke's chest, and at the orc's command, crossed his arms and ankles and tried to keep his body tense—that part wasn't difficult.

Luke flattened a hand between Ethan's shoulder blades and gripped him by the back of one thigh—and the next second, Ethan was lifted into the air. Once, then twice, then three times, Ethan's back lightly brushing Luke's chest each time before he was pushed upward again. It was impossible not to laugh, which made him a worse human barbell—which meant Luke struggled to keep a good grip on him, which made *him* laugh. Soon he'd been deposited on the garage floor, where he slipped onto his butt, still laughing as Luke rose.

"You're more of a wriggler than the bar is," he said with a smile.

"Sorry," Ethan said, pulling to his feet and dusting off the seat of his jeans, "it's my first day."

Luke reached up to take a gentle hold of one of his hands, stroking the backs of his fingers with one large thumb. "You're freezing. Let's get you inside."

"Yes, please," he agreed.

"Pizza?"

"Pizza."

Ethan ordered their dinner while Luke showered, happy to distract himself from picturing that activity. Luke's powerful grip on the back of his thigh had been hard enough to take. If he hadn't started to laugh, Ethan definitely would have embarrassed himself.

They ate in front of the fireplace, one of Luke's spare blankets tossed over Ethan's shoulders. Luke hadn't put his prosthetic back on after his shower, and he sat damp-haired beside Ethan in a simple pair of warm sweatpants and a long sleeve shirt, smelling like eucalyptus shampoo. Ethan showed him some of the latest pages he'd been working on, barely noticing when he leaned close enough that his shoulder pressed into Luke's arm.

"You know, I've been doing so much reading about this stuff lately," he said as he set his tablet down. "And actually, I think it's...really cool. I mean, I know it's better to keep your leg if you have that option, but—the technology has come so far, and some people are getting, like, *magic*-enhanced prosthetics, and there are so many different kinds of knees and hands and everything, all used for different kinds of things. Specialized, you know?"

Luke nodded. "I've actually been saving up for a new knee that's better for riding."

"See?" Ethan smiled. "That's so cool. It's like the next stage of transhumanism is here. People have special limbs that are good at riding motorcycles, hiking, mountain climbing—it's wild. My legs aren't even good at one thing. All I ask them to do is walk, and I still trip on my own feet sometimes."

Luke smiled at him, shifting a bit to bring the hand he was leaning on up to brush through Ethan's dark, unkempt hair. "It's nice to hear someone talk about it like that. Like an opportunity instead of a disability."

"You don't seem too disabled to me," Ethan said. "Not with the way you throw all that weight around like it's nothing."

"Eh," Luke answered with a small shrug, "I only do it to impress cute boys."

Ethan's face flushed, and he curled his knees a little closer to his chest and held onto his ankles.

Luke ran a thumb over the smaller man's jaw, drawing his attention upward again. "Is it working?"

"It's—it's working," Ethan admitted, inhaling sharply as Luke closed the gap to kiss him. It was slow, and soft, and Ethan's skin felt like it might melt off his bones at the gentle warmth of the other man's touch. He found himself briefly chasing the kiss when Luke pulled back, and he looked up into the orc's pale eyes with heat in his cheeks.

Luke hesitated just a moment before a faint smile touched his lips.

"Good."

Ethan pulled his bottom lip between his teeth in a smile.

They picked up after themselves, and once the dishes were washed and the pizza remains safely in the fridge, Ethan checked his watch.

"It's pretty late," Luke said before Ethan could. He leaned against the kitchen counter to support himself on one leg and glanced briefly toward the door. "You could...just stay if you want to."

"Stay?" Ethan squeaked, hands tightening into fists at his sides. "Stay all night?"

"If you want," Luke said again. He lifted one hand against the question Ethan's brain asked without waiting for it to come out of his mouth. "No pressure. Just...it's late. If you don't want to drive."

Ethan looked across at him, standing so casually in his house clothes—it looked a little funny where his cut pant leg ended halfway to the floor with nothing inside it, but to Ethan, it looked like...comfort. It looked like someone who trusted Ethan enough to know he would never look at him and grimace. That Ethan was someone he could ask to grab something from the kitchen because it was easier than hopping. Who understood the desire to want to just *exist* without expectations or performance.

He didn't want to go home.

"Okay," he said, and Luke's lifted eyebrows looked as surprised as Ethan felt.

"Okay?" Luke echoed, and then he subtly straightened, nodding. "Okay. I'll...find you something to sleep in, and bring a towel? If you want to shower. I think I have a spare toothbrush somewhere, too." He turned to start toward the bathroom, scooping up his crutch on the way, then paused and looked back over his shoulder. "Unused."

"Perfect," Ethan said with a laugh. He followed, lingering in the short hallway near the bathroom while Luke gathered supplies. He took the offered towel and folded clothes, then let Luke by into the bathroom to show him the still-wrapped toothbrush in the cabinet.

"You can just—take that chair out of there," he said as he edged back out of the doorway. "Or use it I guess. If you feel like sitting," he added with a chuckle. "Use anything in there you like. Whatever you need."

"Okay," Ethan said, avoiding Luke's gaze so his blush didn't worsen. "Thanks." He shut the bathroom door, laid his borrowed linens on the toilet, and hesitated.

He was about to shower in Luke's house. Wear his clothes. Sleep in bed beside him. What had made him agree to this? What was he thinking? He pulled at his shirt and paused once it was over his head, letting it hang from his elbows while he smiled. His only consolation was that Luke, in his way, seemed a little nervous, too.

Ethan decided to leave the chair where it was and just shower to the best of his ability, which meant occasionally twisting to avoid it, and he allowed himself to linger with the scent of Luke's shampoo suds in his own hair. He hung the towel up on the wall rod to dry and tried to dress himself in the clothes Luke had given him—the t-shirt was baggy but wearable, but the pants...were a no go. Even when Ethan tightened the drawstring at the waist, they were just too large. They fell down his narrow hips almost immediately.

He stood for a while with them pooled around his ankles, frowning down at himself. At least he could put his underwear back on. The shirt came low enough on him that it was *almost* decent. He sighed, folded the pants again, then opened the toothbrush from the cabinet and helped himself to some of Luke's toothpaste. It was cinnamon flavored—Ethan didn't know there was anyone on the planet who *actually* bought cinnamon toothpaste.

When he came into the bedroom, Luke was finishing fixing the comforter and putting a spare pillow into a case, and he froze when Ethan appeared in the doorway.

"The, uh—the pants are too big," Ethan said, and a few quiet seconds went by before Luke answered.

"Right. Sorry. Is that gonna be—"

"It's fine," Ethan cut him off. "I usually sleep in something similar anyway."

"I remember," Luke said, then seemed to remember himself. "When I came to fix the drywall. I figured those were pajamas."

"Right." He hesitated a moment before laying the folded pants on top of the nearby dresser with his own clothes.

"Anyway," Luke carried on, circling the bed again and reaching up into his closet, "here." He took down another blanket and laid it over one side of the bed. "It's supposed to be pretty cold tonight. So." Luke approached him and paused near the door. "I'll be right back. You can go ahead and get settled, if you want."

"Yeah. Thanks," Ethan said weakly. He stepped out of the way as Luke moved past him on his way to the bathroom, and as soon as he heard the door click shut, he shot to the far side of the bed.

This was it. Luke's bedroom. Luke's bed. He was here. He could do this.

He stared at the comforter until the bathroom door knob turned again, then whipped it back and dropped inside, pulling the blanket up to his chin.

Oh, this was such a bad idea.

Luke appeared in the doorway on his crutch, but he didn't have house clothes on anymore—just a pair of soft-looking brown sleep pants, the right leg cut shorter so it didn't hang all the way to the ground. He didn't pay Ethan any mind as he clicked off the light, moved over to the bed, and pulled back the blanket. He just leaned his crutch against the nightstand and slid under the comforter, letting out a small sigh as he settled on his back.

He looked even larger like this, laid out beside Ethan's substantially smaller body, the blanket doing a poor job at covering the curves of his hair-covered chest. He looked over at Ethan with a smile, cementing him in place.

"You good?"

"Uh—yeah. Yeah. Good."

"You...usually sleep with your glasses on?"

"Oh." Ethan grimaced as he pulled them off of his face, but Luke only smiled as he took the folded frames and set them on the nightstand for him.

Luke turned to click off the small lamp on the table, then situated himself again, arms draped lazily over his middle outside the blanket.

The silence in the room pounded in Ethan's ears. Luke wasn't at the edge of the bed, but he wasn't too near Ethan, either—he was in a perfectly normal, casual spot to be when sharing a bed with someone. Ethan laid on his back, staring up at the ceiling with the blanket clutched in his fists at his chest. He would definitely try to make a move, wouldn't he? Now that they were in bed together, both half naked, with the lights off?

Ethan tensed when Luke shifted on the mattress, but after a brief movement, he went still again—just getting comfortable.

Luke really was okay with them just...sleeping? That night on the couch, Ethan hadn't stopped him—Luke had noticed he was nervous, and he'd stopped himself. He'd been fine with it. He'd made sure Ethan knew he was fine with it. It had felt like...whatever the opposite of pressure was. Ethan was used to being the one to make excuses, to feign illness, or just to panic his way out of sexual situations like he had with Nareth. To have someone not even attempt to sleep with him when he was half naked in their bed, for them to let him set his own pace for once, warmed him from the inside out.

There was no way he was going to be able to sleep like this. With Luke *also* half naked next to him? This man who talked so gently to him, who made him laugh, who could pick Ethan up and snap him like a twig, but who always treated him like he was made of glass? Who seemed so cool and aloof, but who was actually thoughtful, introspective, and kind? Who fed stray cats and gave them names? Who made certain Ethan knew that his company was good enough, and that he didn't need his body.

Ethan had never been more turned on in his entire life.

He looked over at Luke, who laid with his eyes closed, breath coming in soft waves, and he sat up on one elbow. He scooted a little bit closer, one hand supporting himself on Luke's chest as he leaned in and kissed him.

Luke briefly tensed underneath him in surprise, but then his arm snaked underneath Ethan and held him close, fingers spreading against his back. He pulled Ethan tight against him and opened his mouth to taste him, and Ethan's fingers curled into the larger man's chest as a soft sound slipped out of him. Luke was solid and warm against him, and his kiss was eager. The orc's fingers slid through his hair, and Ethan felt himself pressing close into him, hands exploring the soft muscle of the other man's chest and stomach. He wanted more of him. All of him.

Ethan let out a quiet yelp as Luke shifted him, turning them both onto their sides, and slid a hand down his waist to his bare thigh. Ethan's body arched against him all on its own, his mouth opening to welcome Luke's exploring tongue. He felt the hard press of him through his sleep pants, and a shiver went up his spine, breath catching in his chest as the other man's hand squeezed his slender thigh. Ethan ran his palms down Luke's stomach, barely brushing the waistband of his pants when the orc clenched around him, and Luke pulled back to break the kiss, looking down at him in the darkness of the room with only space for their panting breath between them.

"Are you okay with this?" he whispered.

"What?" Ethan breathed, his head swimming. "Yeah."

"We don't have to if you don't—"

"Luke," Ethan cut him off, nails biting gently into the other man's stomach, "I think you don't fuck me right now, I might actually die."

A tense second went by, Luke's pale yellow eyes seeming to catch what scraps of light remained in the room—and then he was on Ethan's lips again, devouring him in a kiss. He gripped the waistband of Ethan's underwear and pulled it away from him in such a sudden, forceful movement that Ethan heard the stitching rip. Ethan whimpered helplessly into Luke's kiss as the orc's hand closed around him, large and hot and stroking him with a firm, eager grip.

His hands lost track of what they were doing, his brain muddled by the intensity of Luke's mouth on his. He was pressed into the mattress, his shirt pushed up to reveal his torso to the chilled air of the bedroom, and then Luke's tongue was running over one of his nipples, drawing a shamefully wanton sound from his throat. Every brush of his blunt tusks hitched Ethan's breath, and Luke's hand on him flushed heat all over his body, coiling tension in his belly. This was too much—he was drowning.

"I'm—" he barely managed to get out between breaths, "if you don't stop—"

The low, rumbling growl of encouragement from Luke's chest was the final straw. Ethan grabbed at the orc's broad shoulders, his body arching as he spilled himself over Luke's fingers and his own stomach. He trembled and gasped until Luke kissed him again, melting him into the bed. Luke pressed his lips to Ethan's mouth, his cheek, his jaw, and close to his ear.

Ethan tried to catch his breath as Luke pulled away from him to open the drawer in his bedside table, but it was impossible. His skin was still on fire, and the soft, familiar click of a cap sent another jolt through his stomach. He let Luke spread his legs with a gentle hand, and he sucked in a breath as the cool gel on the other man's fingers touched his skin.

"Are you okay?" Luke asked in a soft voice that did nothing to help Ethan's trembling.

He nodded, bottom lip caught in his teeth. He let out the breath in his lungs as Luke pressed inside of him, fingers tangling in the orc's hair at the thick intrusion. He whimpered and sighed underneath the other man as Luke propped himself up on one elbow, kissing his chin, neck, and chest and laving his tongue over his nipple.

Luke was patient with him, teasing him and easing him into readiness with slow, gentle hands, until Ethan was panting and writhing and pressing down on him, eager for more.

"Please," he begged, and a quiet, longing groan sounded in Luke's throat.

Luke shifted on the mattress, the loss of his hand drawing a whine of desperation out of Ethan. He pulled on the waistband of his own pants, seeming to fight with them for just a moment, and a sudden flash of clarity lit Ethan's brain.

"Are you—without your leg on, will it be—"

Luke turned to press a kiss to Ethan's jaw. "I should have told you you're going to have to be on top for this to work."

Ethan froze, watching Luke for a moment with his heart hammering panic in his chest—then he took a deep, steadying breath and pressed both hands into the orc's chest, forcing him onto his back as he sat up. He wet his lips and brushed Luke's hands away, hooking his fingers under the larger man's waistband. He could do this.

Luke's voice softly murmuring his name like a question steeled his nerves. He'd been so patient and perfect already—Ethan didn't want him wondering now if this was what Ethan really wanted.

That didn't stop his breath from catching in his throat as he freed the orc's erection, though. He was intimidatingly large. It took both of Ethan's hands to hold him, but the soft gasp Luke made at his first touch was worth all the nerves he'd built up until this point. He wanted more of that.

Ethan savored the heat of the soft skin under his hands and the quickening of Luke's breath as he stroked him, only pausing to let Luke tug the oversized shirt up over Ethan's head and toss it away. He tried to slow his breathing while Luke reached into his bedside drawer and tore open a condom from a new box, but even watching the man roll it down himself put Ethan on edge. He supported himself on Luke's chest as he settled on his lap, shivering at the firm grip of the orc's hands at his waist. Ethan took hold of him and drew in a long, preparatory breath, then began to ease himself downward—but all the air immediately left his body. Luke was larger than anything Ethan had been practicing with, and even with the other man's patient, attentive care, he struggled to relax enough to fit him. Tears pricked the corners of his eyes, and he gasped as the very tip of Luke's erection slipped inside of him, but he had to stop there. His breath came in shuddering pants, his fingers splayed against Luke's chest as he paused.

"Ethan," Luke said, his thumb brushing away a tear rolling down his cheek, "it's okay. Let's stop."

"I don't want to," he answered with a shake of his head, but when he tried to push down a little farther and grimaced, Luke made the decision for him. He was lifted free with strong, gentle hands and deposited on his back again, and in the next moment, Luke was over him, holding himself up on his single knee and both hands on either side of Ethan's waist.

"Don't push yourself," he whispered against Ethan's lips.

"But I want to—make you feel good too."

Luke hummed softly into his next kiss, and he shifted himself to hook one arm underneath Ethan's knees and lift them up toward his shoulder. "I'm not letting you off that easy," he murmured. He leaned Ethan's legs against his chest, then paused to reach back for the previously cast aside tube of gel, balancing himself on one arm and leg.

"But I thought you said—" Ethan gasped softly as he felt Luke's weight shifting closer to him. "I thought you said I had to be—"

"I was teasing," he admitted, nipping softly at the smaller man's bottom lip. After a snap of the discarded condom, he pressed himself smoothly between Ethan's thighs, holding his legs tight together with one strong arm. "But I couldn't interrupt a view like that."

"You—" Ethan began to protest, but any trace of irritation left him as Luke started to move. The gel warmed instantly between them, and Ethan gasped at the hot weight of Luke against him.

"Use your hands," Luke murmured as he bent to close his mouth over Ethan's in an overwhelming kiss.

Ethan obeyed; he wrapped his hands around both of them the best he could, whining and whimpering as they slid together at the quickening pace Luke set. Ethan could barely breathe—Luke felt massive over him like this, pressing into him and holding him so easily in place. He wasn't going to last long. Not with Luke kissing him, hips hitting hard against the backs of his thighs, velvet skin slipping under his fingers. Ethan cried out, fingers gripping tighter around them as he finished again, adding further heat to their sticky mess. Luke groaned against his neck and pushed faster, grip tightening on Ethan's trembling thighs until he gave a tight, clenched grunt and spilled his own orgasm onto Ethan's hollowed stomach.

They breathed together like that for a few moments, caught in a long, lazy kiss, until Luke reluctantly pulled free and dropped heavily onto the mattress beside him.

"I'm sorry I couldn't—" Ethan started, and Luke quieted him with an arm around his shoulders, pulling the smaller man into his chest.

"This is more than enough," he whispered into Ethan's hair. He pressed a soft kiss there, then pulled free again. "Stay here."

Ethan waited while Luke rose from the bed, flinching a little in the sudden light from the bathroom. He tried to clean himself with the warm, damp cloth Luke brought back, but the orc refused, urging him back down and sitting on the edge of the bed to gently wipe any trace of stickiness from his body. He tossed the towel into the hamper in the corner and laid down with him again, tugging the blanket up over them both and curling Ethan close against his chest.

Ethan smiled into Luke's shoulder, hesitating just a moment before wrapping his arm around the larger man in return.

He'd never slept better in his life.

Ethan woke up to an empty bed and the smell of cooking. He stretched himself over the edge of the bed to reach the clothes he'd abandoned the night before and pulled the borrowed shirt on over his head—but his underwear was actually torn. Heat flooded his face at the memory of Luke so eagerly undressing him, and he gathered his own pants from the dresser and pulled them on in a rush. He wadded up the underwear and stuffed them into the pocket of his jeans to be disposed of later and grabbed his glasses from the nightstand.

He stood in the bedroom doorway, looking out into the hall to the rest of Luke's house. He'd really spent the night here. He and Luke had actually—well, maybe not *actually*—but they'd—

Ethan covered his face in both hands and took a deep breath. It was going to be hard to look him in the face in the full light of day.

He forced himself to step out into the hallway and around the corner, pausing at the edge of the kitchen. Luke stood on both legs in front of the stove, but he still wore the mismatched pants from the night before, so his prosthetic was fully visible below the cut fabric. Ethan guessed that leg wasn't likely to get cold. At least he'd put a shirt on—that was good for Ethan's heart.

He watched with a faint smile while Luke took two plates from the cabinet and laid them on the counter just in time for two slices of bread to pop up from the toaster. The orc set them carefully at the edges of the plates, then scooped what looked like two monstrous servings of bacon and eggs from his pan. When he turned to pull open the silverware drawer, he spotted Ethan lurking and jumped.

"Hey," he said with a quick smile. "Good morning."

"Good morning," Ethan answered. "Sorry I overslept."

"You didn't. I was kind of hoping to catch you before you got up, actually." Luke set a fork from the drawer on each plate and nudged one an inch in Ethan's direction. "But at the table is good, too."

Ethan's stomach did such a sudden flip that he put a hand on it to stop its escape. This man had been planning to bring him breakfast in bed.

"Coffee?" Luke asked, already pulling down a mug for himself.

"Uh—yes please."

"Milk and sugar, right?"

"Right," Ethan confirmed in a swiftly weakening voice. This wasn't real life. He took the plate Luke offered and sat with him at the small dining room table, thanking the orc quietly as he placed a mug of coffee in front of him.

"Are you feeling okay?" Luke asked as he settled into his own chair.

"Yeah! Yeah. I'm fine."

He took a sip of the coffee, and it was perfect. The eggs were soft, the bacon was crispy, and the toast was a crunchy, chewy brown. Across from him, Luke was casually leaned on one elbow, his thick shoulder hunched slightly while he ate. His hair was bed-mussed, and a day's worth of growth shadowed his jaw. When he looked up with those soft eyes that had stared at him so intensely the night before, Ethan's knees instinctively pressed together under the table to quell the wash of heat that flooded him. It wasn't possible for someone to be this perfect.

"You look like you're thinking serious thoughts," Luke said softly.

"I'm sorry about last night," Ethan answered, then snapped his mouth shut to swallow. That had not been what he'd meant to say.

A faint crease formed in Luke's brow. "Sorry as in you regret it?"

"No! No no!" Ethan's fork clattered to his plate as he raised his hands to wave away the idea. "I'm—sorry about—with—because I couldn't—"

"Oh," Luke mercifully cut him off. He shook his head. "Really don't worry about it. That's—" He shifted in his chair a little and scooted a piece of egg on his plate. "This is going to sound like bragging, but it's not like this is the first time it's been a problem. I know what to expect."

"I just was really worried about it going in—I mean! Going into the situation, not—not going as in going in. In. I tried to practice enough so that I was ready, and then when I got there, I still couldn't, so I guess I was worried you were...disappointed."

Luke had gone still across the table from him. He stared for a few seconds before speaking again. "...Practiced?"

All the blood in Ethan's face drained into his shoes. "Did I say practiced?"

"You did that...because of me?"

Ethan gripped the edges of his chair. "Well I mean, I knew I *wanted* to, and I kept thinking about...I mean—"

He was cut off by a sudden rattle of silverware and the deep scraping sound of the whole dining table being shoved aside, and in the next moment, he was lifted out of his seat by one strong arm and thrown over Luke's shoulder. It only took a few long steps for him to be deposited on the mattress in a brief bounce, where he scrambled back in alarm as Luke planted his good knee on the bed and leaned over him.

"What did you keep thinking about?" he murmured, one hand firmly on the side of Ethan's neck and lips brushing over the corner of his mouth.

He expected him to be able to talk in a position like this? Ethan shivered under the other man's kiss, clutching at the front of Luke's t-shirt with a vice grip.

"Hm?" Luke pressed gently, one tusk prodding the soft flesh under Ethan's jaw as he kissed down his neck.

"I—" Ethan started, breath catching in his chest at the warm brush of the orc's fingers through the hair at the back of his head. "I saw you get hard when we were kissing on the couch that day and I saw how big you were and that's why I left because I was scared I'd get split in half so I wanted to be as ready as I could be before we tried anything."

Luke paused, and Ethan's face scrunched in a grimace of shame as the orc pulled back to look at him. A tense lull passed between them for just a few seconds, and then Luke laughed, pulling Ethan's head toward him and pressing a single soft kiss to his lips. He shifted his weight and sat next to him on the bed, hand still in his hair.

Ethan rubbed at his eyes with the ball of one hand, trying to stay the watery embarrassment threatening to leak out of them, and Luke turned him gently with a hand on his cheek.

"You're adorable," he said, his forehead softly thunking against Ethan's.

"I'm—a disaster," Ethan answered miserably, but Luke just kissed him again and drew him close so Ethan could press his face into his shoulder.

"Will you be my disaster?" he asked after a pause, sounding hesitant. "It probably seems weird to ask now, especially after last night, but...I like to know where I stand with things like this, and I don't like to assume. So do you want to...be my boyfriend?"

Ethan went still for a moment, feeling like someone had just opened a fresh, bubbly can of soda inside his chest, then sat back a little to look up at the man holding him. Luke was...blushing? He definitely was. His muted green cheeks had taken on a soft, dark tint, and Ethan saw the bob of his Adam's apple as he swallowed. He gave a hopeful half smile, bottom lip tucked in his teeth. This man was trying to say *Ethan* was the adorable one.

"I'd like that," Ethan said, one hand worrying the fabric of Luke's shirt near his stomach.

"Yeah?" Luke asked as if it was an unexpected answer.

When Ethan nodded, Luke took his face in both hands and kissed him again, twice, three times, until Ethan laughed and pushed at his chest. Luke smiled down at him, brushing his cheek with one thumb.

"Then, why don't we finish the breakfast your boyfriend made for you before I have to get to work?"

Ethan smiled, his own cheeks flushed. "Sounds good."

17

A few days later, when Ethan and Luke made their fourth drive to the prosthetist office, Luke went through the same motions of trying on the newest test socket, standing around in it, walking a few laps around the room—and, finally, Daniel was satisfied. He lifted all four arms in triumph, then rolled across the room on his stool and retrieved a whole drawer of swatches. There were a dozen colors to choose from for the socket itself, and twice as many samples of skin tones for the prosthetic foot—including a wide range of shades of green, of course. Daniel and Luke chose the one closest to his natural skin color, and Luke decided on the carbon fiber socket.

Luke seemed so much more excited about the process now. Ethan sat in his chair in the corner, holding Luke's bag for him and smiling. It was a relief to see him no longer dreading the idea of a new leg.

"Well," Daniel said as he rolled back from Luke again, "I'll get all your parts ordered. Should be good for a final fitting next week. Did you want me to have that other knee shipped here for you?"

"Yeah; please. I'll want to make sure I'm attaching it correctly."

"Not a problem." Daniel stood and shook Luke's hand, giving the orc's shoulder a warm pat. "I'm glad we'll be able to get you up and running properly. You've come a long way, kid."

"Yeah," Luke agreed softly. "Thanks."

On their way out, Ethan handed him back his bag and looked up at him. "Is the other knee the one you mentioned? That's better for riding?"

He nodded, climbing into the car opposite Ethan. "It's a really fancy one. You can adjust it for different things depending on what you're doing, where you need the stability. And then I'll have the everyday one."

"That's so cool. Legs for every purpose."

Luke smiled, his head leaned back against the seat. "I'll be able to race again."

"Race?" Ethan's brow furrowed.

"Well, probably not with other people very much. But I'll at least be able to get out on the track again."

"Wait, what track? I didn't know you raced anything."

"Oh, yeah. Not on the street or anything—dirt bikes. I used to do it semi-professionally. I was trying to move up and make a living out of it, but then...things changed." He sat up a little straighter in his seat and looked over at Ethan, a hesitant look on his face. "I actually...wanted to thank you."

"Me?"

"Yeah. I know you're going to say you didn't do much, but just being around someone who never makes my prosthetic a big deal, and hearing the way you talk about it like it's just a change, or an opportunity, even...I've been thinking about it a lot. I was so worried about trading in this leg. But you helped me see that this isn't another loss, and it doesn't have to feel like one. So thank you."

Ethan's whole face went hot. He gripped the steering wheel tight and was glad for the excuse of needing to keep his eyes on the road, because if he'd looked at Luke just then, he definitely would have said something stupid. "I'm...glad I could help."

"I don't talk about racing a lot." Luke looked down at his lap and picked at a stray string on his bag. "It's been kind of a sore spot. I was pretty good. I had some chances open up for me. But then Aunt Lena died giving birth to Riley, and Rob needed help, so I started spending a lot more time at home, you know? Family always comes first. Then when I lost my leg, it felt like the final nail in the coffin. Just a dream I had to give up." He reached across the gap between them and took Ethan's hand from the steering wheel, lacing their fingers and giving him a soft squeeze. "But even though things are different now, I get that

I don't have to stop doing something I love just because my situation changed."

Ethan bit his bottom lip, hard, but it didn't stop the warm swell of tears pooling in his eyes. He spoke so honestly, so openly. He was so *good*. "I didn't really—"

Luke shushed him and brought his hand to his lips to press a soft kiss to Ethan's knuckles. "You did. So just let me say thanks." He paused as Ethan sniffled, and he leaned forward to look him in the face. "Are you crying?"

"I'm sorry," Ethan whimpered, pulling his hand free from Luke's grip to wipe at the tear falling down his cheek. He stopped at the next red light and pressed the balls of his hands into his eyes to try to stop the flow, but Luke gently pried them free, smiling at him and touching his hair as he leaned across the gap.

"I didn't mean to make you sad."

"You didn't!" he insisted. "I just—I'm really glad. You've been through so much, and you're still so—so—"

Luke pulled him closer by a hand at the back of his head and cut him off with a kiss. Ethan melted against him, savoring the warmth of the larger man's hand on his cheek and the slow brush of his tongue. A brief honk from behind them reminded Ethan that he was supposed to be driving, and he jolted upright and clamped his hands on the steering wheel again, shouting out a definitely unheard "Sorry!" to the driver behind them as he started off again.

Ethan took a few deep breaths before trying to speak again. If he wasn't careful, he'd let slip the thought that was really on the tip of his tongue—that he was more in love with Luke in this moment than he'd ever been with anyone in his life.

Luke saved him yet again by talking first. "So tell me how the book's coming."

Ethan's shoulders relaxed into his seat, and he smiled. That was easy to talk about, at least.

Luke's interest and constant encouragement, as well as Maya's texts demanding updates on Ethan's story, spurred him into work. His productivity usually came in waves like this—much to his editor's frustration—so he tried to channel his enthusiasm while he could.

Mostly that involved shutting himself in his house and forgetting to get up from his desk for days at a time.

When he did force himself to stand and take a walk around the house, get another energy drink from the fridge, and flex his sore hands, he spotted Evie out the front window, helping Carlos unhitch from his delivery cart. She'd been around a lot the last few days, in and out of Carlos's barn and helping him in the yard. They were *illegally* cute together—they were always laughing, or blushing as Evie adjusted Carlos's scarf for him—once Ethan had even caught them holding hands. He was glad. Carlos deserved someone who made him smile like that.

Luke brought him dinner in the evenings, either from the diner or something he'd cooked himself, and forced him to take small breaks. He didn't seem to mind hanging out while Ethan ignored him—he cleaned up after dinner so Ethan could return to his artist nest in the office, and he picked empty cans of Red Bull off the desk around Ethan while he worked. When Ethan pulled off his headphones to crack his back and stretch, he could hear Luke downstairs, watching television at a low volume, and he smiled. When it got late, Luke would come up behind him, gently pull one side of Ethan's fat headphones away from his ear, and murmur a warm, soft goodnight into it. He would remind Ethan to get *some* sleep, his tusk pressing into Ethan's cheek as he kissed it, and he'd let him get back to work.

After four days of work and very little sleep, Ethan had completed and sent a few more pages off to Dee, but he wasn't finished. He wanted to at least get through the second act before he ran out of steam, and he wasn't there yet. When he texted Maya a screenshot of a panel he was particularly proud of, she replied immediately.

I love it. But I gotta say, this is a whole lot of art-ing you've been doing lately. You remembering to eat?

Ethan paused, pulling his headphones down around his neck before picking up his phone to answer. Downstairs, the sink was running, and the soft clink of gathered silverware drifted up to the office door. Ethan pulled his legs up into his chair to squish his fluttering stomach into behaving properly.

Luke brought me dinner, he typed back. *He's here now.*

Holy shit, the answer buzzed onto his screen. *You're letting him see you in filthy cave hermit mode?*

I guess so? Is that what you call it?

Ethan, this is serious. You guys are officially serious.

He chewed his lip and looked over his shoulder at the open door. She wasn't wrong. It would have been awkward to have anyone else there—Ethan had only opened the door a crack to let in Carlos's food offerings before, ashamed to be seen in his pajamas and two-day-old bed head—but he didn't mind it with Luke. He could almost forget Luke was there entirely, except...knowing he was downstairs was even better than just being left alone. Ethan had never been *more* comfortable around someone else than he was on his own.

I guess it is a little serious, he answered, unable to keep the smile from his face.

He set his phone face down on the desk at the sound of Luke's uneven footsteps on the stairs and smiled as he appeared in the doorway, a small plate in one hand. Luke plucked an empty can from Ethan's desk and laid the plate in its place—an offering of pecan pie from Ophelia's. Before he could thank him, Luke's arms were folded around Ethan's small shoulders, engulfing him in the warmth of his body and nuzzling the crook of his neck. Ethan smiled and reached up to curl his fingers into the sleeve of Luke's hoodie. "Thanks," he said softly, tensing a little as the orc touched a kiss to his neck.

"I just wanted to touch you," he murmured against Ethan's skin, squeezing him tight. "I can go if you're in the middle of something."

Ethan shook his head, allowing himself to sink into the embrace and tilting his head to make more room for the orc's gentle caress. "I like you here," he answered.

Luke's chuckle rumbled against him, flipping his insides. "Then I guess I'll stay a while."

Ethan reached a hand up to run his fingers through Luke's dark hair, and the orc's grip tightened on him.

"If you do that, I'm really going to interrupt you."

"Promise?" Ethan whispered before his brain caught up to his mouth. A second later, he was spun in his chair so fast that he lurched sideways, and Luke's lips were on his, urging his mouth open as the orc tugged Ethan's headphones free and dropped them carelessly onto his desk.

What had Ethan said? Why had he said that? Since when did he even think things like that, let alone say them?

It was hard to be too angry at himself when Luke's hand pressed into his side, thumb running over one of Ethan's nipples over his shirt. The orc broke their kiss only to shift himself down into kneeling in front of Ethan's chair, his fingers immediately hooking into the elastic of the smaller man's pants and pulling them down his thighs. Ethan's fuzzy teddy bear slippers were discarded on the way, and when Luke slid his arms underneath Ethan's knees and fastened his grip on the arms of the chair, he was forced to grab onto the back of the seat to keep steady.

"Luke," he breathed with growing panic, "I haven't—I should shower first—"

"Too late for that," the orc murmured against the skin near Ethan's hip as he laid a hot kiss there. "Shouldn't have teased me."

Ethan didn't have time to protest further—he was enveloped in the heat of the other man's mouth, and his breath left him in a shuddering sigh. He tensed, legs tightening where they hung around the orc's thick arms, but that was the only movement he was allowed. Luke kept him precisely where he wanted him, drawing gasps and whimpers from him with every firm, eager movement of his tongue. He was exceptionally good at this. Unfairly good, considering Ethan would have to unhinge his jaw to return the favor—but he wasn't about to stop him now.

He gripped the back of his chair so tight that his hands ached, and he couldn't help the slight buck of his hips as Luke drew him so deep into his mouth that the orc's tusks scraped softly against the skin at the crease of his thighs. Ethan wet his lips and bit his cheek to try to keep in his moans, but it was pointless. Luke was so gorgeous, and his massive body barely fit between Ethan's thighs. Ethan had never been wanted like this. He panted out a warning that he was reaching his limit, but Luke ignored him, only inching closer to him and bending him into a deeper arch in the chair. One of Ethan's hands fastened into Luke's hair in desperation, and the larger man's growl of satisfaction pushed him over the edge. He cried out as waves of pulsing ecstasy washed over him, and his fingers tightened in the orc's dark waves as he spilled his orgasm into Luke's waiting mouth.

Luke finally released him once he finished twitching, but Ethan still trembled and slumped into his seat as the orc pulled to his feet.

"You shouldn't have—" Ethan protested weakly, cut off by the loom of the large body above him as Luke leaned one arm on the back of the chair above Ethan's head. He watched with a fresh thump of excitement in his chest as Luke unbuckled his belt and pushed low his jeans and underwear, freeing his erection with a faint sigh of relief. Ethan sucked in a sudden breath at the sight of him—this was very different from the darkness of Luke's bedroom. Here, in the light from Ethan's desk, he could see Luke perfectly—the darker green skin leading back to a nest of black hair that trailed up and under his shirt, where Ethan knew it made a line up the orc's firm stomach to meet the dark curls on his chest.

Before Ethan's brain had a chance to focus, his hands were already moving, both reaching for Luke and brushing fingers over velvet skin. Luke's large hand covered one of Ethan's, urging him on at an eager pace.

"Hold up your shirt," the orc rumbled, and Ethan obeyed, tugging the hem of his shirt up to bunch up around his armpits in a panting haze. Luke almost enclosed him in the chair, he was so broad, and Ethan heard the faint creak of the plastic chair back under his tightening grip.

He stroked and squeezed at the rhythm Luke set, his eyes on the other man's face. Luke's yellow eyes ran over Ethan's bare, flushed torso, and his jaw tightened as he pulsed in the smaller man's grip. Then, with a sudden, easy movement, Luke lifted him closer by a hand at the back of his neck, crushing him into a kiss.

"You're so beautiful," he murmured against Ethan's lips, and when Ethan gave him a long, firm squeeze in response, he let his forehead fall to the other man's shoulder, a tight groan catching in his throat as hot ribbons streaked across Ethan's stomach and chest. Luke had to release him to catch himself on the back of the chair again, taking a few shaky breaths before he was able to push himself to standing.

Ethan managed to put his feet on the ground as Luke took a step back, successfully preventing himself from sliding fully from the chair like the liquid his bones had become. Luke was all over him—literally—and his swiftly-cooling brain was on the verge of replacing passion with panic when the orc reached out a hand to gently brush through Ethan's hair.

"Stay put," he said, and he crossed the hall into the bathroom, returning shortly with his jeans safely fastened again and a warm cloth in his hand.

"Thanks," Ethan mumbled, doubly awkward as Luke carefully wiped the mess from his torso. When he was clean, he pulled his shirt down and his pants up, then peeked upward at Luke where they stood close together in the cluttered office. "Do you, uh...want to stay? The night?"

Luke tilted his head at him, one hand cupping Ethan's jaw as he considered. After a moment, he gave a soft, smiling sigh. "I'd better not. You seem like you're in a groove here."

"Because I'm supposed to concentrate after what you just did?"

Luke chuckled and bent down to kiss him. "I believe in you. I'll see you tomorrow?"

"Yeah," Ethan answered with a smile, holding onto the sides of Luke's hoodie.

"Eat your pie," Luke ordered as he touched another kiss to the smaller man's hair. "And get some sleep."

"I will," he promised. He didn't let go until Luke moved fully out of his reach and stepped toward the door.

"Good night, Ethan. I'll lock the door behind me."

"Good night," he echoed, standing still while Luke made his careful way down the stairs and only slumping back into his chair when he heard the thud of the front door. He reached for his headphones again, but waited until the sound of Luke's motorcycle had faded down the road to put them back over his ears.

He definitely wasn't going to be able to concentrate now.

18

When Ethan finally emerged from his hermitage and made himself presentable enough to head into town, his first stop was the library. He had a number of pages mostly-finished that he just couldn't make himself happy with. When that happened, he needed to see them on paper instead of a screen—and his printer had bitten the dust before his move.

Nareth sat at his desk near the stairs, right where Ethan expected him, and he smiled as the door swung shut.

"Hello, stranger," the elf said, laying down his pen and leaning on his elbows to look up at him. "I was beginning to think you were avoiding me."

"Sorry," Ethan answered as he slipped his bag from his shoulder into the nearest conference table chair. "There's been a lot going on."

"So I see. Did you need something librarial, or did you just come to rub my defeat in my face?"

"What?"

Nareth lifted his white eyebrows and tilted his chin toward Ethan, who paused, then looked down at himself with a frown. He'd left the house in one of Luke's hoodies, his small body almost disappearing in it.

"Oh! Geez," Ethan sighed, his face flushing bright pink as he pushed awkwardly at the oversized sleeves. "I'm sorry—I didn't mean to—I wasn't even thinking—"

Nareth laughed and waved away his rambling. "So I take it you sorted out your matter of ratios, then?"

"I don't, uh—" Ethan turned away to dig through his bag rather than let Nareth see the embarrassing shade of crimson he could feel himself becoming. "It feels inappropriate to—"

The elf hummed over the top of him. "Perhaps not."

Ethan slumped with both hands inside his bag, chin falling to his chest. He took a breath, grabbed his thumb drive from its pocket, and turned slowly back to face the librarian. "Listen, I'm sorry; I'm trying not to make it weird, but—"

"Oh, enough," Nareth scolded him. "At what point did I give you the impression I was forlorn and sulking these past weeks? Are you having a good time with your large new boyfriend or aren't you?"

"I—I am," Ethan admitted with a small nod.

"Excellent. Now let's move along. Tell me what you came here for, if it isn't my cheerful disposition."

Ethan paused, watching the elf's sharp, waiting face. Then he let out his lungful of air and smiled. "I need to print some things."

Nareth held out his hand without further question, and Ethan dropped the drive into his palm. After a brief back and forth about dimensions, Nareth got Ethan's pages printing and sat back in his chair to wait for the aging printer to do its work. A long silence stretched between them while Ethan stood off to the side of the desk, rocking slightly on his heels.

"So you've been...good?" he said when the tension became too much, but when Nareth looked up at him with a casual raise of his eyebrows, Ethan wondered if he'd been the only one feeling it.

Nareth adjusted his glasses with one delicate knuckle, subtly swinging the thin gold chain dangling from the arms. "Of course. Have you been worried about me, dear? There's no need. I told you I was fine, didn't I?"

"I know, I just mean...like...in general, you're good? I'm trying to have a normal conversation. It's not going great, is it?"

The elf smiled. "In general, I am good, yes. I appreciate your concern."

"Have you been...you know. Seeing anyone?"

"You won't tell me about your successes and/or failures, but you want to know about mine?"

"It's a general question!" Ethan insisted, hiding his face in his hands. "General!"

"Oh, I've missed you," Nareth said with a quiet chuckle. He leaned his elbows on the desk and his chin on the back of his laced fingers, peering up at Ethan over the gold rims of his glasses. "You and Luke aren't perhaps looking to form some sort of polycule, are you?"

"What—no. No thank you," he corrected himself. "One person putting up with me is lucky enough."

"Ah, so then you *are* planning to allow me to be your gossipy confidant?"

"Nareth," Ethan groaned, but it turned into a laugh as he fell into the seat closest to the elf's desk.

"Well, there's hardly any gossip. I've been irritating Ophelia again. She hasn't much cared for me ever since Zoe and I started seeing each other casually a couple of years ago. I suppose she felt some relief when you came along, but she can blame Luke for that reprieve coming to an end."

"Zoe?" Nareth and the young satyr had seemed fairly close the few times Ethan had gone with him to the diner, but—seeing each other for a couple of years was a level above that. "When you say casually, you mean..."

"Oh, yes. Purely sexual," he answered with such a cavalier tone that Ethan recoiled. "We're very compatible, but she doesn't have much patience for my personality, I think."

"Right," Ethan said softly, his brow furrowed in disbelief. If he could ever be half as confident in himself as this elf, he would be leaps and bounds ahead of where he was now. "Isn't she...a little young for you? She's only, like, twenty-three or something, right?"

"*You're* too young for me," Nareth pointed out. "How old do you think I am, Ethan?"

"I think you'll be mad at me if I guess wrong."

He laughed. "You've forgotten that my kind age so much slower than yours. I'm fifty-three."

Ethan stared at him for a few seconds. "Wow," he said. "I am too young for you."

Nareth crumpled a piece of paper on his desk and chucked it at

Ethan's face. "That's how you get banned from the library."

"But my pictures!" Ethan laughed.

"These are for your new book?" Nareth turned to check the pages waiting on the printer, flipping through them as he rolled his chair back toward Ethan.

"Yeah. It's been going really well lately, actually. Dee hasn't yelled at me in a while."

"These look good." He ticked one eyebrow, his lips curling into a smirk as he handed the pages over. "You know, I've got copies of your other two in here now. Hot commodities."

"What, really?" Ethan said with a grimace.

"What is that face? You want to make comic books, but you don't want anyone to read them?"

"I mean, that's ideal."

Nareth hummed softly. "A shame. I got to charge a late fee for the first time in years."

Ethan chuckled as he tucked the pages into a folder from his bag. "Glad to contribute, I guess?"

"I had to *call* Luke on the *telephone* before he would bring them back," the elf drawled, unplugging Ethan's flash drive and holding it out to him across the desk. "He's worryingly obsessed with you. You're sure you're safe? Blink twice if he locks you in a basement at night."

Ethan smiled as he took back the drive. "Thanks, but I think I'm good."

"Well, to each their own, I suppose." Nareth tilted his head, toying idly with one of the rings on his slender fingers. "Let's have a drink soon. I'll start to feel neglected if this keeps up."

Ethan pulled his bag back over his shoulder and puffed his cheeks out in an uncertain exhale, eyebrows lifting as he started toward the door. "I don't know; you sound *worryingly* obsessed with me."

"Get out of my library," Nareth shot back with a laugh, and Ethan raised a hand in a brief wave on his way out.

The entire ride to the prosthetist for his final fitting, Luke fidgeted with his bag, full of excess energy. It made Ethan's whole body warm to see him actually excited for a new leg instead of dreading it.

In the little room, Daniel helped Luke with his new socket, pointing out the differences between it and the previous one and showing him how to replace and attach both of his new knees. One of them, what Daniel called Luke's "walking-around leg," was very similar to the one Luke had before—matte silver and dark blue coated metal, and a solid-looking attachment for the black steel foot—but the new one looked like it had been stolen from an actual robot. A black metal rig with heavy silver bolts supported an inner hydraulic system that Luke said could be adjusted to varying tensions depending on the activity the wearer intended to participate in. There was even a piston in the foot.

"Try not to hurt yourself with it," Daniel said, but he was smiling as he watched Luke reattach his everyday knee to do some test laps around the room.

"It was more expensive than my real leg," Luke pointed out. "I'll be careful."

Daniel clapped his patient on the back with both of his left hands. "Call if you have any troubles, got it? But hopefully I won't have to see you back here for a good while."

"Right. Thanks, Daniel. I'll try not to wait until this one's falling apart next time."

"See that you don't," he agreed with a nod, and he pointed one meaty finger at Ethan. "I expect you to hold him to that."

"Yes, sir," Ethan said. He bit his lip as Luke threw him a warm smile, and they walked together back to Ethan's car for the drive home.

"Are you free the rest of the day?" Luke asked as they drew close to home.

"I can be," Ethan answered. "I got another page sent off last night, so Dee should be happy."

"Do you want to go take a walk? Just in the park or something. To give the new leg a test run."

Ethan pulled his lips between his teeth to keep from smiling too broadly. Did he want to take a walk in the park in mid-December with his handsome boyfriend? What a difficult choice.

"Sure," he said, doing his best to sound nonchalant.

He parked the car along the side of the park near downtown Adelbury, and he pulled his oversized jacket up tighter around his neck to better keep out the cold. He should have brought a scarf. He tugged on a knit beanie from his back seat and stuffed his hands into his pockets, but as soon as they stepped onto the sidewalk together, Luke reached for him, lacing their fingers and squeezing him gently in a grip warmer than Ethan's pocket.

They walked the winding path through the large park, Ethan's heart jumping in his chest as they skirted close to the main street and were spotted by a pair of holiday shoppers, who smiled at them in passing.

"You okay?" Luke asked when his hold tensed.

"Yeah, just—holding hands like this, it's—"

"Sorry," Luke said with a solemn shake of his head. "There's no avoiding it today. I've got this new leg, you know. What if I lose my balance? You'll have to help me. I'm just a poor cripple, after all."

"Oh my god," Ethan laughed, "don't say that!"

"Or maybe I just want everyone to know you're mine."

Ethan looked up at him with fresh heat in his cheeks, thankful they were already pink from the cold. Luke said things like that so casually—so confidently. His smile as he looked down at Ethan out of the corner of his eye was so gentle it made Ethan's own legs far wobblier than the orc's prosthetic.

Luke stopped walking and turned to face him, cupping Ethan's cheek with his free hand and bending down to press a long, slow kiss to his lips. "I want everyone to be jealous that you chose me," he murmured with their noses touching.

Ethan took hold of the front of the orc's jacket and let out a soft snort of laughter. "It's cute that you think *I'm* the one anybody would be jealous of in this relationship."

"Of course," Luke said as he straightened. "Surly orcs are a dime a dozen."

"Is surly what we're going with to describe you?"

"Sometimes," he said with a shrug. He watched Ethan's face for a few hesitant moments, then glanced back the way they'd come. "Anyway, this leg works." He grinned down at him. "Want to help me try the other one?"

Trying the other one, it seemed, was more complicated than Ethan expected. They met Rob at Luke's house, and the two older orcs rolled Luke's dirt bike from his garage up onto the bed of the truck, where they secured it with canvas straps and buckles while the children raced around the yard. Ethan rode in the passenger seat of Luke's truck without question once the bike had been loaded, no longer trying not to be obvious about watching the way the hand controls worked. Luke noticed him looking and pointed out the different modifications he'd made, smiling while Ethan typed notes and took pictures with his phone.

"It was actually a lot easier to do it to the bike," he said. "Rob's been helping me get them installed on this one, now that I have a leg I can actually ride it with."

Ethan smiled at the look on the orc's face. He was so excited. This was a side of him Ethan hadn't seen before—the calm outer shell was completely broken. He liked it.

They unloaded the bike at a broad field of dirt in the middle of the woods, and Ethan frowned as he looked out over the low, sharp hills and patchy brown scraps of grass.

"This is the place?" he asked as Luke circled the truck, tugging off his overcoat and tossing it into the cab.

The next few words out of Luke's mouth fell on deaf ears—Ethan was too busy taking in the sight of him. He'd swapped out his leg and changed clothes back at the house, but now that Ethan could get a good look at him, his stomach had pretzeled itself. Luke's grey pants were snug around his hips and thighs, tucked into knee-high black boots, and his racing shirt fought against the expanse of his shoulders, the nine-tailed fox logo spread tight across his chest. He flexed his fingers into a pair of highlighter-yellow gloves and hauled a matching helmet from the bed of the truck, tucking it under one arm. This person—*this person* expected Ethan to believe *he* was the lucky one.

"I'm just glad the ramps seem to have held up pretty well," he said with his eyes on the clearing past Ethan's shoulders.

"Held up, my ass!" Rob called from the front of his own truck. "You think it was spirits got this place back into shape for you?"

"Wait—ramps?" Ethan cut in, looking between Luke and the dirt behind him—which, he was now realizing, was a track. "Those are ramps? Is it normal for there to be ramps?"

"Well, yeah," Luke answered with a chuckle. "You've never watched motocross?"

"I have not. And this is—this is okay? I mean—this is what this new knee is for, right? So it's fine?"

"Don't worry," Luke said, taking a light hold of the back of Ethan's head to draw it closer so he could touch a brief kiss to his hair. "I know what I'm doing."

Ethan nodded, but he still wrung his hands as he took up a place beside Rob and the kids. They didn't seem concerned at all—the children watched with interest as Luke mounted the blue and white bike, pulled his helmet on, and secured a pair of dark goggles over his eyes. He shooed them away once he'd settled himself, and they scattered and cackled as the engine zipped to life. Luke gave them a couple of revs at their urging, then shifted on the seat and tore onto the track in a spray of dirt from the rear wheel.

Ethan jumped and clenched his hands at the speed with which Luke took off, but he did seem to be being careful—at first. By the third lap, he looked like he was at about twice the speed he'd started at, much to the delight of the kids cheering and whooping at the edge of the track.

Rob put a heavy hand on Ethan's shoulder the first time Luke's bike left the ground completely, as if anticipating his nerves.

"He's fine," the orc assured him. "Kid's practically half motorcycle."

Ethan's knit brow softened, and he managed a small smile as Rob gave him another reassuring pat.

Then Luke revved his way through a tight corner, showered clay into the grass, and thudded to the ground, his bike's engine buzzing angrily as he skidded sideways. His back hit one of the stacked hay bales making up the outside edge of the turn, and he came to a stop with the bike half on top of him.

Ethan raced across the track immediately, followed closely by Rob and the kids, but by the time they reached Luke, he had already pushed himself up on one elbow and was pulling his goggles up to rest on the visor of his helmet.

"Are you okay?" Ethan called in a panic as he drew close. Was Luke—laughing? He was laughing. Ethan slowed to a stop a foot away from the bike and sighed as Rob hauled it upright and dropped the kickstand.

"Good thing that was the leg I already lost," Luke said, laughter muffled by the mouth guard of his helmet. He accepted Rob's offered hand and hauled himself up while his cousins pushed at him, and he paused only to dust off the leg of his pants before stepping over to the bike again.

Even half-hidden by his helmet, Ethan could see the crinkle in Luke's eyes and the smile on his face—a beaming grin unlike any Ethan had ever seen on him before. Ethan had never seen him this *happy* before. A suddenly quickened heartbeat fluttered through Ethan's chest as the orc's eyes turned on him.

"I'm good," he promised.

"I know," Ethan answered with a faint smile.

Luke grinned at him and pulled his goggles back into place, and Ethan retreated with the rest of the family back to the sidelines. After a few more laps, Rob tapped Ethan on the arm to get his attention.

"I've got to get these monsters fed. Can you help him get the bike loaded up when he's done?"

"Oh—sure. Of course."

The orc herded his children back into the cab of his pickup, waved a quick goodbye to Ethan through the window, and pulled out down the narrow lane toward the main road. Ethan climbed up to sit on the hood of Luke's truck and tucked his hands into his armpits to warm them, content to watch his boyfriend make jumps and take turns that surely would have made Ethan himself pee his pants. Luke deserved this—after the sacrifices he'd made to help his family, and the hard times he'd had learning to adjust to his new reality as an amputee, it was about time he got to have this kind of joy again. Ethan would stay there all night if that's what Luke wanted.

Ethan had started to hunch his shoulders against the deepening cold of sunset by the time Luke roared his bike to a stop a few feet from the truck. He smiled as Luke leaned a hand on the side of the pickup and eased himself off of the motorcycle, taking a few hops to balance himself once he'd put down the kickstand. He tugged off his goggles and helmet, dropping them heavily onto the hood of the truck beside Ethan, and took a long, deep breath. His dark hair was a mess, sticking up in damp waves now that it had been freed from his helmet, and there was sweat running down his temples despite the cold. He looked up at Ethan with a warm smile.

"Sorry. I didn't mean to keep you waiting so long."

"It's fine," Ethan said, dropping down to the ground to approach the bike. It still gave off heat that steamed in the cold air. "I told Rob I'd help you with this, but I'm really hoping you can take the lead, here."

Luke laughed softly and led the bike around to the back of the truck himself, then slid out the built-in ramp from the bed and rolled the motorcycle up it. He directed Ethan toward the straps on the opposite side, and he managed to do his part, though he had to stand on the top of the back wheel and bend over the side to do it. Once the bike was secure, they both climbed into the cab, and Luke tossed his coat over Ethan's shoulders to help warm him until the heater kicked on. He leaned back in the seat with an air of contented exhaustion and drove toward the road.

"I guess you had fun?" Ethan said after a pause, and Luke let out a soft snort of agreement.

"Yeah. I had fun. Thanks for coming with me. You must have worried."

"Am I so obvious?"

"Only a little," he teased.

"It was fine. You could have warned me you were likely to wipe out like that, though."

"Oh, yeah, like I'm going to admit to my cute boyfriend the first time he sees me ride that I might eat shit." He smiled sidelong at Ethan's laughter. "It just sucks that it's going to start snowing soon. I just got going again, and now I'm going to have to wait."

"I'll keep my fingers crossed for an early spring," Ethan promised him, and the smile the orc gave him put bubbles in his stomach.

Ethan was definitely, inescapably in love with him.

19

Ethan paced his living room with his phone in his hand, head hanging back as Maya called his name. He finally rolled his head forward again with a miserable whimper and frowned into the screen, where his best friend stared back at him. Her hair was all dark shades of blue and green today, but the exasperated face she was making at him was the same as always.

"I thought we'd be done having this kind of meltdown now that you guys are boyfriends."

"But I wasn't thinking this far ahead!" he protested. "I was just going along, one step at a time, like an idiot. Now it's almost *Christmas*, and he's going to take me out to see the *lights*, and it's going to be *romantic* and *amazing* and—"

"And you're moving back home in a few weeks?"

"And I'm moving back home in a few weeks!" Ethan slumped into his sofa, leaving Maya to look at the ceiling as he dropped his arms limply onto the cushions.

"Listen, this might sound like a wild idea, but have you considered maybe *not* moving back home?"

He turned his head and tilted the phone enough to look at her. "What do you mean? My apartment—"

"Your apartment is sublet, and if the guy in there now doesn't want to stay, you can find another one until your lease is actually up. And what, you think Carlos is going to kick you out at the six-month mark?"

"Well, no, but..."

"Get your notebook."

"Maya, I don't want to get my notebook—"

"Get. Your. Notebook," she commanded, glaring straight back at him when he frowned at her until he gave a grunt of frustration and carried her up the stairs to his office. He pulled open one of the desk drawers and retrieved one of many small spiral notebooks, dropping into his chair with a huff and flipping through to a blank page.

"Okay," he said, propping the phone up on his desk.

"Pros and cons of staying in Adelbury," Maya said. "Pro number one. Luke, obviously. Write it down."

Ethan did as he was told, drawing two columns on his paper and writing Luke's name under one side. "If I list everybody I'd miss, I may as well just put the whole town," he grumbled, and Maya tutted at him.

"Well, doesn't that tell you anything? Friends. Friends is a big one. More friends than just me."

Ethan paused, frowning at his paper, then made a mark on the other side of the page.

Maya stared at him. "Did you just write my name down, you absolute goob?"

"You're a con!" he shot back. "For staying here. I'd miss you. I do miss you."

"You're literally talking to me right now, Ethan. And I'd visit. If you think I'm not getting my hands on your boyfriend's beefy chest again, you are sorely mistaken."

"Please don't plan in advance to assault my boyfriend."

"The point is you're not really losing me by staying. Especially now that I know I can trust Carlos to feed you. Next pro—you won't get roped into going to any parties again."

Ethan chewed his lip and tapped his pen against the desk. "I do hate parties."

"And Ophelia's cooking. And not having an upstairs neighbor who lifts weights. Having a boyfriend who does lift weights. These are a lot of pros, here. You should probably underline Luke, like, three times."

He folded his arms over the notebook and buried his face in them with a heavy sigh. "Listen, I just—I can't do this. I have to actually talk to Luke about it."

Maya was silent for a few beats, then let out a dramatic sob. "My baby is—is all grown up and—trying to communicate with his significant other!" She pulled a blue handkerchief from thin air and blew her nose into it.

"Give me a break. I'm trying."

"I'm serious! I'm really proud of you! *Please* go talk to Luke."

"I will. Maybe—after romantic looking at Christmas lights. Or before? Is before better?"

"After," Maya said with a decisive nod. "And don't think about it until then. Just go, drink hot chocolate, look at lights, hold hands, and kiss under the moonlight. Have a good night. Don't let something that might happen ruin what's already happening now. You know?"

"Yeah," he agreed softly. "You're right."

"Someday you'll realize I'm always right."

"Someday," Ethan echoed. He sat up when a knock sounded from the door downstairs. "He's here."

"Have a good time, Ethan. Stress as little as possible."

"Right," he said. "Right. I'll talk to you later."

"Grab his ass for me," she said, and he hung up on her mid-cackle. He could do this. He could talk to Luke like a grown-up—and he could enjoy their time together now no matter what happened.

He could do this.

When he opened the door downstairs, he found Luke filling his doorway, a faint, warm smile on his face.

This was definitely a "pro."

"Ready?"

"Ready," Ethan confirmed, pulling his other sleeve up his arm as he shut the door. He'd prepped as best he could—warm sweater, long jacket, scarf, knit toque, and gloves. He could already feel a shiver coming on as he crossed the yard, but Luke looked fine, of course. He'd just thrown on jeans and a long-sleeved shirt under his brown leather shearling bomber, and he didn't seem to be suffering in the slightest. Ethan would have to stick his hands up the orc's shirt later.

The drive out to Glen's farm wasn't bad, but it was at least far enough for the truck to get warmed up. Carlos hadn't stopped talking about the farm for what felt like a month—how Glen had really gone all out this year, how hard he and Evie and Joe had worked to help put up the lights and decorations, and how thrilled he was to be put in charge of the hot chocolate stand this time.

The lights were visible for at least a mile before they parked. Arches, trees, and icicles in every color spread across the field, and Ethan couldn't keep the smile from his face as he climbed out of the truck.

Carlos hadn't undersold the spectacle—as they drew closer, Ethan saw animated displays, painted murals with moving spotlights, and a miniature train that chugged along with laughing children in each little car. Soft music was playing from speakers Ethan couldn't see, and the whole broad field was alight with shifting and blinking colors. Glen himself was wandering the open area, dressed up like Santa Claus. He wasn't especially convincing—he had opted to leave his dark beard visible rather than put on a fake one, and he hadn't bothered to make his belly look any bigger—but that didn't seem to be the point. He had a wide smile on his face, and kids constantly ran up to him to accept the candy canes he handed them from a red bucket.

It wasn't only Christmas on display, either—whole sections of the farm were lit up with blue and white menorahs and Stars of David, or the red and green candles of the Kwanzaa Kinara. There were pentacles decorated with wood and berries and dried orange slices, a nativity display made of carefully-painted wood figures, a collection of wooden dolls with horned, feathered faces and Indigenous designs, and even a huge, red ribbon-wrapped goat made of straw. Glen had clearly made an effort to represent every holiday of the season. It made for a bit of a mish-mash, aesthetically, but that didn't seem to matter to anyone in attendance. All the lights were beautiful, and it was hard for Ethan to find anything to criticize about the evening while he was walking hand-in-hand with Luke.

Carlos waved at them when they approached the hot chocolate stall. He had a warm red coat snugged up high enough on his chin to meet the earflaps of his fuzzy hat and a tasseled blanket draped over his back and haunches, and he beamed as they stepped close.

"Hey guys! I'm so glad you could come!"

"It looks great, Carlos," Luke said, and Ethan nodded enthusiastic agreement.

The centaur poured two paper cups of hot chocolate from a metal dispenser on the table and offered them with a smile. "Make sure you do the whole walk," he said. "Don't miss the part on the right between the two candy canes." He gave Luke a conspicuous wink that warmed Ethan's cheeks.

"Good looking out, buddy," Luke answered with a chuckle.

They thanked him for their drinks and smiled as Carlos waved before turning his attention to the next person waiting. Luke gave Ethan's hand a gentle squeeze and opened his mouth to speak, but they were interrupted by Glen stepping in front of them with a loud, deep Santa Claus laugh, one fist on his hip and the other extending his bucket.

"Happy holidays, boys!"

Ethan laughed and reached out to take a candy cane for both of them. "Thanks."

"Nothing spooky this time," Glen promised, clapping Ethan so hard on the shoulder that he swayed. "Have a good night!"

"Don't worry," Luke said as the werewolf wandered off to ho-ho-ho at someone else, "I'll protect you in there."

"Oh, like you did last time? I'm onto you now—you have a new leg and everything. No more excuses."

"Sorry, boss. Won't happen again." Luke glanced down at him with a smile that made his tummy feel prickly, and they wandered together into the long, winding maze of lights.

Everything was tinted blue, then pink, then green, then gold as they walked, each section of empty field transformed into colorful arches with hanging balls of light, framework polar bears, or whole tunnels made of twinkling white. The hot chocolate helped heat Ethan's insides, but he hardly needed it after all—Luke's steady gait and easy grasp on Ethan's hand made him warmer than the drink. He didn't even mind the people that saw them—until they rounded a bend in the lit path and came upon Nareth, Piri, and Tia, lingering under a display of blinking ribbon-wrapped gifts.

Oh, this would be awkward. Ethan's ex—was Nareth even an ex? Did they ever establish whether they'd been boyfriends or not? Unclear. That didn't matter right now. He was right over there, no matter what he was—if not an actual boyfriend, a person who'd had his tongue down Ethan's throat a few weeks ago—and here Ethan was walking up to him holding hands with someone else, who definitely *was* Ethan's new boyfriend.

"Too late," Luke murmured, clearly sensing Ethan's panic as his grip grew tight.

Nareth had seen them. He smiled, and as he lifted his hand in a brief wave, Piri and Tia turned, too.

"Look at you two!" Tia said with a laugh.

"See, Nareth," Piri added, "that's why you didn't match. Ethan needed to do his shopping at the big and tall store."

Ethan wished he could melt into the floor. It was like high school again—the cool kids looking over their shoulders at him. Nareth looked exceptionally fashionable in his eggplant turtleneck and calf-length black coat, because of course he did. Ethan tried to smile, but it faltered as the elf took a few steps closer to them. He didn't seem bothered in the slightest—neither by Piri's teasing nor Luke's presence.

"Happy Christmas," Nareth said. He held up his own paper cup. "Hot chocolate?"

"Uh, we—I have some—thanks," Ethan managed to get out, and Nareth gave a low chuckle.

"But ours have Irish cream in them."

"Of course they do," Luke said with a light sigh.

Nareth ticked a brow at him. "Does that mean you don't want any?"

Luke stared at him for just a beat, then held his cup out. "Well, go on."

The elf gave a conspiratorial cackle as he pulled a small bottle from his jacket pocket and poured a dose into Luke's waiting drink. Nareth lifted his eyebrows at Ethan and shook the bottle at him like a treat bag, so Ethan relented with a soft laugh and allowed the other man to add liquor to his cup, too.

"Thanks," he said as Nareth tucked the bottle into his elbow and screwed the lid back on.

"Anytime."

"I didn't think you came to things like this."

"Because I didn't want to trod through the mud at a pumpkin patch?" Nareth snorted. "I happen to quite like Christmas, thank you very much. Don't I radiate a merry, good-will-towards-men sort of disposition?"

"You don't want the answer to that," Luke said, so Ethan didn't have to.

Nareth's lips curled into a sly smirk, and his eyes flicked briefly between the two men. "Come for New Year's. The both of you."

"Are you inviting people to my house?" Piri spoke up from behind him, and Nareth shot a look over his shoulder.

"Are you *un*inviting Ethan and Luke from your house?"

Tia smacked her brother's arm with the back of her hand, so the fairy rolled his eyes and took a drink from his cup instead of answering.

Nareth returned his attention to the men before him. "Do come. I'm making lamb and risotto. Extra helpings," he added with a pointed look down Luke's body.

Luke glanced over at Ethan, leaving the answer up to him. It would be awkward—but it was clearly only awkward for Ethan. Nareth had said from the start that he wasn't heartbroken, and he seemed to be making an effort to be clear he was happy for them now. The least Ethan could do was try his best to match the elf's energy.

"Sounds good."

"Of course it does." He smiled and gave Ethan a quick wink before turning to go back to the others. "Good luck with your ratios," he said over his shoulder, and Ethan squeezed Luke's hand painfully tight and half dragged him farther down the path.

"Ratios?" Luke asked once they were a safe distance away.

Ethan couldn't look at him. "It's nothing," he said first, but when he could still feel Luke's eyes on him, the rest of it spilled out. "He was just giving me shit a few weeks ago about you being so much bigger than me. And he—I mean, bigger was the joke, you know, but he—you know how Nareth is. He always makes it about—"

"Oh," Luke said, and when Ethan dared to peek up at him, the orc's cheeks were darkened in a blush. "I didn't know you talked about...that kind of thing. With him."

"*He* talks about it," Ethan clarified quickly. "There's no stopping him."

"Right," Luke answered with a chuckle. "Anyway—you're okay with going to a New Year's party, really? Not just because he asked you?"

"Really really," Ethan said, nodding. "I think it'll be good. He's trying to be a friend."

"I do like lamb," Luke admitted with a faint smile, and Ethan chewed his bottom lip and briefly bumped his shoulder against the orc's arm.

"Are you blind?" a voice said loudly from behind them, and they both stopped to glance back for the source.

A tall sun elf man in what looked like a very expensive coat stood near Piri, Tia, and Nareth, flanked by a human and a man with pale purple skin, hooves, and horns curling from his dark hair. Tia had a hand on her brother's back as if she'd kept him from falling, and one of their cups was on the ground.

"You bumped into him!" Tia argued, her green moth wings fluttering irritably. "An excuse me would be nice."

"He shouldn't be standing in the center of a walking path, perhaps," the sun elf said dryly, a faint, sneering curl in his lip as he glanced between them. "I'll accept your apology," he added, and the horned man beside him snickered.

"Why don't you go fuck yourself instead?" Nareth suggested, his voice calm as always.

The sun elf gave him a slow look up and down. "Who let you out of your cave?"

Luke gave a sigh that sounded like resignation, releasing Ethan's hand as he took a step forward and started to pull his coat from his shoulders. But before he could get any farther, a Southern drawl Ethan recognized called out from the bend in the path.

"Now, buddy," Joe said as he appeared behind them, slapping one hand each on the elf's and the human's shoulders and forcing himself between them, "I think you ought to come on back with me now. People are here to have a good time."

The other elf looked down at Joe's gloved hand like it was filthy, and he visibly recoiled as he took in the sight of Joe in his trapper hat and camouflage jacket. He brushed Joe's touch from him and dusted his shoulder once it was gone. "I think I'll stay wherever I want."

Joe shifted, subtly placing himself between Nareth and the stranger. "I don't know you," he said, "so I don't know how you was brought up, but around here, we don't treat each other like that. So you and your friends'd best come along with me now."

"What is this?" the elf scoffed as he glanced at his companions. "Farm security?" He tipped his chin at Joe. "Mind your business, hillbilly.

Surely even you have better things to do. Maybe get back to the goat you were fucking."

"Nah," Joe shot back immediately. "Turns out I done squeezed out just enough time in my day for dragging racist pricks in knockoff Burberry coats out of Christmas get-togethers."

Ethan squeezed Luke's sleeve and looked up at him with an anxious grimace. "Should we do something?" he whispered, but Luke only shook his head with a faint snort of amusement.

"Sounds like Joe's handling it, actually," he murmured back.

The sun elf's cheeks tinted pink, and he took a step forward to put himself more directly in Joe's face. "You really want to talk to me like that? Aren't you ashamed? For the sake of a fairy and some cavern-skulker?"

A beat of silence passed, and in the next second, Joe's fist shot out and connected with the other elf's jaw, sending him flat on his back on the frosty path.

"Shit," Luke said, and now he did move forward.

The people on either side of the elf gasped in alarm as they scrambled to grab their friend, but Piri and Tia gave laughing cheers. Luke stood beside Joe and put a warning hand out when the human shot to his feet with anger on his face—and seemed to wither immediately as the orc gave a calm shake of his head.

"Now, you're gonna want to put some comfrey on that," Joe said. "Keep the swelling down."

Ethan rushed over, ready to ask Nareth if he was all right, but he paused a few steps from him. Joe had reached back and now had a firm, protective grip on Nareth's opposite wrist, and the dark elf seemed to be unable to decide whether to look at the other man's hand or his back. He watched as the strangers gathered up their racist friend, who was now bleeding profusely from the mouth, and pulled him stumbling back down the path.

Joe turned back to look at Nareth, still holding his wrist between them. He had a frown on his lips and a furrow in his brow as he scanned the smaller man's face. "You good?"

"Good," Nareth confirmed after a brief pause, his voice sounding a little dry.

"Well. All right." Joe seemed to realize he still had a hold on the other man and let him go with a laugh that was just a little too loud. "I'd better make sure they go all the way out." He gave Luke an appreciative nod and took a step back, lifting his hand in a wave before turning away. "Y'all have a merry Christmas."

Ethan inched a step closer to Nareth and leaned forward to get a look at his face, which seemed to have blanched to a slightly paler grey. Was he—flustered? Nareth? About *Joe?*

Nareth startled as he noticed Ethan beside him, and he cleared his throat and straightened his coat, brushing invisible somethings off his sleeves. "I ought to—" He hesitated, glancing sidelong at Ethan's face. He gave a pointed sniff and straightened his shoulders, ignoring the growing smile on Ethan's face. "Oh, shut up." He pushed Ethan lightly by the chest and brushed by him, following the other elf back down the path.

"We'll carry on without you, no worries," Piri called after him, and Tia bent to pick up the now empty paper cup.

"Thanks for pulling the intimidation card before that got worse," she said with a smile at Luke. "Hope Joe doesn't catch a charge."

"Ah, Glen'll smooth it over," he assured her. "You guys good?"

"Don't let us interrupt your date," Tia said, shooing them along with one hand.

Luke took the out and turned back to continue down the path with Ethan, reaching out immediately to hold his hand again. He seemed to be keeping an eye out for something while they walked, which Ethan took as lingering vigilance after the interruption—but after they'd ambled a while longer, he tugged Ethan gently by the hand and ducked between two illuminated candy canes on the side of the lane.

"Is this—should we be—" Ethan started, and Luke gently shushed him.

"It's fine," he promised. "Through here." He led Ethan through the gap between some wires and into a small clearing made by walls of trellises lined with white lights. Above them, snowflakes made of lights and tinsel softly twinkled where they hung from dark archways almost invisible against the night sky.

Ethan let out a breath as he tilted his head back to look up at the lights. They really looked like they were floating. "How pretty," he murmured. He blinked back downward when he felt Luke stop walking, and he smiled as the orc stood facing him.

"I asked Carlos for a hot tip," he admitted with a warm smile.

"Insider trading on the Christmas lights scene? In our town?" Ethan flushed warm as he realized what he'd said—*our* town. Luke hadn't missed it either; his expression softened, and he reached a hand up to gently tug Ethan's toque a little lower over his ear.

"I wanted to get you alone," Luke said softly. "So I could tell you something important."

Panic flared in Ethan's chest, but he tried to swallow it down. Had he done something wrong? Should he not have agreed to go to the party? Maybe he'd overstepped with how often Luke was at Ethan's place lately? He had been leaving empty cups around. Or he'd put something offensive in the book without realizing? Maybe Luke was dying. Or Ethan was dying. Wait—why would Luke be the one to tell Ethan he was dying? Had someone else died?

Luke's hand settled at the side of Ethan's neck, fingertips in his hair and thumb brushing his cheek. He seemed to be hesitating—and Ethan's extremities grew more prickly with each passing second. "I had a whole lot I'd planned on saying, but—I think I'll chicken out if I try. So I—" He took a quick breath, his gentle grip tensing just a little at Ethan's jaw. "I love you, Ethan. I know it might seem soon to say, and you don't have to say anything back, I just—"

"I love you too," Ethan blurted out over the top of his attempted explanation. He covered his mouth with his fingers for a moment, trying to close the barn after the horse had already bolted. His next words came out half muffled by his hand. "I think I knew...a while ago."

Luke laughed, and he gently pulled Ethan's hand from his mouth so he could kiss him. Ethan was pulled up on tiptoe by the orc's arm around his waist and held tight against the larger body. When they parted, Luke kept his forehead against Ethan's, the steam of their breath mixing between them.

"I guess I deserved that for making you ask me out first, huh?" he murmured.

"We're square," Ethan whispered. He pushed up a little higher on his toes to close the gap between them, holding himself up with his hands on Luke's jacket as he pressed a kiss to his lips. What had he been worried about a minute ago? Luke was perfect. They were perfect.

This was perfect.

"Will you come back to the house with me?" Luke asked when they finally broke apart again, and Ethan nodded.

"Yes please."

They walked together through the rest of the lights, fingers laced. Luke dropped their empty hot chocolate cups into the trash on their way back to the rows of parked cars, but a dull, quiet thud made them pause when they neared Joe's lifted pickup.

"Listen," Joe said from the other side of the truck, sounding a little out of breath.

Ethan and Luke both froze, as if he was talking to them, and they shared a brief glance before hunching over in unison to listen to the two pairs of legs visible under the tall truck.

"I've thought about this for—years," Joe admitted in a hushed voice, "and I don't mean to talk you out of it, but—you remind me of a— prayin' mantis, a little bit. The type whose partners disappear under mysterious circumstances, you feel me?" He gave a sudden, startled jolt of a sound that made Ethan blush.

"Just get in the truck, hillbilly, before I change my mind." That was Nareth's voice.

"Yessir," Joe relented immediately, and Ethan and Luke backed up a step, peeking around the next car in the row as the truck door swung open.

Both pairs of legs disappeared up the step, and when the door slammed shut again, they waited for the engine to start—but it didn't. Ethan couldn't see into the raised cab from this angle, but he did catch Joe's hat hitting the front of the dashboard before the cabin light went out.

"I don't...think they're driving anywhere," Luke said.

"...Yeah."

"Why don't we just..." Luke trailed off, leading Ethan the long way around the next row of parked cars to reach his own truck.

They made it into the truck and out of the parking lot before they both started laughing.

20

Back at Luke's house, Ethan shrugged out of his coat and let the other man hang it up for him, then tried to smooth his hair as best he could once his toque was stuffed in a pocket. The mood was tense, despite the romantic evening and heartfelt confessions. Ethan wasn't an idiot—he knew that they both knew what they'd come back here for. Luke had held his hand for as much of the drive as he could, his thumb brushing Ethan's knuckles, and Ethan's stomach had clenched every time a wave of goosebumps prickled up his arm. Now they were here. Together. Alone.

He'd told Luke he was in love with him less than an hour ago—so why did the orc's soft smile at him now send him into a panic?

"I should wash," Ethan said, way too loudly, arms flat at his sides.

Luke blinked at him and paused with his own jacket halfway down his shoulders. "Okay," he said after a moment, then hung up his jacket.

"We were walking a lot," Ethan explained, completely unnecessarily. He hoped Luke could read his mind for the rest—that he was obviously going to stay the night, and that he was nervous about what that meant and was looking for a way to delay the most anxiety-inducing part of the evening. Which he didn't even want to delay, really. He'd daydreamed about Luke pressing him into the office chair so many times since it happened that it felt disrespectful. But when he thought about making that part clear, his whole throat tightened up, and his stomach hurt. Why was he like this?

Luke stepped close to him and put a gentle hand on the back of Ethan's head. "Why don't we go together?" His voice was soft and low, and it made every drop of Ethan's blood drain into his feet.

The next couple of minutes were a blur. Somehow, Ethan had communicated his agreement, and now he stood naked in Luke's exceptionally well-lit bathroom while the orc started the shower. The upside of the lights being on was that Luke was also naked. The soft lines of muscle in his back and arms held Ethan's attention—until he bent over to turn the faucet on. God, Luke had a good butt. Illegal. When he turned around, Ethan's eyeline was perfectly positioned for an even better view. He snapped his gaze back up to Luke's face, his whole body already hot, and saw the orc smirking faintly at him as he sat down on the closed toilet to unlatch his leg.

"My eyes are up here," Luke teased, and Ethan felt the flush of heat wash up his chest to his cheeks.

He kept his mouth clamped shut while Luke removed his prosthetic and laid it aside. He watched the orc shift himself into the sturdy chair in the bathtub, and his heart began to race. Was Ethan supposed to...wait?

Luke patted his thigh, exceptionally casual about the whole situation. "Saved you a seat."

"You're joking," Ethan said before he could stop himself.

"Only if you need me to be."

It was impossible not to look. Luke's dick was just *there*, resting against his thigh, waiting for Ethan to come and sit naked on the orc's lap. Ethan's hands instinctively went to cover himself as his own stomach gave a clench of anticipation. He could do this. He wanted to do this. He just had to go. He just had to get his body to move and stop standing and staring like an idiot until it got weird. Go. One foot then the other. The hottest man you've ever seen, the man you're in love with, is asking you to come sit on his lap and bathe together, Ethan. Move your legs, Ethan.

With a rush of determination, he stepped over the rim of the tub and into the spray of warm water. He didn't have to do much else— Luke's hands found his waist immediately and settled Ethan on his one solid leg, holding him easily steady as they traveled up Ethan's stomach and chest.

"You don't have to be nervous," Luke murmured, barely audible over the hiss of the shower as he touched a pair of soft kisses to Ethan's shoulder. "I want you to be comfortable with me."

"I'm trying," Ethan admitted weakly, and Luke's grip on him tightened briefly. Ethan kept a hold on the grab bar for stability, but he gingerly moved his other hand to touch Luke's arm as it wrapped fully around him, pressing his back into the orc's chest. "I just—I get in my head so much, and it's like my brain won't stop."

Luke held him tight with one arm and reached around him with the other, taking up the fresh washcloth he'd laid out and pumping some eucalyptus soap into it from the bottle on the shelf beside him. He let it warm under the water, and then gently began to run it over Ethan's chest. It smelled like him—cool and soothing.

Ethan relaxed a little under the other man's slow attention, but he tensed again immediately when Luke pressed a kiss to the back of his neck.

"Then you take care of your brain," he said softly against Ethan's hairline, "and let me worry about your body."

Ethan must have moved, because Luke's fingers curled against Ethan's skin where he held him, and he let out a soft grunt. Ethan felt Luke stir against him and shivered, his own grip tightening on the orc's arm.

"I'm trying to take my time," Luke said, lips at Ethan's hairline as he dipped the washcloth down to the smaller man's inner thigh. "You don't make it easy."

Ethan twitched to life as the cloth brushed close to him, his breath catching in his chest as he fought the urge to squirm. He couldn't answer—he didn't have the air. Anything he said would have definitely just embarrassed him, anyway.

Luke ran silky soap over Ethan's legs, which spread for him instinctively, and he soon abandoned the washcloth on the floor of the tub and began to rinse the suds from Ethan's skin with his hand alone. By the time he got to his stomach, Ethan was already trembling and hitching up his hips in anticipation, and the next little nip the orc gave his shoulder brought a pitiful, begging noise out of him. Luke was merciful as always; his warm grip closed over Ethan's aching erection, and his other hand moved down Ethan's stomach.

"Put your leg up," he commanded softly, and Ethan obeyed without thinking, lifting one foot to press his heel into the cutout shelf on the wall.

He panted while Luke stroked him, the orc's other hand brushing down his inner thigh to press a thick finger to his entrance. Ethan gasped, and his free hand went automatically to the back of Luke's head, gripping him by the hair for stability. This had the unintended side effect of drawing a growl out of Luke's chest and tightening his grip, which pulled Ethan's next breath from him in a rush.

Luke stayed gentle and slow with him, clearly with great restraint. Ethan's head grew foggy as steam filled the room, and he allowed himself to rest his weight against Luke's body. With only the warm water keeping him slick, Luke didn't even try to actually put even a finger inside of him, but the soft, rolling pressure and the steady pump of his grip were enough to push Ethan to the edge. The brush of the orc's blunt tusks against his neck as he kissed and licked at the sweat that began to bead there made him shiver, and the press of his growing arousal against Ethan's back was almost too much to take. He was going to be the only one feeling good again at this rate.

"Stop," Ethan finally whispered. "Wait."

Luke paused immediately, tilting his head to get a look at Ethan's flushed face. "You okay?"

Instead of answering, Ethan dropped his foot back to the tub and shifted unsteadily out of Luke's lap, twisting to rest on his knees with the water against his back. He took Luke in both hands and wet his lips as he raised his eyes to the man in the chair. This was ambitious. But the heated look in Luke's eyes was worth it. Ethan had very little chance of actually fitting any significant portion of the orc in his mouth, but he did his best, using his hands and tongue on the warm, smooth skin until Luke gripped the edge of his chair so hard the plastic creaked. Ethan wished he didn't need two hands—he was suffering from lack of touch himself.

Luke noticed his squirming and put a hand in his hair, gently guiding him back. "I think it's time to get out," he said with a slightly breathless smile that put an instant knot in Ethan's stomach.

They turned off the water and climbed out of the shower, and Ethan tried to protest that they were still dripping, but Luke wasn't listening—he urged Ethan out of the bathroom ahead of him and scooped up his laid-by crutch on the way. He let it drop to the floor with a clatter as soon as they reached the bed, and Ethan bounced onto the mattress as he was pushed down, Luke dropping over him and crushing him in a heated kiss.

Ethan was still fighting to center himself when he heard the click of the cap from Luke's nightstand, and an embarrassingly wanton noise fell from him as Luke pressed a slick finger into him. Ethan whined and rocked against him, clinging to the now damp blankets underneath him, desperate for more. Luke was calmer than him, but only just—Ethan could feel the urgency in his touch and the hot, biting kisses Luke left on his chest. He let out a soft, shaky cry as Luke brushed over the tender bundle of nerves inside him, and he ran a hand through the orc's hair to draw his attention up.

"I want to try again," he whispered.

Luke studied his face for just a single heartbeat, as if checking that Ethan was sure, and then he lifted himself up to sit back on his heel, balancing with one hand on the bed. "Turn over," he said, and when Ethan complied, Luke took him firmly by the hips and hauled him up onto his knees so easily that Ethan yelped.

Ethan hid his face in the comforter, every inch of him tense and burning hot from the vulnerability of his position. There was no hiding from Luke like this—but his anxiety melted away as the orc ran a soft, slow palm up Ethan's spine. He kept his face buried, listening carefully to the mattress shifting behind him. Then he jolted, crying out as the heat of Luke's tongue ran over him, the orc's hands keeping him firmly in place with a grip on his legs. Luke's tusks scraped pleasantly against the sensitive skin at the backs of Ethan's thighs, and he shuddered, no longer even attempting to keep his moans in. His legs quivered under the attention, his belly clenched tight.

"Please," Ethan sobbed when he felt like his body would give out. "Luke." He went a little slack at the other man's retreat, but he didn't have long to catch his breath. He felt the mattress dip again a moment before Luke's hands found his hips again.

"Tell me if it's too much," Luke murmured, and Ethan nodded without raising his head.

He tried to breathe through the tick of tension as he heard the tear of a condom wrapper and another drop of cool gel touched him. Luke's gentle hand on his hip kept him steady. Ethan shifted his knees a little farther apart when the other man urged him, and he purposefully exhaled as Luke pressed against him. He went carefully, moving at slow increments, until Ethan gasped as he slipped inside. Luke paused while Ethan breathed, fingers clenched into the bedding—but he didn't want to stop this time.

Ethan shifted back against him, and Luke's fingers tightened on him, both men letting out soft moans as Luke pushed deeper. Ethan felt stretched to the limit, his breath coming in quiet pants, but Luke gave him time, not moving again until Ethan peeked back at him and nodded. The fullness was overwhelming. But Luke was so gentle, so steady, that soon Ethan was pushing back against him to set a faster pace. The orc's uneven breath behind him made his heart skip, and each quiet sound Luke gave was like a wholly separate thrum of pleasure.

Ethan let out a little squeak of alarm as he was suddenly shifted to his side, landing with his back against Luke's chest and his head on his bicep. Luke held his leg up with one arm and curled the other around him to cup his jaw, turning his head until he could kiss him.

"I wasn't close enough to you," Luke murmured against his lips.

Ethan shifted just enough to accept a deeper kiss, whimpering into the orc's mouth as he began to move again. His back arched, and when Luke found the angle that made Ethan cry out, he held the smaller man tight with a flattened hand on his collarbone and quickened his pace. Ethan's whole body turned into electricity. He made sounds he would be ashamed of later as the orc held him still against the force of his own hips.

When Ethan approached his limit, he couldn't form more than a half-babbling sound to communicate with, but Luke seemed to understand him just the same. He kept the demanding rhythm while Ethan panted and mewled into the bed, until Ethan let out a sharp cry, fingernails digging into Luke's skin wherever he could reach him as he emptied himself onto the blanket.

Luke growled into his ear and let go of his leg to grab him tight by the hip instead, pinning his overstimulated body down and pressing into him. He went so hard and fast Ethan thought he might black out, but he still gasped and held tight to the man behind him until he heard the surprisingly soft, gentle moan Luke let out as he suddenly stilled, pulsing deep inside of him.

Ethan couldn't tell if it was him trembling or Luke—or maybe both of them. They slowly relaxed in each other's arms, both panting for breath.

"I love you," Luke whispered, bringing up a fresh set of goosebumps on Ethan's arms.

Ethan snorted out a faint laugh of warm disbelief and turned his head enough to kiss him again. "I love you, too."

Luke touched a second kiss to Ethan's lips and brushed his thumb lightly over his jaw. "You okay?"

"I'm good," Ethan promised, though he was still a little breathless.

Luke gave himself another few moments of stillness before he eased his way back and out of the other man. Ethan let out a puffing exhale as Luke left him, and as he heard the sound of latex, he twisted to take the freshly-tied condom to throw away himself. He managed to turn and start his scoot to the edge of the bed before he let his eyes bulge out. How much was in there? It looked like a water balloon.

By the time he got back from the bathroom, Luke was already balancing himself on his crutch to change the sheets. How did he have the energy? Ethan felt like a newborn giraffe. He did his best to help anyway, but he was happy to collapse into the bed when they were done. Luke's arm was a pleasant weight across his middle as they settled under the blankets together, the orc's whole body seeming to envelop him. Warmth spread through Ethan's chest as Luke softly nuzzled his hair and whispered one more sleepy "I love you" before both of them drifted off.

21

It was even harder to bring up the inevitable conversation of Ethan moving in the days that followed. He and Luke both agreed not to get each other Christmas gifts, as they were required to participate in Carlos's yearly gathering and Secret Santa. Ethan got Evie, who he gave a pair of earrings with mushrooms on them, and he received an entire fresh-baked pumpkin pie from Ophelia, which he refused to share. The laughter and cheer that filled Carlos's house hurt Ethan's heart—the prospect of leaving town seemed more and more impossible. Maybe he really didn't have to.

He went with Luke to Nareth's party at New Year's, which was actually much more low-key than he'd been expecting. Nareth had apparently invited Joe, but despite Piri's whispered teasing, the dark elf had refused to acknowledge that this was out of the ordinary in any way.

For his part, Joe seemed boisterous as always—happy to be included. He'd brought a 24-pack of canned beer that only he was interested in drinking, but when he passed around a large glass jug of clear alcohol, everyone had a taste. The smell alone almost knocked Ethan on his ass, but the moonshine had a sweet peach flavor that coated his tongue and throat and seemed to lift the tension from his shoulders. It was a little like the anti-anxiety liquor Joe had given him when he first arrived, with fewer amphetamine-like qualities. When Ethan smiled, the elf winked at him and passed the jug along.

They ate dinner, chatted, and Nareth played the piano so expertly that Ethan asked to take a few videos of his hands for reference material. It was a fun night—and Ethan had never had a better New Year's kiss. He even pretended he didn't see Nareth tug Joe into a corner.

But now that the new year was here, the time to make a decision was even closer—and Ethan still hadn't brought it up to Luke. How could he, without knowing what the right answer was? Had he even mentioned to Luke that his lease was only six months? He couldn't remember. If he hadn't mentioned it, had Carlos? Carlos mentioned everything.

But if Luke knew already, why hadn't *he* said anything?

Ethan tried to put it off as long as he could, despite the constant, gnawing anxiety this avoidance put in his guts every day. He worked in his office with his headphones at a volume that would definitely damage his eardrums, he hung out at Luke's house, and he pretended this wasn't a conversation he had to have. He sent a couple more pages to Dee, and he lamented his plight to Maya via text almost constantly. She was not as sympathetic as he hoped.

He took a deep breath as he stood on Luke's porch with his hand hovering by the door. Guilt chewed his insides. He couldn't keep doing this. He let out his lungful of air in a slow puff and knocked. As tense as he was, he couldn't help smiling as Luke opened the door. The orc had on a soft waffle-knit shirt with the sleeves pushed up to his elbows, and a kitchen towel decorated with daisies was flung casually over one of his thick shoulders. The whole house smelled like cooking, and Ethan's mouth watered immediately.

"Hey," Luke said, stepping back to let Ethan inside and bending to give him a quick kiss as he pushed the door shut. "You're early." He moved back into the kitchen to stir the pot simmering on the stove, and when Ethan had hung up his jacket, he took another deep inhale. He knew these smells.

"What is that?" he asked, hoping he was guessing right as he took a step closer. The counters were covered in open jars, bottles, and plastic containers, and cutting boards and bowls had been piled in the sink.

"It was supposed to be done before you got here," Luke said. He glanced sidelong at Ethan with a slightly sheepish smile. "I know it's not a big deal, but today is a month since we really started dating, so I asked Maya what your favorite food was, and...I'm sorry if it's no good. We can order pizza if it sucks. I've never cooked anything like this before; I'm afraid to even say it out loud because I know I'll say it wrong."

Ethan felt rooted to the spot. Luke had been...counting things like month anniversaries? Had cooked him dinner? Had contacted Ethan's best friend to ask for advice about *what* to cook him? Ethan held his own elbows to try to keep his stomach from oozing out onto the floor. "It's...doenjang jjigae?" he said softly, and Luke perked up.

"That's it. Maya sent me a recipe, and I've just been doing my best," he said with a laugh. "There's also—" He let his ladle clunk against the side of the stew pot and turned to peel the lid from a large plastic container, holding it out for Ethan to see. "I think it was called yakgwa?"

"Really?" Ethan took hold of the box without thinking so he could get a better look. The syrupy little cookies glistened in their nest—they looked a little misshapen, but the smell made Ethan's stomach rumble.

"These were really hard," Luke admitted. "I bought Oreos in case they're bad. And the kimchi I bought. But I think the stew came out pretty well."

Ethan looked up at this man watching him with a hopeful half-smile that shifted pleasantly around one tusk, his dark hair pushed haphazardly back from his face with only a single soft curl against his forehead. This was too much. Ethan wet his lips and tucked them between his teeth, trying to sniff back the tears building in his eyes without giving himself away. When he gave a little hiccup, Luke set aside the container and cupped Ethan's cheeks.

"What happened?"

Ethan shook his head and wiped at his eyes with the cuff of his shirt. "Nothing. You're just amazing," he said miserably.

Luke laughed and pulled Ethan close with a hand in his hair, curling over him to rest his cheek on the smaller man's head. "You dummy," he said with such soft affection that Ethan hiccuped again. "Don't say that until you've tasted it, at least."

Ethan smiled and nodded, sniffling as he pulled back from Luke's embrace. After dinner. He would definitely say something about moving after dinner.

The meal was delicious—more so because Ethan was able to picture Luke dutifully slicing vegetables and folding cookie dough. Maybe he'd wiped at his face with floury hands and left some on his cheek. Ethan wished he'd been able to see it. They talked about progress Ethan made with his book, how well Luke was adjusting to his new leg, and which movie they'd take to Carlos's next. Evie was supposed to come this time.

When they were done, Luke reached over to take Ethan's hand, running his thumb lightly over him. This was the right time. This was when he should say something. It was a conversation they had to have—but it felt too practical and pragmatic for a moment like this, with Luke softly smiling across the table at him.

Then the next thing Ethan knew, he was in Luke's bed again, making a mess of himself as he knelt at the edge of the orc's bed with his chest held upright by a pair of strong arms, his head leaned back against Luke's shoulder where he stood.

That didn't seem like the right time, either.

But when he lay wrapped in a warm blanket, his forehead tucked against Luke's chest and his fingertips brushing through dark chest hair, Luke's gentle voice cut through the growing darkness in the room.

"I want you to stay here," he said, his soft grip on Ethan's shoulder tightening ever so slightly. "In Adelbury, I mean. When your lease is up."

Ethan pulled back just a little, trying to make out the orc's face in the dim light.

"I know this was supposed to be a temporary thing for you," Luke went on in a murmur. "And we haven't been together long. But I think it would be a shame to give this up before we even give it a chance."

"Of course I'm staying," Ethan answered, as if it had been the obvious answer all along. Maybe it was. He'd been an idiot before.

Luke squeezed the air out of him as they kissed. Ethan held tight, smiling against the orc's lips. Luke made everything so easy.

Ethan tried to hide his hobble out of Luke's house the next morning. He was adjusting to the demands of their difference in...body size, but there was only so much a body could take. He kissed Luke goodbye, told him to have a good day at work, and gingerly took his place in the driver's seat of his SUV.

He'd have to talk to Carlos about his lease.

His phone rang as he was pulling into the long path up to his farmhouse, and Ethan grimaced as he glanced down at the screen on his dashboard. Dee. Had she sensed his intentions? Read his thoughts?

Ethan let out a small sigh as he reached to tap the screen and answer the call. Treat it like a Band-Aid, right?

"Hello?"

"Ethan," Dee began, sounding much brighter than he'd ever heard her. "Are you sitting down?"

"Uh, I'm in the car, so, yeah."

"I got a call last night from Oswyn Bromlow at Studio Aegirine. You know them?"

"Um—"

"Yes you do," she cut him off. "Oswyn Bromlow is the reason *The Gryphon Prince* exists. You've heard of *The Last Waterweaver*?"

"Oh. Wow, yeah. I love those shows." He shifted the car into park in front of his house and turned off the engine. "What did he want?"

Dee let a few seconds pass for dramatic effect before she said, "They want to make *Wildlight*."

Ethan sat in silence for a bit, waiting for her to explain what this had to do with him—and then he ripped the charging cord from his phone so he could put it to his ear. "*Wildlight*? My *Wildlight*."

"That's the one," she confirmed. "They want you to come to a meeting next week. This is big, Ethan. Many figures big. The meeting's set for first thing Monday morning," she went on, leaving Ethan no time to comment. "I'll book you a flight, and we can worry about bringing your things back down later."

"Wait—what? My things?"

"Ethan," she said with maternal patience, "if this deal goes through—which it will—you'll need to be here. They want you on the writing staff."

"But—"

"I know you still have a few weeks left on your lease, right? Don't worry about it—I can have you put up in a hotel until you're able to get your apartment back or find a new one."

"But Dee, I—"

"This is such an opportunity for you. Who knows? Maybe if you tell

Oswyn about this new project of yours, they'll be interested in that, too."

"Dee!" he shouted, and she finally went quiet long enough for him to speak. "I was—I wasn't going to come back."

"What do you mean? You've had your sabbatical; you're working again; it's a good project—this little adventure has served its purpose, hasn't it? Oh, Ethan," she said, interrupting her own train of thought, "tell me this isn't about your small town crush."

"It's not just that!" he protested. "I really like the town, and I'm happy here, and I've made real friends. And—I have a boyfriend here now."

"So bring him with you. What sort of job does he have? Is he a farmer? A local grocer?"

"He's...a mechanic," Ethan admitted, and the harpy sighed.

"Oh, good lord. Of course he is. Well people here have cars that need repairs also, Ethan, but with the sort of money they're going to offer you, you could keep him as a pet. But not if you turn them down. Are you hearing what I'm saying?"

"Yeah," Ethan answered softly. He frowned at the steering wheel, his head feeling foggy.

"I'll send you the flight details shortly. Make sure you bring something businesslike to wear. Nothing with frogs on it."

"Okay."

"This is good news, Ethan," Dee said, more gently. "Try to see it that way."

"Right. Yeah. Thanks, Dee."

"I'll see you soon. Check your email."

Before he could agree again, she hung up. He let the hand holding his phone drop into his lap, and he sat for a long while as the car chilled around him. He'd barely noticed that he'd begun to shiver when a sudden knock on the car window startled him. He turned to see Carlos's frowning face framed by the furry flaps of his USPS hat, his puffy jacket zipped up to his chin.

"Ethan?" he said, a little muffled by the closed window. "You okay?"

Ethan let out a huff and opened the door as Carlos stepped back, and after a few failed attempts to take steady, deep breaths, he latched his arms around the centaur's middle and whimpered into the nylon of his jacket.

Carlos's hooves shuffled as he steadied himself, but it only took him a moment to recover and wrap his arms around Ethan's shoulders, holding him snugly without question until his breathing slowed. "Come inside," he said, and Ethan nodded.

22

Carlos got Ethan settled on his couch with a cup of hot chocolate in his hands, then seated himself on the low cushion beside him. He listened patiently while Ethan poured his guts out, he asked gentle questions, and he sympathized. He even made some breakfast once his tenant had calmed down.

Ethan was very glad he was here.

He couldn't sit on this information, though. The longer he went without saying something to Luke, the worse it would be. But Ethan had just told him last night, wrapped in a warm post-coital cuddle, that he was going to stay. Even the possibility of leaving now made him feel like a liar. But it wouldn't do any good to wait—and Luke deserved to know right away.

So, Ethan washed his face, took a deep breath, and drove to the garage. Rob was leaned over a little two-door sports car engine in one of the open bays, and Luke was in the other, in front of a car with its hood up, wiping oil from his hands on a rag that he half-stuffed back into his coverall pocket as Ethan parked. The way the orc's face lit up when he turned and spotted him made Ethan's heart clench in his chest, but he forced himself to climb out of the car.

"Hey," Luke said, but the smile on his face dropped into a faint frown as Ethan approached. Ethan could never hide what he was thinking from anyone—but especially not from Luke. "What's up?"

Ethan fidgeted with the zipper of his jacket. "I'm sorry to bother you at work, but—can we talk for a minute?"

"Of course," he answered immediately, and he gestured toward the office door, calling over his shoulder to his uncle that he'd be inside. The other orc only grunted, not even looking up from his inspection. Luke shut the door behind them once they were in the garage's back room.

Ethan had never been in here—there were a couple of lockers against the wall, a water cooler, a cheap table with metal folding chairs, and a small, well-loved looking bed for Manny the oil-eater underneath the framed photo naming him Employee of the Month. All three of Rob's kids were at the table, reading or bent over homework, and when Luke shooed them out, they obeyed after each giving Ethan a brief hug. This wasn't getting any easier.

He sat down in the chair Luke pulled out for him and waited until the orc had settled beside him before speaking. "I got a call from Dee," he began, fingers laced tightly together in his lap and his eyes on the peeling vinyl of the table.

"Is everything okay?"

"An...animation studio wants to make a show out of my book."

"What?" Luke laughed and reached over to touch Ethan's hand, making his shoulders tense. "That's amazing! Congratulations."

Ethan shook his head, briefly squeezing his eyes shut to prep himself for the next thing he would have to say. "I have to go home. I have to go—back. Like to live. Dee says I need to be in the city to work on it with them." He hesitated, only slowly turning his gaze to Luke's face.

Luke's brow furrowed, and he leaned back a little, letting his elbows rest on the table. "Oh," he said softly. "When...do you have to leave?"

"Tomorrow."

"Oh," Luke said again, even softer this time. He paused a moment, scanning Ethan's face. "This is a huge opportunity for you, though, right?"

"It is," Ethan admitted. "The company that wants to do it is really famous. I don't know a lot of details yet, but Dee says it's probably going to be...a lot of money."

"And more people will see your story, right? It's a foot in the door."

"Well...yeah."

"So...I guess you have to go." Luke wasn't looking at him now. He leaned into his elbows with his eyes on the table.

"But I don't—want to go," Ethan said, scooting forward in his seat. "I want to stay here. I want to stay with you."

"Ethan," he answered softly without looking up, "you can't turn this down for me. This is your dream, right? Making comics, telling stories—this could be your whole future."

"I know, but—"

"You'd never forgive me if you stayed," Luke said flatly, finally raising his eyes to Ethan's face. "It's non-negotiable as far as I'm concerned. You have to take this offer."

"Then—why don't you come with me?" He gripped the edge of the table when Luke frowned. "You're a good mechanic—you could get a job in the city for sure. But even—even if you didn't, Dee says this deal is for a lot of money! I could—I mean, you could—you could stay with me." His cheeks heated as Luke stared at him. It was early to even suggest moving in together, but these were weird circumstances, weren't they?

The silence stretched between them, and Ethan's heart hammered in his chest—until Luke's next word stopped it cold.

"No."

Ethan wasn't sure he was even breathing for the next few seconds. "No?" he whispered, and Luke shook his head and ran a hand through his hair.

"I can't just pick up and leave. Rob is here, and the kids. I've lived here my whole life. My doctor is here. If I'm not here, Rob will have to run the garage on his own, and there'd be nobody to help with the kids. I can't just—go."

"Oh." Ethan retreated into his seat, clutching his stomach with both arms. "Yeah, I—I guess not. Stupid to ask."

"Ethan," Luke sighed as he turned in his chair to face him better. "This isn't about—"

"What was that last night?" he interrupted, his voice strained by a tight throat. "I love you, I want you to stay— it would be a shame to give this up before we even give it a chance. Isn't that what you said?"

"I did—"

"But that's okay when it's *me* uprooting my whole life to be with you?"

"What?" Luke let out a faint scoff of disbelief. "You'd *already* uprooted your whole life yourself to come here!"

"And when you asked me to stay, I said I would!" Ethan was aware of the wavering timbre of his own voice, but he tried to swallow down the tears he knew were coming.

"That's not the same thing, and you know it."

"You don't even want to try? You don't even want to talk about it, or—or ask Rob, or—"

"Of course Rob would tell me to go with you. But that doesn't make it the right thing to do."

"But now you won't let me stay!" Ethan shouted, gripping the sides of his jacket painfully tight.

"No!" Luke shot back, briefly lifting his hands and letting them drop back to the table. "No, I don't want you to give up your dream career for somebody you've been dating for a month!"

Ethan went silent and still then. That was the truth, in the end. They'd only been together a month—they'd only *known each other* for five. Maybe Ethan had been the only one feeling things so intensely. How well did he know Luke, after all? How easily did he tell someone he loved them when they were dating? How affectionate and gentle was he with everyone he had a relationship with?

Ethan had overestimated his importance.

"I get it," he said, and he pushed quietly back from the table and stood. He wiped the hot tear from his cheek with the cuff of his jacket and tried not to breathe, fearful of letting even more escape. He swallowed the heavy lump in his throat with some difficulty.

"Ethan—"

"Bye, I guess," Ethan cut him off, and he fled out the backroom door, striding through the garage as quickly and nonchalantly as he could on the way back to his car. He heard Luke call after him again, but he didn't stop—if he stopped now, he'd do something even more stupid. He pulled out of the parking lot and caught sight of Luke in the open bay door as he turned the corner.

He'd been such an idiot.

Luke texted asking to talk and called a few times over the course of the evening, but Ethan didn't answer. He saw the email from Dee with his flight itinerary and focused every scrap of brainpower he had into packing his things. He would have to fly tomorrow to be there for a meeting Monday morning. He did pick up when Maya called, and when she said Luke had texted her, Ethan lost it. He blabbered into the phone for probably close to an hour while he threw clothes into his suitcase, wandered the house, and sat cross-legged on the floor. When he'd cried out all the fluid in his body, he took a deep breath and tried not to whimper as he spoke.

"So can I stay with you?"

"Oh, you idiot," Maya sighed. "Of course you can. But I think you ought to talk to Luke again before you leave, don't you?"

"I can't. He's right. He can't leave, and I can't stay. If I talk to him, I'll just feel bad, and he'll try to explain again, and he'll tell me not to stay again, and I—I can't. I was wrong again, Maya."

"Okay," she said gently. "Just tell me when to come pick you up tomorrow, and I'll be there."

"Thank you," Ethan whispered. At least when he got back to the city, he would be able to pretend he didn't feel alone.

Carlos kept his sniffles mostly contained as he hugged Ethan goodbye, but he asked about a hundred times if he was really sure he had to leave. He tried to ask about Luke one last time, but he relented when Ethan teared up himself.

"I'll come back to sort out the rest of my stuff soon," Ethan promised. "And I'll come visit for sure."

"You'd better." Carlos turned to look over his shoulder as Nareth's car pulled into the yard, and he gave one final sniff and held out a care package from Ophelia. "Let me know when you land?"

"Yeah." Ethan held the box of pastries and bread close to his chest and reached for his suitcase once Nareth parked. "Thanks for everything, Carlos. For real."

"Stop," the centaur protested in a wobbly voice. "Come back soon."

"I will."

The trunk of Nareth's car clicked open, so Ethan gave Carlos one more smile and loaded his suitcase in, choosing to hold the box of treats in his lap as he climbed into the passenger seat.

Nareth gave Carlos a brief wave and pulled the car back to turn out of the driveway without a word to Ethan, and they drove for a few minutes in silence before either of them spoke.

"Thanks for driving me," Ethan said, unable to bear it any longer.

"It's not a problem. I like an excuse to go into town." Nareth's warm golden eyes glanced sidelong at Ethan over the rim of his glasses. "Is this decision sitting right with you, dear? You look miserable."

"I...am pretty miserable," he admitted. "I don't really want to go. But this is too big to ignore."

"Seems so," Nareth agreed softly. "I assume you and Luke exhausted all possible avenues before arriving at this one?"

"Kind of." Ethan shifted in his seat and looked out the window at the passing fields and forest so he wouldn't have to look Nareth in the face. "I was going to stay to be with him, but he didn't want to move to be with me. He didn't...care enough, I guess. And he said if I gave up this opportunity because of him, I'd...never forgive him."

"He's right. This is the sort of thing that would chew what-ifs into the back of your brain until you'd built up a world of possibility without Luke in it, and you'd regret him keeping you in this one. Better to end things amicably, if you must."

"We didn't do that either," Ethan whimpered. "I got mad and left, and I haven't talked to him since."

Nareth paused. "Well. Perhaps you both need a bit of distance."

Ethan let his head thump heavily against the car window.

"Ethan, I'm certainly not the one to come to for relationship advice, and you didn't ask for any—but in the end, you're being sensible. Some breakups feel like the end of the world, but they really aren't. You'll get through. But I don't think you ought to come away from this thinking that Luke just didn't care about you enough. You couldn't see what I saw."

Ethan frowned over at Nareth as he lifted his head. "What's that mean?"

"He's disgusting. The way he looks at you. It's even worse than the usual new relationship lovey-dovey eyes."

"No," he protested automatically, curling up a little in his seat and holding the diner box tighter.

"What do you mean, no? I saw it. Like he'd been struck by lightning." Nareth exhaled softly when Ethan grunted his disagreement. "I know a bit about how your brain works, and all I'm saying is that you shouldn't take this situation to mean that your worth is in question. You're a catch; do you understand?"

Ethan shook his head, but he couldn't help smiling a little. "Thanks, Nareth."

"And make sure you tell me if you need anyone to help with rebounds, revenge, et cetera. Joe will understand."

"You're top of my list," Ethan agreed with a sage nod, and Nareth smiled sidelong at him as he reached to turn on the radio.

23

Maya squeezed him tight as he came out of the airport gate, forcing him to take a deep, shuddering inhale to keep from weeping at the terminal. He called Carlos and Dee to let them know he'd gotten in, then he let Maya bundle him in blankets and fill his stomach with takeout. She did what she could to keep his mind off of what he'd left behind and instead asked him about his flight, his meeting the next day, and what he planned to wear. Ethan had precisely one suit, but it still fit him pretty well, so Maya approved it after a brief inspection.

He slept on the futon in her small office, underneath a large window and surrounded by plants. Gertie stayed with him through the night, curled up into a tiny, ghostly ball in the space between his neck and shoulder. When he rolled over and checked his phone in the morning, he half expected to see more missed messages from Luke—but there were none. Guilt gnawed at his stomach. He shouldn't have left the way he had. He shouldn't have ignored him. But if he called now, he would just make a mess of himself—he had to make it through this meeting without being an embarrassment, or the whole argument would have been for nothing.

So, Ethan showered, dressed, and let Maya help turn his hair into more than an overgrown mop on his head. She fixed his tie knot for him, gave him some toast and eggs for breakfast, and poured some coffee for him into a thermos with cicadas on it. Then she gave him her Pronto card for the trolley, kissed his cheek, and sent him on his way, wishing him good luck as he started down the hallway.

It felt strange to get on the trolley again, surrounded by people and buildings and concrete. Everything was so much busier than in Adelbury—and he knew now which he preferred, for sure. Maybe, if this job paid as well as Dee thought it would, he could afford to visit a lot. Or get a less crappy apartment in a less crowded part of town, at least.

Ethan announced himself at the front desk of the office building Dee had sent the address for, and he waited in the lobby with his visitor badge clipped to his lapel, feeling like he didn't know what to do with his hands. Should he have brought something? Dee hadn't told him to bring anything—but showing up without his tablet, or a portfolio, or anything else felt weird. The suit was uncomfortable. Everything here was glossy marble and glass, and everyone who passed through the lobby looked so put together, all sleek jackets and updos. Ethan hoped he didn't look like too much of a trainwreck in comparison.

"Ethan," a familiar voice called, and he shot to his feet. Dee was coming out of an elevator across the room, her long, birdlike feet clicking on the stone floor. She had on a trim grey skirt suit, and the large, deep black wings at her back tucked a little less snugly behind her as she emerged from the enclosed space of the elevator. Dee cut a striking figure among the humans, elves, and halflings that filed out into the room with her—at well over six feet tall, she stood head and shoulders above most people she encountered, and she was intimidatingly beautiful otherwise, too. Straight black hair hung in a tidy cut around her ears, which were feathered with the same oily black as her wings in a mottled line down her neck and shoulders, and her skin was a warm, umber brown, a contrast to the sharpness of her black sclera and shining blue eyes.

Ethan had thought she might swallow him whole when they'd first met, but it hadn't taken long for him to find the soft heart she tried so hard to hide.

She smiled with full, darkly rouged lips as she crossed the lobby to greet him, showing sharp teeth. She accepted a brief, professional hug before tilting her head back toward the elevator. "You look nice. Have you been waiting long?"

"Not really."

"I won't ask if you're nervous," she went on, already leading the way across the room. "But try not to show it. Bromlow asked for you specifically—you're here because *they* want *you*. Don't just agree to whatever they ask—if I look like I want you to shut up, then shut up, and let me argue about the numbers."

"I'll just try to shut up most of the time," Ethan said, and Dee nodded, seeming to agree that this was the wisest course of action.

When they entered the small conference room Dee led him to, two men rose from their chairs to greet them—and Ethan knew immediately which one was Oswyn Bromlow. They were human— taller than Ethan, with an even slighter build, and they wore simple black slacks and a matching black turtleneck, the sleeves pushed up pale, slender arms. They had distant, sad grey eyes and a sharp face with a dark scar on their left temple and cheek, only half hidden by the fall of soft, dark hair at their cheekbones.

Was this a real person, or a comic book character?

"Mr. Kwon," they said in a quiet, faintly raspy voice, coming around the table to offer their hand. Their grip was gentle, but between the two of them, Bromlow looked far more likely to break. "I've been excited to meet you. I'm a big fan."

"Uh, me—me too," Ethan answered. "I really love *The Gryphon Prince.*"

"Do you? That's great to hear." They gestured to a seat, so Ethan took it while they shook Dee's hand and returned to their own chair across the table. They smiled, but even that looked sad. "This is Arthur Warwick," they said, gesturing to the older man beside them. "You can think of him as my studio's version of Ms. Grivas. They've come to talk about contracts and paperwork—but I want to talk to you about *Wildlight*, and how we can make it come to life."

"I wanted to—thank you for this opportunity, Mr. Bromlow," Ethan said in his best imitation of a professional business person, but his words were waved away.

"Please call me Oswyn. Can I call you Ethan?"

"Please," he agreed, some of the tension easing out of his shoulders as Oswyn leaned their elbows on the table.

From then on, the two conversations happening at the table barely overlapped—Dee handled the numbers, like she promised, and Ethan and Oswyn talked story arcs, voices, and music. It was the broadest of opening meetings, and Ethan had no idea if that was normal, but he could have stayed and chatted with Oswyn all afternoon. Oswyn never quite got worked up, exactly, but they occasionally looked at Ethan with a faint smile that just barely crinkled their nose. They were easy to talk to and excited to get to work, and by the time Dee and Mr. Warwick shook hands, Ethan and Oswyn had already worked out the broad strokes of an entire season.

Oswyn walked them both down to the lobby, and when they saw that it had begun to pour with rain, they asked the clerk at the front desk to call a car. Dee refused the gesture, claiming she had other business nearby anyway, but when the black sedan pulled up to the front of the building, Oswyn walked onto the sidewalk with Ethan. Oswyn lifted their hand, forming a barrier over the pair of them that dripped water as if from an invisible umbrella. They walked Ethan to the car and offered him a small card as he opened the door.

"This is my cell," they said. "Don't hesitate to use it anytime. I'll see you Thursday?"

Ethan nodded, knowing full well he definitely would hesitate, but he slipped the card into his pocket, shook Oswyn's hand and thanked them again, then climbed into the car. He gave a long, heavy exhale as the car pulled away. This was going to be good for him.

So why did he still feel like shit?

24

Luke sat against the back wall of the garage, his hoodie zipped up around Noodle's fat, stripey body as she snoozed in his lap. The mug of coffee on the ground beside him had long ago gone cold; he'd been sitting for some time, staring at the blinking cursor of an unwritten text message to Ethan. All four of Luke's prior messages sat read but unanswered. He couldn't try again without coming off desperate—even though that's pretty much how he felt.

He'd said all the wrong things. Hadn't explained himself. And Ethan had been hurt. Maybe if Luke gave him some more time, let the wound heal a little—but even so, what then? It wouldn't change anything. Smooth things over with him, and become, what—friends? That had been agony enough the first time. Now that Luke had seen that smile in his eyes that he only showed when they were alone, held him, listened to the sound of his breathing while he slept, smelled his citrus shampoo on the pillowcase—he couldn't go back to being friends. Impossible. Better to just accept his loss. It would be better for Ethan that way, anyway.

Knowing that hadn't made the last two weeks any easier, though. He hadn't even gotten to say goodbye.

Luke turned off his phone screen and tucked it back into the pocket of his coveralls, exhaling steam slowly though his nose into the cold morning air. Eventually, Noodle began to wriggle inside his jacket, so he unzipped it to release her and pushed himself up to standing. He poured the cold coffee out into the grass and made his way inside, leaving the empty mug on the table in the back room.

He didn't even have anything to do until the afternoon, when Ms. Cribbins had an appointment for an oil change. Rob was in the garage handling an alignment and had already shooed Luke out when he'd offered to help. Luke stood in the empty room for a minute or two, not quite knowing what to do with himself. Nothing he'd tried over the last few days had seemed like enough to take his mind off of Ethan. What had he done before he came?

He hadn't been this pathetic, probably.

Luke sat at the lunch table and scrolled on his phone for a while, trying to pass the time until there was work to do. Rob kicked the door open some time later, wiping his hands on a rag and walking over to his locker to grab his paper bag lunch.

"Still moping?" he asked, tugging the chair beside Luke out with his heel and dropping into it with a warning creak.

"I'm not moping."

"The hell you're not. It's been weeks, kid. You either got to sort this out for yourself, or you need to move."

"I can't move," Luke protested. "You know that."

"Why not?"

"Because of you! Because of the kids." He paused at the frown on his uncle's face, and he sighed. "I'm not saying it like blame. But you're my family. Family has to come first."

Rob unrolled the top of his paper bag, taking his time digging inside and laying a banana and a bag of baby carrots to the side. He chose a small bag of potato chips instead and tore it open, all without looking at Luke. He plucked a chip from the bag and crunched it loudly, then slowly raised his eyes to stare across the table at his nephew while he chewed. "Is that the reason?"

"Of course it's the reason. If I left—"

"We'd get by," Rob cut him off. "How long are you going to keep your own life on the back burner because of us?"

"It's not like that."

"It's not?" Rob slouched in his chair and draped one arm over the back. "Then how long are you going to use us as an excuse?"

Luke drew back slightly, his brow creasing into a frown. "What does that mean?"

His uncle took a deep breath before speaking. "I know why you stayed when Tariq left town back then. You two really liked each other, but you wouldn't go when he asked you. You said the same thing then—you had to stay because we needed you. But that's not the whole truth, is it?"

"And what other truth do you think there is?" Luke leaned an elbow on the table, ready to brush off Rob's psychological probing, but the other orc's next words stilled him.

"You're scared."

Luke hesitated, watching his uncle's patient face without answering.

"You're scared to be in a big city again, aren't you?" When Luke stayed quiet, Rob sighed and sat up straighter to look at him properly. "You think I don't know you, kiddo?"

"I'm not—scared," Luke protested, but it sounded weak even to him.

"Listen. What you went through as a kid—nobody ought to have that happen to them."

Luke's chest tightened, and he dropped his eyes to the table. He'd pushed the memories out of his mind for so long that they only came in occasional nightmares now—but he remembered. He remembered the radio in the car cutting off, the thunderous noise of the crash, the acrid smell of smoke, and his view from the back of the crumpled fiberglass that used to be the front seat. He remembered his mother's hair, dark curls hanging from her slumped head. He remembered sitting in a hospital bed, his own sparse cuts bandaged, listening without understanding to the woman telling him his parents were dead. He was seven. It was supposed to be a fun family trip to the big city—but only Luke had come home.

"I know it shook you," Rob went on. "You might not remember the months after that so well, but I do. I remember how quiet you were. You wouldn't even go out in the front yard for the longest time, and every engine that revved too loud brought you running back in. I thought when you got into riding, that was the best thing for you— getting over that fear. Then—"

"Then I had my accident," Luke finished for him. "In the city."

"Yeah," Rob agreed with gentle weariness in his voice.

Luke ran a hand over his face, slouching his elbow into the table with his hand over his mouth. He hadn't said any of this to Ethan. He hadn't even wanted to admit to himself how the idea of moving to a city like that had made his heart pound. He'd pushed those feelings down for a long time, too. But Rob was right—it was the reason he'd broken up with Tariq years ago. Between a move with the guy he was dating and staying put, Luke had chosen safe.

"I'm not going to tell you how to live, kiddo," Rob said, "but even an old idiot like me noticed that Ethan was the reason you finally got your new leg. The reason you got riding again. I haven't ever seen you the way you were when he was around."

Luke looked up at him, his shoulders feeling heavy as he let his hand drop to the table. "I think I've already fucked it up."

"So what? Un-fuck it up."

"Some things you can't just un-fuck up."

"You definitely can't if you don't even try."

"He won't answer me," Luke countered, gesturing to his phone where it lay on the table. "I texted, I called, and he ignored me. Now he's gone. If he doesn't want to talk to me, what am I supposed to do? I have to respect his decision."

Rob shook his head, and he let out a small grunt as he pushed to his feet, grabbing up his bag of chips on the way. "It's up to you, kid. But I'd do whatever it took if it meant not losing your Aunt Lena. Some people are once in a lifetime." He gave Luke's shoulder a warm pat as he passed him, letting the door to the garage swing shut behind him.

Luke sat at the table for a long time, staring down at his folded arms. It wasn't only his decision. Even if he got over himself, pushed through this dread that ate at him, it wouldn't make Ethan forgive him. It wouldn't take back the things Luke had said, and it wouldn't fix how he'd hurt the person he loved. Some things you couldn't un-fuck up.

25

Ethan sat in a conference room on the twenty-somethingth floor of the glass building that housed Studio Aegerine, wearing a second suit Dee had forced him to buy and wondering how much he could loosen the tie before he started to look unprofessional. Oswyn just had on slacks and a sweater again, but they were the big name around here—they could wear whatever they wanted.

Ethan had no idea how starting work on an animated show usually worked, but things seemed to be progressing. He had a small team of writers working with him, and they'd begun to sketch some things out. Writing a show with a whole group of people was very different from writing a graphic novel all on your own. It was a lot—there was always someone coming or going, questions to answer, decisions to make.

The whole experience was exciting, humbling, and not a little bit surreal—all of these people were working to make something new out of a story Ethan had written. If he thought about it too much, that fact alone was enough to send him into hyperventilation.

Oswyn made it easier. They seemed to have a sixth sense for when Ethan was getting overwhelmed, and they always showed up at the right moment with a coffee or a request for a "little chat" that was really just an excuse to get Ethan out of the room. He didn't know why Oswyn cared if he was feeling in over his head, but Ethan appreciated the consideration all the same.

And it was, as it turned out, a *lot* of money, with more to come once the show was actually released—if it did well. Oswyn seemed positive it would.

Ethan was still staying with Maya for now—he was looking for his own place, a little, but the idea of being so isolated again made his stomach hurt. Maybe if he waited long enough, the apartment next door to Maya's would open up. Ethan had gotten too used to being a stone's throw from a very chatty neighbor. He'd talked with Carlos over the phone a couple of times since he'd left, promising to come back for the rest of his things as soon as he had a place to put them, but he hadn't asked what he really wanted to know. He hadn't asked how Luke was doing. Maybe he didn't want the answer. He didn't want to hear that Luke was missing him—or worse, that he was fine.

Being here was a tremendous opportunity. It was exciting, fulfilling work for great pay, and it meant things for Ethan's future that he'd never imagined. But every day was a little bit awful, too. Ethan hated the crowded trolley, the bustling street, the way baristas always seemed to rush him, and how it never quite got dark outside at night. He'd been in a city his whole life—it was silly to think he'd gotten used to small town living in such a short time.

"Ethan?" Oswyn said from the doorway, snapping him back to reality. "Lunch?"

"Oh—" Ethan glanced at the clock on his tablet screen and closed the case as he pushed away from the table. "Yeah. Sorry. I didn't know it was so late already." He followed Oswyn down the hall to the elevator that would take them to the cafeteria and waited beside them, rocking awkwardly on his heels.

"How's it coming in there?" Oswyn asked.

"Good, I think. I don't really feel like I know what I'm doing. I probably shouldn't tell you that, huh?"

They smiled faintly. "I understand. This is new territory for you. That's actually why I wanted to talk to you today."

Ethan's whole body tensed, and he followed stiff-legged into the elevator as the doors pinged open. Oh no. He'd screwed up already. What had he done wrong? Had he done anything right at all? Ever?

"You haven't done anything wrong," Oswyn said, pale eyes glancing sidelong at him. "I think you're adjusting very well."

"Oh. Thank you?" Ethan watched them with a crease in his brow.

"You didn't say it out loud," they went on. A small frown touched their lips as they turned to look at him. "I'm sorry. I try not to pry, but you're so—expressive."

"Sorry?"

"I'm an empath," Oswyn explained. "I'm usually able to stay out of people's business—and I try not to let them know. It...tends to make people uncomfortable."

"But I'm just nervous so loudly you can't help it?"

"Well—yes." Oswyn paused, watching him, and when Ethan laughed, they smiled.

"I won't tell anyone," Ethan promised. "And I'll try not to be so loud."

"I'm hoping that I can help with that part, actually." They gestured for Ethan to lead the way out of the elevator as it came to a stop.

Ethan paused as he reached the corner of the hall and saw Dee sitting at one of the hightop tables near the window, back talons tucked daintily into the footrest of the tall chair. He looked up at Oswyn with a frown, but they only carried on toward the table themselves, so Ethan followed.

"I thought you said I wasn't in trouble?" Ethan asked, hitching up to slide onto the seat beside Dee.

"Ms. Grivas reached out to Arthur about your living situation, and he brought it to my attention," Oswyn said as they took their seat much more gracefully. "You're staying with a friend right now, aren't you?"

"I've—been looking for a place," Ethan said in a rush, hands gripping the edges of his seat as he came to his own defense.

Oswyn shook their head. "Don't misunderstand. I'd noticed myself that you've seemed...wistful? Perhaps—distracted."

"You're miserable," Dee cut in bluntly. "And it's not because you're living with your witch friend."

Ethan stared at each of them, mouth slightly agape, but no words came out. Had he been so obvious?

"I asked for an...accommodation," the harpy continued.

"Ms. Grivas mentioned you'd recently moved back to the city from a small town up north?" Oswyn asked. "She thought, and I wondered, if perhaps you were—missing something there. Something that might make it easier for you to concentrate on your work."

Ethan looked into Oswyn's grey eyes and saw the same distant sort of sadness he'd come to expect there, but this seemed...kinder.

"Mr. Bromlow has generously arranged for you to work remotely," Dee said. "You'd still have to fly back for meetings for a couple of days each month, but for the most part, you'd be able to communicate with the other members of your team from...wherever you choose to be."

Ethan sat silent for an awkwardly long time, his brain working so hard he practically heard the cooling fan start up in it.

"Stay with us, Ethan," Dee said, briefly waving a slender hand in front of his face.

"Are you serious?" he finally managed, glancing between them as he tried to slow the quickening pace of his heart.

"I'd rather have you working than moping, so if this makes that happen, I want to make *it* happen. You've been like a wet rag ever since you got here."

"Dee," Ethan said, earnest despite her sniping. "Thank you."

"If you cry at this table, I'm taking it back," she said, but he saw the faint touch of a smile just at the edge of her lips.

"Thank you, too," Ethan said, leaning forward in his seat to look Oswyn in the face.

"It's not a problem. I'm sure you'll be communicative, and you aren't the only one we'll have telecommuting. I'm glad Ms. Grivas mentioned it."

Ethan was definitely going to cry. He felt his cheeks heating up and tried to push down the prickling in the backs of his eyes, but his next breath was still shaky.

"Why don't you gather your things from your desk?" Oswyn mercifully suggested before actual tears could spill. "We'll sort out the details this afternoon."

"Thank you—thanks," Ethan repeated, desperately fighting the urge to hug the harpy as he slid from his chair. He retreated from the cafeteria, lunch forgotten, and took swift steps back toward the elevator—but as he approached the small desk that had been his workspace on the upper floor, the smile fell from his lips.

Could he really go back? He missed the little farmhouse, and Carlos's company, and late dinners at Ophelia's diner—but—

Ethan dropped slowly into his desk chair, hands in his lap and fingers curled against his thighs. He might not survive seeing Luke again. The orc hadn't tried to reach him since he'd left, which was to be expected, Ethan guessed. As clean a break as anyone could ask for. He'd been right about thinking he meant more to Luke than he actually did. Some people just weren't so careful with their "I love you"s.

Dee had been looking out for him better than he deserved to even bring the subject up, and he was grateful. But even if Ethan went back to Adelbury—the person who'd made it hardest to leave might not be waiting for him. Maybe he should just...accept the way things had gone. No matter how the thought turned his heart inside out.

Ethan shifted his messenger bag on his shoulder that evening while he waited for the elevator. He'd asked Oswyn for some time to make arrangements, but really he was indecisive. If Oswyn had noticed, they hadn't said anything.

He needed to talk to Maya. He needed to think. He needed someone to tell him the right thing to do—the thing that would make him stop hurting so much.

He filed out of the elevator with some other workers from his floor and crossed the lobby, taking a deep breath to steel himself against the long walk and public transit awaiting him. As he moved down the stone steps from the building's entrance to the sidewalk, a high-pitched sound caught his ear over the general noise of the traffic. When he turned with a curious frown, he spotted a familiar motorcycle skidding into what hardly counted as a parking space along the front of the building.

Ethan froze across the small stone courtyard, both hands clutching the strap of his bag as he watched a figure he knew brace himself on the ground and dismount the bike.

Luke pulled off his helmet and strapped it quickly to his seat, then turned toward the building with a determined step—but he stopped as he locked eyes with Ethan.

Was this real? What should he do? He forced his hand to grip his bag tighter so he didn't wave like an idiot. He stood still for so long that Luke approached him again, stopping a step or two away from him.

"I fucked up," the orc said before Ethan could bring any air into his lungs. "I shouldn't have let you leave like that."

"Luke—"

"I was afraid," he carried on, seeming unaware of the people on the street who had to skirt them. "I was afraid to come because every shitty thing that's happened to me has happened in a place with more than a thousand people in it, so I lied, and I made excuses. I know I hurt you, and I get it if you just tell me it's over, but if I let you go without telling you that you're the reason I started thinking I had anything real to live for again—" He stopped, swallowing to steady his voice. "Ethan, you're more important than any of my stupid hangups, and I'm sorry I made you think you weren't. So I'm here, and I'll stay. I'll stay if you want me to."

Ethan looked up at him, fingers tingling from their grip on his strap. He could only take short, shallow breaths, and they crept up into his throat until one became a soft hiccup. If he spoke now, it would come out as a whimper, not a voice. So he just nodded, and Luke closed the gap between them, enveloping him with a thick arm around Ethan's shoulders and a gentle hand in his hair. Relief flooded him, loosening a tension he hadn't even realized he'd been feeling, and he gripped the back of Luke's riding jacket with such sudden force that his bag slipped down to the crook of his elbow.

Luke squeezed him so tight he could barely breathe, but he didn't care. He sniffled into the orc's chest and only pulled back when Luke's grip relaxed. Ethan's heart thumped at the warm smile on the other man's face, and he finally opened his mouth to speak—only to snap it shut again when realization poured down his spine like ice water. They were standing on the sidewalk. Downtown. Pedestrians avoiding them—or stopping to watch. Oh no.

"Can I drive you home?" Luke asked softly, and Ethan nodded.

He tightened his bag across his chest and accepted the spare helmet Luke offered, resting his head against the orc's back with his arms tight around his middle. It was the best Ethan had felt in weeks, but when Luke turned to look over his shoulder at him, he had a frown on his face visible through his lifted visor.

"I don't know where that is," he admitted.

Ethan's laugh was muffled by his helmet. "I'll direct you."

"What the hell is this?" Maya shouted down from the balcony where she was watering her plants, leaning over the rusty railing to peer down at Ethan as he tugged off his helmet. "You won't get on my broom, but you'll ride a *motorcycle?*"

There was a brief pause—then, as Luke laid his own helmet aside, recognition split the witch's face into a cackle of delight, and she abandoned her watering can with a rolling thunk and swung herself over the railing. Hissing whispers filled the air around Ethan's ears as her fall was slowed by a sudden rush of wind, allowing her to drop with her arms around Luke's neck at a less injury-inducing speed. He caught her with only a brief step back to brace himself, chuckling as he lowered her feet to the ground.

"Hey, Maya."

"This is news!" she said, pulling back to take Ethan by his jacket sleeve and shake him. "This is good news! Right?"

"I hope so," Luke answered, and the touch of uncertainty still in his voice made Ethan's stomach twist.

Maya looked between them with skepticism creasing her brow, and she threw a thumb over her shoulder. "I suddenly feel like Thai for dinner. You guys like Thai? I'm gonna go get Thai. You know how that place is, Ethan; I'll be waiting for ages. Long walk, too. You guys go on in. I'll be back later. In a long time. Taking my time." She waved before Ethan could give her more than a grateful look, and she turned to stride off down the sidewalk away from them.

Ethan peeked up at Luke, suddenly self-conscious, but he led the way into the building and up to Maya's apartment. He hung up his jacket and Luke's, then sat with him a safe distance apart on the sofa.

"They said I could go back," Ethan blurted out, arms flexed straight and shoulders scrunched high as he gripped his knees. "To work remote. And just come for meetings. But live—wherever I want."

Luke's eyebrows lifted, but he didn't speak right away. He looked hesitant, like he was trying to guess what Ethan most wanted to hear. "Whatever your decision," he began slowly, "I just want to be with you. Wherever you are. If you still want to be with me."

"I hate it here," Ethan admitted, the floodgates open now. "I hate the noise and the crowds and the bus and I just want to sit at your house and watch movies and go to Ophelia's in the middle of the night, but I thought I was feeling more feelings than you were and that I wasn't as important to you as I thought and maybe I was stupid for asking you to move, and to *move in with me* after just a month, and then when you *said* it had been just a month, I—I thought—"

Luke moved closer to him, taking Ethan's hands in a warm, gentle grip and bringing them up to touch a few soft kisses to his knuckles. "You thought too much," he murmured. "And I didn't think enough. I'm sorry, Ethan. I'll tell you everything, but—for right now, just...can we start this whole conversation over?"

Ethan's cheeks flushed, and he swallowed hard in an attempt to slow his heart. "I want to stay in Adelbury," he said. "I'll have to work a lot, and I'll have to fly down for meetings sometimes, but I want to do it if it means I can stay. And I want to keep dating you. And I love you."

Luke laughed softly, the low, rumbling sound almost vibrating Ethan's insides. "I want that, too. And I love you, too, and I'll be more honest from now on. With myself and with you."

Ethan nodded, tears welling up in his eyes despite his smile and the warmth in his chest.

"Can I kiss you?"

He nodded a little faster and let out a small sound of surprise when Luke closed in on him, cupping his cheek and pressing a long, slow kiss to his lips. Ethan grabbed at his shirt with both hands, keeping himself close to the orc as the brush of tusks at the corners of his lips sent a shiver down him. He'd missed him so much—how had he ever gotten along without him before this? How had he thought he could now?

He never wanted to try again.

Maya's key scraped in the apartment door a while later, and she nudged the door open with one foot, balancing an overstuffed plastic bag of takeout in her other arm. As she sidled through and nudged the door shut again with her heel, her eyes locked onto Ethan on her sofa— stiff-backed, red-faced, and top shirt button missing. Luke was only mildly more composed, his hair tousled and one of Maya's couch pillows held far too casually in his lap.

She snorted. "Glad you got it worked out."

26

Ethan practically fell out of the truck as soon as Luke parked, walking ahead a few steps before he remembered to shut the door behind him. The noise of the fair was loud already even from the parking lot— chatting voices, laughter, screaming, and the rumble of fast-moving carnival rides. The weather was warm now; even Ethan could get away with canvas shorts and a loose t-shirt. He wasn't sorry that Luke had taken to shorts and cutoff sleeves, either.

"Come on!" Ethan called, bouncing on the balls of his feet while Luke made his way around the truck.

"Take it easy, champ, or you'll tucker yourself out before sundown," the orc teased. He took Ethan's hand in his to walk with him toward the entry gate, and Ethan waited with an eager smile while the attendant strapped their wristbands on for them.

"That one first!" Ethan said, shaking Luke's hand in his grip as he pointed to one called the Zipper—a tight oval of rolling, flipping cages.

"Better get all these out of your system before we eat," Luke said with a chuckle, but he didn't argue. He barely fit inside the cage, but he was laughing along with Ethan the whole ride.

They rode everything they could find that flipped, twisted, sped, or spun, until Ethan was dizzy. Luke sat him down at a picnic table near the food trucks and came back with a hot dog for each of them and a funnel cake to share, and they sat together in the late afternoon sun, watching people go by while they rested.

The last few months had been hectic, and it had taken some time to adjust, but Ethan had finally gotten into a routine of work at home, online meetings, and flights for three day trips at the end of each month. The show was coming along well—and Oswyn had been asking questions about Ethan's latest project, too. In a lot of ways, it was ideal—he got to spend most of his time in the little town he now thought of as home, and he still got to visit Maya. Luke had even come with him once, and Ethan had taken him to a few of his favorite places in the city.

Most importantly, Luke came home to him every evening. When Ethan's lease with Carlos had officially run out, Luke had invited him to move into his little cabin house. He'd cleared out his spare room to make an office for Ethan to work in, made room in his closet and dresser, and stocked his fridge with Red Bull by the time Ethan brought his first box through the front door. It had given Ethan palpitations to even consider living with a boyfriend full-time, but now he could hardly sleep on the nights he was on his own in a hotel or on Maya's futon.

Ethan leaned his head against Luke's shoulder with a smile while they sat at their little table, mopping up the remains of the powdered sugar with the last piece of funnel cake. Across the laneway from them, he saw Nareth stumbling off of a ride called the Ring of Fire, his black skin somehow looking faintly green. Joe held him up with an arm around his waist, laughing as he led him off. He was glad Nareth had finally found someone who gave him butterflies.

They ran into Carlos later in the evening, who was exceptionally pleased that the chair swing had provided a proper weight-bearing harness for him to ride in. Ethan had to bite the inside of his cheek to keep from laughing at the image.

When night fell, Luke and Ethan found a place to sit in the grass just outside the fairgrounds. Luke leaned back on his hands, and Ethan nestled himself in the small gap under the orc's arm, his head pillowed against his shoulder. Summer fireworks cracked in the sky above them, painting the field and townsfolk below in reds, blues, and golds. This was where he was supposed to be. Here in Adelbury, and here next to Luke. This was home.

Luke turned his head to press a soft, lingering kiss to Ethan's hair. "I love you," he murmured, little more than a rumble near Ethan's ear.

Ethan turned his head to press his cheek into the orc's chest with a smile. "I love you, too."

ABOUT THE AUTHOR

Tess likes to write about what makes people tick, whether that's deeply-rooted emotional issues, childhood trauma, or just plain hedonism. Throw in a heaping helping of action and violence, a sprinkling of steamy bits, and a whisper of wit (with alliteration optional but preferred), and you have her idea of a perfect novel. She believes in telling stories about real people who live in less-real worlds full of werewolves, witches, demons, vampires, and the occasional alien.

Born and bred in the South, T.S. started writing young, but began writing real novels while working full time as a legal secretary. When she's not writing, she reads other people's books, plays video games, watches movies, and spends time with her husband and daughter. She hopes her daughter grows into a woman who knows what she wants, grabs it, and gets into significantly less trouble than the women in her mother's novels.